NO WAY BACK

A SHANNON AMES THRILLER

TJ BREARTON

INKUBATOR
BOOKS

Published by Inkubator Books
www.inkubatorbooks.com

Copyright © 2022 by T. J. Brearton

T. J. Brearton has asserted his right to be identified as the
author of this work.

ISBN (eBook): 978-1-915275-29-5
ISBN (Paperback): 978-1-915275-30-1

For Bob Guth

PROLOGUE
SUNDAY

Kristie Fain crossed the avenue with a small group of pedestrians. Most of them stayed with her, moving east toward the train station. Behind them, the setting sun spread orange over the New Jersey skyline, sending long shadows up the Manhattan street.

She wore her traveling clothes: comfy New Balance sneakers, black yoga pants, a white T-shirt. She'd need the hoodie tied to her waist once she was on the train.

Everything else she had with her was in the suitcase she pulled behind her.

Mateo had made fun of it before she left: "You look like a stewardess from the 1980s pulling that thing."

What would he know about the 1980s? He hadn't even been born yet.

"Why don't you get a backpack? You're not Avon calling."

Mateo made regular references to bygone eras, in part because he'd learned English from watching American TV as a boy. He sometimes displayed a distorted sense of American culture. True, Avon still "called," but the company – with its indelible image of a middle-aged woman in a matching mauve outfit standing on your doorstep with her own rolling suitcase of powders and creams – still had that yesteryear feel.

Mateo was Peruvian and had been her boyfriend for three years. Almost three years – it would be at the end of August, which was coming up fast.

Anyway, backpacks made her sweat. And both New York and DC could be brutal in the summer. You spent more time walking in DC than most people thought.

A rolling suitcase was fine.

Until the wheel broke.

Kristie slowed a little but kept walking, looking back at the suitcase as it scraped along the sidewalk. She was no longer rolling it, but dragging it. "Oh, what the hell ...?"

She went back to it and got a look at the wheels. As she did, the small group of fellow commuters, who'd gathered at Eleventh Avenue and accompanied her for the past minute or so, were passing her. One woman slowed like she might offer to help. But Kristie smiled, and the woman kept going.

Both wheels appeared intact. Kristie pinched one between her fingers and it turned, no problem. But the second one was stuck. Peering closer, she deduced the problem.

The pebble was small, bits of mica sparkling on its triangular surface, the perfect wedge to stop a wheel. She pried at it, but her fingernails scraped the surface. Not that her nails were long; they were medium length. She kept digging, thinking of how many years she'd been dragging around this suitcase – it had gone with her to Peru, Ecuador, India – until at last she got the pebble free. Without a second thought, she chucked it aside, righted the suitcase, and resumed walking. By now, the group was half a block ahead of her, closing in on Tenth Avenue, nearing Penn Station.

The 500 block on Thirty-Third Street was long and a bit

of a mess. Half of the street was sectioned off for construction. All the workers were done for the day, gone to wherever construction workers went when they weren't jackhammering concrete. The bar, some of them, obviously. The others ... to the gym? Straight home to their families?

She always wondered about people. It was her secret obsession, really. What they were like, where they went, what they did. This obsession was both what had attracted her to journalism and the reason it hadn't worked out. Her focus on the banal, the everyday, was at odds with a business model requiring the more lurid and sensational. Studying the micro-neighborhoods of New York's five boroughs in detail worked as a single weekend piece, not a body of work.

Why do we only get one life? She wanted to sip coffee from a terrace on Central Park West. Not to be rich, but just to have a moment to exist in that life. To know what it was like to grow up in the Bronx, or in Chelsea, or way out in Bed-Stuy. To love your neighborhood like your family. To fly its flag like your country. Life was too abundant in its diversity – it wasn't fair to get just one.

A noise behind her derailed her thoughts. She glanced over her shoulder at a man who was walking a few yards back. His shoe had scuffed the sidewalk.

Apparently, not everyone who had crossed Eleventh Avenue with her had passed her when she was fixing the wheel. But the rest of them were up ahead – that group had just made the light and were hurrying across Tenth. *Bye, friends.*

Continuing on, Kristie gave a sideways glance at a gantry crane, the cables dangling listlessly in the evening heat. This heatwave had to give out sometime. Every summer seemed hotter than the last. At least the train would have AC. And she'd have three hours to read.

She relished these trips. She didn't come back to New

York every weekend. But last Thursday had been a big event. And she'd needed to talk to Mateo. To tell him a few things about how she saw their future unfolding.

Which was that, basically, she didn't. Not the way things were going, anyway. The long distance wasn't working. Even though it was only three and a half hours by train, he never made the trip down to see her – she always came back to see *him*. Because he always had a show, or a painting to finish, or some other reason he couldn't travel. It certainly wasn't for lack of funding.

She shrugged it off for now. She'd said what she'd needed to; it was time to let him figure it out. She had a lot ahead of her this week.

Concrete berms blocked the closed side of the road, laid out end to end. On the other side were three large corrugated metal storage containers. She wondered what was in them. Construction supplies, probably. Small offices for the men.

So much life in this city. So many stories. You saw a hundred strange and wonderful things a day. People said you got used to it; you became inured to it. She'd been here three years. And so far it was still–

Another scrape of a shoe off the gritty sidewalk. The sound of it stiffened the hairs on the back of her neck. Just a typical reaction, though. Progress was being made in the world, but women still had to watch their backs.

She quickened her pace.

Tenth Avenue was getting closer.

God, this was a seriously long block.

She heard another footstep. Much closer. Someone with longer strides than hers. Easy to accomplish – she was five feet five, not exactly long-legged. She gave another quick glance over her shoulder.

The man had his hands in his pockets and his head down.

A baseball hat concealed the upper half of his face. The lower half was both oddly white and oddly shadowed.

All kinds of things in New York. All kinds of people. Street performers and homeless people and the mentally ill. Masters-of-the-universe businessmen and hot-dog vendors and celebrity movie stars all jostling together at any given moment. Mostly walking their dogs, it seemed.

Still, the sight of that guy stirred anxiety. No doubt about it. That and the man-sized shape that seemed to be moving along with her on the other side of the covered fencing that bisected the road. Probably just the construction foreman staying late. But still.

She took out her phone. It was instinct: the phone was a comfort, a lifeline to family and friends. Police.

She'd just been texting with her roommate in DC; Rachel's name popped up when Kristie opened the text app. She was able to do it all while she pulled the suitcase. A one-handed texting wonder.

There. Just a few lines to Rach. It made her feel better to make fun of the situation. And maybe it would give the guy behind her a second thought.

Watch out, man, this lady's got a cell phone! And with more twenty-something white women at the other end of it, too!

Kristie let herself smile a little. The intersection was just twenty yards away. A vehicle turned in and started rolling toward her. An SUV, oily black. Only the third vehicle to come down the long block since she'd started walking it.

At last she reached the end of the covered fencing to her right. As she did, the man who'd been on the other side of it crossed the street just ahead of her.

Something was wrong with his face, too. The shadows too big and deep, the white too pale and misshapen.

Oh, God ...

He turned and came straight at her. The SUV sped up, then screeched to a halt.

Kristie let go of her suitcase. She took a step back, then another. When she turned to hurry away, she ran straight into the man who'd been behind her.

His head was raised now, the visor clear of his face.

His horrible, twisted face.

Oh God ... Kristie thought again.

... Not this.

She tried to cry out for help, but hands seized her, and everything went black.

1

The sound of a scream rose and fell – just the squawk of a chair being dragged into place. The agent pulling it blushed and murmured apologies. Standing at the head of the conference room, Shannon sipped her coffee. She studied the group of men and women seated in the chairs arranged classroom style. The agent late to arrive sat and smiled and hoped to be forgotten.

Monday morning. New office building. Sun spangling over the Hudson River in the distance, shining through the twenty-fourth-floor windows. Mark Tyler presided over the lectern beside her. What Tyler lacked in size, he made up for in personality. And style, she supposed. The creases of gray in his suit could cut paper. He wore his black hair pompadour style. He'd shaved probably an hour ago, but by lunch, he'd have a shadow.

He gripped the lectern and cleared his throat. "Good morning, everyone."

The group returned the greeting.

"I've met a lot of you already. Shaken your hands, gotten to know you. And you represent only a fraction of this great office. We have over two thousand agents, support staff, and task force members. Our territory has a population of thirteen million people." Tyler paused, letting that sink in. "So I guess it's true what they say – there's the New York FBI ... and then there's the rest of the Bureau."

People chuckled, and some made faces, wiggled eyebrows. The New York Office wasn't one planet in the FBI solar system – it was its own solar system.

Tyler said, "Some of you have done your homework and know me. Some of you don't, and that's okay. Your boss, Ronald Moray, has retired, stepped down as ADIC, and I have been fortunate enough to take the reins. Before coming here to the NYO, I was the supervisory agent in charge at the Brooklyn-Queens Resident Agency. I was there for nine years, and I've overseen some of the finest agents in the Bureau. We've had our challenges, and we've had our triumphs. So, again, you may have heard my name; we may have worked together, or maybe not." He pointed to Shannon seated on the dais beside him. "But who you probably *do* know are the women – and man – to my right. Special Agent Shannon Ames, Special Agent Charles Bufort, and Special Agent Jenna Reese. They've come over on the *Mayflower* with me, so to speak. This was a team I knew I needed to have."

Shannon bit her nails as Tyler continued; she didn't relish attention. Bufort saw her doing it, and she dropped her hand away.

Tyler said, "A little over a year ago, Agent Ames, still in her probationary period, helped to take down one of this city's worst serial murders. The very next month, one year ago, she was on a case when former federal prosecutor Lucy Donato went missing. She did undercover work that led to the capture of a brutal South Bronx killer, and she just recently helped the Bureau, working with US Customs and Border Patrol, to take down an enormous piece of an immigrant-smuggling operation." Tyler paused, then faced her as he continued. "And you won't find anyone more sincere, more authentic, with more integrity, than Special Agent Ames. So I hope you show her all a warm welcome."

There was scattered applause, and Shannon felt herself blush. Mercifully, Tyler moved on.

"Then there's Special Agent Bufort."

The way he said it caused more laughter. Bufort made a face of mock offense: "Hey ..."

"Agent Bufort comes to us from the Midwest. He was with me at C-18 for five years – is that right, Charles?"

Bufort nodded. While Tyler went on, Shannon took Bufort in, as if seeing him for the first time. It wasn't, of course – she'd been working with him for a year. She knew he was from Missouri, but the shaggy blond hair had always suggested California. And no matter how finely tailored his suits, how combed his hair or smoothly shaven his round face, the tall Bufort had an ineffably shambolic nature. Like a surfer who'd wandered in from the beach in a sun-drenched daze, to somehow wind up at the FBI.

He'd been working in the domestic terrorism unit when she'd started at the Brooklyn-Queens Resident Agency. But soon after that, Tyler seemed to be assigning him to the same cases Shannon was working. The Donato case, then those two months in the Bronx.

Reese, too.

Shannon had never seen Jenna Reese lose her cool; but that was the thing. You sensed this coiled energy beneath her meditative demeanor. Reese had a calm, calculating mind. Excellent pattern recognition. She did deep research with smooth efficiency. She wore her hair short and eschewed jewelry, yet in remembering her you would have sworn she had her nose pierced or a tattoo showing somewhere.

Then again, maybe she did, and it was hidden away.

Shannon had grown fond of her colleagues. No – that wasn't strong enough. After a year, she was beginning to think she trusted them with her life.

Bufort smiled at her as if he read her thoughts. But then he clapped. He was reacting to something Tyler said; they all were. The group of men and women gathered high in this building in downtown Manhattan were laughing again and clapping and breaking up. It was over. It was official. After talking about it for a year – really since she'd started working – Tyler had done what he'd set out to do. He'd taken over for Moray, the assistant director in charge. They were no longer limited by the Resident Agency. All major investigations went through the ADIC's office, and the New York Office was that office. Some of the cases that would now reach her would never have reached her in Queens. She could wind up investigating a spy case, a top ten fugitive, or a huge white-collar crime. It honestly made her a little nervous. But she could handle it.

"Ames," Tyler said after everyone had been milling around for a few minutes. There would be several of these introductions for Tyler, but for Shannon, it was just today. This was her floor; these were her people – agents who took on a variety of cases, as opposed to other floors where the focus was highly specialized.

After calling her name, Tyler picked his way through some chatting agents until he reached her.

"I appreciate what you said, sir," she told him.

"Well, I like facts. They have the benefit of being true. Come here with me for a minute, would you?" He took her gently by the arm and led her to an empty corner. There, he glanced around and smoothed back his hair. A nervous gesture, it seemed. Like her nail-biting. "Okay, we're jumping right into the deep end. I got a call this morning from the

USA's office before this meeting, and then a follow-up just now."

Tyler meant the US Attorney's office. For Manhattan, that was the Southern District of New York.

"We've got a missing persons case, and it's going to be top priority. Do me a favor and round up your team; meet me in my office."

"Yes, sir."

His gaze touched hers a moment, and then he worked his way back through the throng of agents and support staff. The morning meeting was essentially over, but the coffee and donuts encouraged a bit of lingering.

Shannon found Reese first, standing with a group of agents who talked while she listened. Reese caught her gaze and nodded when Shannon mouthed, "Tyler's office."

When she spotted Bufort, it was the opposite – he was the one talking while the agents with him nodded along and smiled. One looked a bit like she'd been caught in a tractor-beam and wanted to wriggle free.

Five minutes later, the three agents entered Tyler's corner office. The windows faced northeast, with views of Manhattan stretching out, then Brooklyn to the right, a slice of Queens beyond. A slice of nostalgia, too, if she was honest.

But this was good. This was really good. This was the center of the universe.

"Okay," Tyler said, pushing a file across his desk, "Kristin Fain is a congressional aide. She works for Joel Nickerson, the US senator from New York."

Shannon was familiar with Nickerson, and a quick glance to read her colleagues' expressions confirmed they were, too. She picked up the file and began leafing through it as Tyler continued.

"Fain is currently missing. Supposed to take the seven o'clock train out of Penn Station to DC last night. Her roommate in DC says she never made it. In fact, Fain sent texts around quarter of seven that suggest she was being followed."

Shannon read the texts:

On my way. Can't wait to get back.

I might need to talk to Cutter about setting me up with something else up here.

If I ever make it out alive – I think there's someone following me ...?

The first two were close together, 6:39 and 6:40. The last one came at 6:46.

Shannon spread the file open on the desk so her colleagues could see.

"This is the Acela Amtrak train," Tyler said. "It's nonstop. A straight shot down, three hours. We've been able to verify she bought a ticket online in advance. And we know she didn't get off in New Jersey or anywhere else. The roommate – she's right there on that first page – Rachel Lockhart – she claims they do the same thing every time Fain comes back to DC. They meet, get a pie at the diner, and return to the small house they rent. But Fain never showed up."

Shannon studied the information on Lockhart, including a picture. A redhead, round faced, pretty.

"The roommate called 911, which put her through to WPD," Tyler said, meaning the Washington, DC, Police. "WPD took a statement by phone, including the texts – which is how we have those. They advised Lockhart to call up to NYPD, which she did. NYPD sent a car by Fain's place, where she lives with her boyfriend. At least part-time, when she's in town. Ah, I forget his name ..."

"Mateo Esquivel," Shannon read from the file. Esquivel

looked young in the picture accompanying his information, a photo from a Village Voice article on his being an up-and-coming painter. He was brown skinned, black haired. Striking blue eyes. Handsome.

Bufort whistled to that effect. "Looks like your man, Ames. Mr. Caldoza."

His observation caused her to blush, to tighten her jaw. Luis Caldoza was an NYPD cop she'd dated. And it was over. Not that it was Bufort's business.

"Hey – let's stay focused," Tyler said. The tone in his voice seemed to freeze everything in the room, the way a loud noise in a pasture silences the crickets. Shannon could see it weighing on him: pressure.

But why? Other than the texts, it seemed nothing suspicious was found in New York. Fain was an adult and could come and go as she pleased. Not quite twelve hours had passed since Lockhart had expected her roommate to disembark the Acela and share some pie.

Of course, Fain's connection to the senator *would* give the Bureau a good reason to get involved, though ...

Tyler kept his gaze on Bufort, who looked away. Tyler said, "But neither Esquivel nor Fain were home when NYPD stopped by, and neither have been answering calls."

"Okay," Shannon said, "so she sends this suspicious text at 6:46; she seems to have missed the train that left Penn Station at seven on the dot. If she's missing, if something happened, then she was somewhat close to the station. If she was used to taking the train, she would know how much time she needed to get there and board. Do we know when she bought the ticket?"

"It should be in the file. Last night, I think, according to Amtrak. Anyway, what's in there is just basics from NYPD and WPD, put together by the desk agent this morning. Since Fain keeps a residence in both places, because she works in

DC, multiple jurisdictions are involved. The commanding officer at Midtown North is Gale Warren. He's handling some of the basics – he'll do a press conference at some point."

Again, Shannon guessed there was more to it than multiple jurisdictions. Judging from the file, NYPD hadn't even assigned a detective. The FBI didn't take over cases. But she felt no need to press Tyler on it right now.

She pulled the sheet with Fain's Manhattan address: 649 West 41st Street. "This is the Silver Towers," she said. "Not far from Penn Station."

"That's right."

"I'd say priority number one is to find Esquivel and talk to him. Unless he's missing, too."

Tyler seemed anxious for them to get started.

Shannon grabbed the file and stood. "I'll have something preliminary for you in a couple of hours, sir."

"Even sooner if you can." Tyler held her gaze. "I'm hoping for everyone's sake she's just got some work stress and blew town for a couple of days. But with that text ... If this thing looks like it's going to go the distance, the DOJ want to be notified. Immediately. And the Southern District. They'll assign an assistant US attorney."

"That's good," Shannon said. "The more hands, the better."

Tyler just kept watching her, then broke eye contact and nodded. "Right." He seemed unconvinced.

Shannon glanced at her partners, who also stood. "We're on it, sir."

2

The map of Manhattan covered a wall in Shannon's office. Unfurled, it was four feet high. Fain's address was Hell's Kitchen – just west of Midtown and north of Hudson Yards, and about one-third of the way up the map. Shannon traced her finger from the Silver Towers, at Eleventh and Forty-First, diagonally down to Seventh and Thirty-First, or Penn Station.

Reese said, "Do we know she didn't take a cab?"

"We don't."

Bufort added, "When someone says they're being followed, usually it's a vehicle situation."

"Not necessarily," Reese said.

"It's New York City," he said. "You're being followed all the time."

Reese made no response. Shannon focused on the wording of the text. It seemed almost flippant; she reread it again, aloud. "*If I ever make it out alive – I think there's someone following me ...?*"

"Sounds like hyperbole," Bufort said. "You know, 'I'll never get out of this alive ...'"

"Well, it's enough that the roommate considered it alarming. And she probably understands the context better than us. We need to know Fain's pattern, though – does she usually take a cab ride? Or does she walk it?"

"We don't even know that she was headed to the train," Bufort said.

Shannon identified the first text. "She tells Lockhart she's on her way."

"That could mean, what? She's still putting on makeup in her apartment."

"And being followed six minutes later?"

He shrugged.

Shannon handed Reese the sheet with the texts and with Fain's cell phone. "We've got Fain's number; let's get started on the trace. Contact the carrier; see if we can get the pings."

"On it." Reese headed for the door.

"Charlie, if you could do due diligence with NYPD and WPD, just make sure we've got everything there is. Or if there have been any updates over the past hour or so."

"Yes, ma'am." He rose from the chair, unfurling his six-foot-two frame. "Is it just me, or is the stick up Tyler's butt deeper than usual today? He called me 'Charles.' Twice."

Typically straight edge, Shannon had learned some of the give-and-take expected – maybe even required – of Bureau agents. "He only wants people whistling at his appearance, Charles. No one else's."

"All I said was Esquivel looked to me a bit like Caldoza."

"Luis Caldoza is Puerto Rican. Mateo Esquivel is Peruvian." She still felt uncomfortable that Bufort had brought up her ex-boyfriend in front of Tyler and Reese. "But you're right, there are some similarities. Anyway, let's keep calling; see if we can get him on the phone. Does he have a job? Some other place we can try to reach him? If the two of them went off somewhere together, this will be a nice, quick case."

"Got it. What are you gonna do?"

Shannon moved to her desk and picked up the phone.

"I'm gonna call the roommate."

RACHEL LOCKHART STUDIED law at Georgetown University. She held down two jobs – one at an upscale restaurant in downtown DC, one as a litigation intern for Strauss and Associates. Shannon was somewhat surprised when she answered so quickly.

"Hello?"

"Is this Rachel Lockhart?"

"Oh God ... Did you find something?"

"I'm Special Agent Shannon Ames, with the FBI in New York."

"I saw the number. I figured that's why you were calling. Is Kristie okay? Do you know anything?"

Lockhart was keyed up; Shannon needed her to pump the brakes. "Okay – is this a good time? Do you have a minute to answer a few questions?"

"I told everything to the Washington DC Police Department." Lockhart paused. "I'm sorry. I'm just ... I'm in class, and all I can think about is Kristie."

"You're in class now?"

"Well, I stepped out. To take your call. Like I said, I recognized the number."

A fast reaction. Her phone had only rung twice.

Lockhart said, "Is there anything? You probably just got started. Oh, poor Kristie ..."

"Ms. Lockhart, listen – it's because of your quick action – your care and concern for your roommate – that we know what we know right now. So, first of all, thank you."

"Listen, I appreciate that, but I don't need you to placate

me. If you could just tell me, right away, if she's dead. And please don't say, 'Why would you think that?'"

Shannon almost said it anyway. But instead: "We haven't found any evidence Ms. Fain is dead."

The roommate let out a breath that rattled over the connection. "Thank God. I just ... okay. I needed that out of the way. Your mind starts going to all of these places, you know?"

"I do know. And I'd like to hear more. Why you're so concerned."

"Do I really need a reason? In the world today? A beautiful woman like Kristie, New York City, telling me she thinks she's being followed? Then she never shows up, never answers her phone?"

"I guess I'm wondering why you assumed she was killed instead of abducted."

"I didn't assume. I worried. Because that's what I do; I fear the worst. If she's abducted, at least she's alive. Oh God, I don't know. That's terrible, too ..."

"Ms. Lockhart, it's okay. But if this *is* an abduction, time is critical."

"Right. Right. I'm sorry ..."

"It's okay. Let's just take a moment. Okay? We don't know anything. I'm not keeping anything from you. But I need your help, here."

More rattling breathing on Lockhart's end. Some faint voices in the background. A chirrup of laughter.

"Okay," she said, sounding calmer.

"Let's start with the basics. How long have you known Kristie?"

"Three years. Well, two and a half."

"Friends first? Or roommates first?"

"Roommates first. But we hit it off right away. Kristie is

just ... she's smart. She's the smartest person I know. She could do anything."

"I understand she works for Senator Nickerson."

"Yes."

"Any other jobs?"

"No. No ... she ... no."

"But she lives in New York. As part of her work?"

"Well, yeah. He's a New York senator. So, you know, he's got to keep a residence in that state. He's got to put in appearances, cut ribbons, attend dinners – all that stuff. And it's an election year, so he's campaigning. He's there a lot."

"So it helps that she has a residence here in the city."

"Yeah. For sure."

"Do you know about her living situation here in New York?"

"She lives with her rich boyfriend. The artist."

"You don't sound like you like him very much."

"He's the most self-obsessed man I've ever known. She's too good for him. But the living situation – like you said – it's good for her to have a place there. And he pretty much foots the bill."

"As an artist?"

Lockhart laughed, a short trilling sound. "No. God no. He doesn't make any money from his painting. Or his music."

Shannon could practically hear the quotation marks around "music."

"He's rich," Lockhart said. "Gianmarco Esquivel is his father." The subsequent silence suggested she expected Shannon to know who that was.

"I'm sorry, I'm not familiar."

"They live in Lima? He won the Latin Grammy Award for Best Singer-Songwriter Album three times ..."

Shannon waited for Lockhart to continue.

"He's sold his songs all over the world to huge companies

that use them in commercials, everything like that. If the family isn't billionaires, they're close."

Shannon jotted some quick notes. *Wealthy. Lima. Left country?* "Maybe it's possible that Ms. Fain and her boyfriend took an unexpected trip there?"

"No. I mean … I don't think so. No. She was definitely on her way to the train. I know that. And she never got here, because I was waiting."

"Did you communicate over the weekend other than the texts you shared with Washington PD?"

"I told them they could take my phone. Go back through all the texts. But they said they'd let me know. No, we didn't talk this weekend. The last we spoke was on Friday morning. This past Friday. She had a package show up at the house, so I sent her a text asking if it was anything urgent. We look out for each other. She said no, it could wait. I asked her how things were going. She said good. I asked her about Mateo. She sent me a gif that … it's from a movie. An old movie. *Deer Hunter.* Do you know what movie that is?"

"I do."

"Yeah. The gif shows the guy putting a gun to his head."

"What did it mean?"

"What did it mean? She wants out of that relationship. She's trying to figure it out."

"And what does she say the problem is?"

"That he's self-obsessed. That he drinks all the time; he's high all the time. He has a bunch of lowlifes he hangs out with. Guys who think doing drugs makes them artists. And he sleeps around. He doesn't know what he has with her because he's a spoiled rich kid. She's gorgeous, independent … she just deserves better."

Shannon was writing again. *Drugs. Friends. Infidelity …* "Has Mateo ever gotten physically violent with her, that you know of?"

Lockhart didn't respond.

Shannon checked the connection. Still seemed good. "Hello?"

"She never told me he did. Sometimes the sex got a little ..."

"What?"

"She said he had some kinks. He'd maybe choke her a little."

Uh-oh. "Have you ever seen bruises?"

Lockhart paused. "It's more like ... emotional abuse. He's subtle. He manipulates her. He makes her feel bad about herself. Makes her feel guilty. She'd say that sometimes he'd get drinking and he'd just, you know ..."

"No, I don't."

"He'd get this look in his eyes. This bad look."

"Is there anything else you could tell me?"

Another pause. "If I'm honest ... talking to you ... you're different than the police. I didn't know what to say to them ... I stuck to the facts. I didn't speculate. But if I'm honest about what I'm feeling?"

It felt like a request for permission.

"Please," Shannon said.

"When Kristie told me she thought she was being followed, I thought it was him. That she left the apartment, maybe she'd said goodbye, and this time it was goodbye for good, and then he followed her." Lockhart's voice grew tremulous near the end. "And he hurt her. This time physically."

3

"Southern District," said the voice on the other end.

Shannon explained who she was and what she was after – a warrant to search Kristie Fain's apartment. Mateo Esquivel's apartment, really. It was in his name.

"Special Agent Ames," said a different, deeper voice. She'd been passed to the assistant US attorney, James Galloway. She'd never met Galloway in person, but he regularly worked with the New York Office, so she'd probably be seeing a lot of him. "I've been expecting your call."

It took her a moment. Did he want an update so soon? She'd barely gotten started. "I'm sorry, sir, I, ah ... it's been pretty crazy here, settling in ..."

"That's okay. I guess Tyler didn't mention it. He's got a lot on his plate. He'd just said we'd touch base, get to know each other a bit. But if this is not that call – that's okay." Galloway had a nice, smooth laugh, which seemed genuine. "What *can* I do for you, then?"

"Well, it's nice to meet you. Over the phone."

"Do you prefer Special Agent Ames or–?"

"Shannon is fine."

"Okay. Good. Call me Jim."

"I'm actually calling about a warrant to search Kristin Fain's residence here in Manhattan."

"Excellent, yes, I see that she's over at the Silver Towers."

"The boyfriend could potentially give consent to search the common areas in their home, and that could include the bedroom, if they share one. Which they probably do. But we haven't been able to reach him."

"That's what I'm seeing here. Well, Shannon, you've got your warrant."

This also threw her off. "I haven't even written up the affidavit yet."

"That's fine. I've been looking at all of this since early this morning. I already had the warrant typed up. My office sent it to the US Magistrate for review, and she signed it. Of course, you'll need to return it to her after the search with receipt for any items seized, and leave a copy of that same receipt and warrant on the premises. The basic stuff."

"Okay," Shannon said after a moment. "Thank you."

"Are you headed there now?"

"As soon as I have it in hand."

"I'll send it via courier. It should reach you momentarily." The US Attorney's Office was just a block away, on Park Row. They were basically neighbors. "Stop by any time, and don't hesitate to call with anything you need."

"Thank you, Jim."

"My pleasure." He added, "Be careful out there."

She hung up. Standing, she pulled her gun and holster from her desk. She affixed it to the small of her back and slid the Glock into it, secured it with a Velcro latch.

She inhaled sharply, let it out smoothly, and left.

THE NEW YORK OFFICE was located in the Tribeca area of lower Manhattan, walking distance from the US Attorney's Office. The Bureau occupied floors twenty-two to twenty-eight of the forty-one-story building, which also housed Health and Human Services, US Immigration Services, the Army Corps of Engineers, and the Social Security Administration. One big happy family.

By the time she had collected Bufort and reached the lobby, the courier had arrived from Galloway's office. She grabbed the warrant and headed out, saving the courier the time and trouble of security.

In the adjoining parking lot, she and Bufort approached her Chevy Impala, a vehicle provided by the FBI.

"You driving?" Bufort asked.

"Yes, I am."

The car was hers for the duration. She could even take it home at night, which was still in Queens. Even though her pay had changed to reflect the cost-of-living adjustment figured by the government, she had yet to make the move. But there was no mandate to do so, and she might not. She liked her little apartment with her calico cat and windowless bedroom for prime sleeping. And she lived closer to work than many agents, anyway. Most agents assigned to the NYO lived in Jersey, Westchester, or even Pennsylvania, with the average commute ranging from one to two hours. She could be to work in twenty minutes – given optimal traffic.

The security gate lifted, and she pulled out of the parking lot onto Broadway, turned onto Reade Street, over to Hudson, and then got on the West Side Highway going north.

As she did, Bufort cracked the window.

"I've got the air on," she said.

"Yeah, but the breeze is nice."

She shot him a look, then shut off the car's AC, buzzed down her own window. He was right. She cruised along in the fast lane, making the lights. To their left, the Hudson River was flat and pale blue in the heat.

"So what do you think?" Bufort asked.

"I think Attorney Galloway was very helpful this morning."

Bufort smiled. "I knew you were going to say something like that."

"I'm not a Pollyanna," Shannon said. "I just don't see the point in always hunting for ulterior motives."

Now Bufort laughed. "Are you kidding me? We're federal investigators. Our job is to look for ulterior motives."

"Our job is to help people and keep them safe."

Bufort's chuckles tapered off. He ran his fingers along the edge of the passenger door. "All I'm saying is senators vote on DOJ appropriations. There's a reason this case is already moving along like greased lightning."

The traffic light ahead changed to yellow, and she slowed.

Bufort continued, "I can't overstate how much political pressure a senator could apply if needed, and how much a high-ranking Bureau official would work to accommodate that senator. I'm not saying in a threatening way, but the message would clearly be heard."

Shannon brought the Impala to a full stop and idled at the light. She watched the bicyclists, joggers, and dog-walkers moving along the strip of trees and grass between her and the river. She thought of the pressure she'd seen expressed in Tyler's eyes. In his voice. In the way he'd snapped at Bufort. Bufort, now, was digging at Tyler a little for that. But he wasn't wrong. A senator's aide was missing, if only for a short time. It was more attention than almost anyone else would get, and it wasn't fair, but Fain was a person like anyone else. Hopefully, the quick and robust response would serve her.

The light changed, and Shannon hit the gas.

"Anyway," Bufort said, "when I said, 'what do you think' – I meant about the boyfriend."

She turned it over in her mind for a few seconds. "We're going to find out."

"You're like a fortune-teller. Did you know that?"

"I am. I'm practically psychic."

They merged right onto Tenth Avenue when it came, and continued to catch the lights for several more blocks north until they hit a red. Shannon looked left up the long block, which was relegated to one lane due to some big construction project. Thirty-Third between Tenth and Ninth was more open. The light changed, and she got up to speed. After a year of driving in the city, she knew: You had to be on your toes.

They continued to Forty-First Street and took a left. Half a minute later, she slowed in front of the Silver Towers.

"This probably gets choked with traffic for the tunnel," Bufort said, referring to the Lincoln Tunnel. "That's where you get on, right up there."

"It seems fine now." She pulled up to the curb just ahead of a delivery truck. The car in park, she checked her reflection in the mirror for any stray eyelashes or boogers. All good. A few light freckles dotted her small nose, her eyes were a lighter brown than her hair, and smooth edges defined her jaw. People said she resembled the actor Kate Mara. Or Emma Watson. She saw herself as the female version of Toby, the youngest of her four older brothers.

She exited the vehicle and headed inside, noting the camera above the entrance. Bufort followed.

The woman at the concierge desk smiled flatly at their approach. "Good morning."

Shannon showed the concierge her picture ID and shield as she introduced herself and Bufort.

The concierge wore a similar white button-down top to

Shannon's, but under a gray vest. Her nametag read Brianna. "How can I help you?"

Shannon returned the black leather billfold to her pants pocket. "We're here to speak with Mateo Esquivel. Do you know if he's home?"

"I believe ... yes, Mr. Esquivel is home. But I can call up and check."

"That would be great."

"Is he expecting you?"

Shannon glanced at Bufort before replying, "No. I don't think he is."

———

THEY WAITED while the concierge called upstairs, and spoke quietly to each other about the additional cameras in the lobby – two of them behind the large front desk, two in the adjoining elevator section. Video could tell them exactly when Fain had left the building. If, in fact, she had.

Brianna hung up the phone and shook her head. "Mr. Esquivel is not answering."

Shannon pulled the paper from the inside of her black blazer. "That's okay. This is from the US District Court."

Moments later, the agents were rising to the thirty-fifth floor. So far, the whole place felt more like a hotel than an apartment building. But, she figured, that was what "luxury apartments" meant. And she understood it even more when she stepped off the elevator into the thirty-fifth-floor lobby and had a look at the view of the city. Her work building was as tall, but this was just west of Midtown, amid towering skyscrapers. Their presence was quite something. As if height conferred power.

"Fancy," Bufort said. He started hunting for the apartment.

Shannon followed him down the hallway, in presumably the right direction. Everything seemed very clean – gleaming floors, freshly painted walls. Decorative wall sconces lit the way.

Bufort slowed.

"What is it?" Shannon got a look past her large colleague at an apartment door slightly ajar. 3513.

Bufort's left hand went to his service weapon holstered on his hip. Shannon touched the grip of her own weapon as Bufort gave the door a gentle push. "Hello?"

Their eyes met and communicated: He would cover her; she'd lead the way in.

Bufort drew his Glock.

Shannon got just two steps in the room, breath drawn to announce herself, when out of nowhere the figure rushed at her.

4

The man hit Shannon low and to the side, knocking her off balance. As she fell, she reached out to brace herself but cracked the side of her hip on a table just inside the doorway. A bowl of keys fell. Time seemed to slow.

After colliding with the table and bouncing off, the momentum carried her down. The man was still holding onto her. His lowered head gouged her ribs while his arms hugged her waist. Like a damn form tackle. They completed the fall onto the hard floor, him on top of her, the bowl shattering when it hit, keys clattering away.

"Hey!" It was Bufort yelling. "Hey! Hey!"

Shannon struggled to get out from under. The man lifted his head and saw her, his mouth opening in surprise. Shannon could've hit him, but instead she was quick, pushing him back as she escaped his weight and gained her feet. It left him there on his hands and knees for a moment, his neck twisted around to try to see behind him.

"Don't move, buddy," Bufort said, holding the gun on

him. "Let me see your hands. Nice and easy. Keep your back to me."

The man raised his hands as instructed, staying on his knees. Though he faced away from the door, Shannon could see his profile.

"Now put your hands behind your head. Slowly. Interlace your fingers. Good."

Shannon wanted to confirm it: "Sir, are you Mateo Esquivel?"

On his knees, hands laced behind his head as instructed, he made a small nod. Shannon could see his chest vibrating with a hard-beating heart. Hers was going at a good clip, too.

She also noticed his disheveled appearance: white tank top, cargo shorts, brown sandals. The tank top was stretched and twisted. And as she moved in front of him for a better look, she thought she saw blood on the fabric.

His lip was swollen, with blood there, too. But it had already dried – whatever had happened hadn't happened just now.

He looked at her with glassy, bloodshot eyes. "I'm sorry."

"Stay right where you are," Bufort said. "Is anyone else in the apartment?"

Esquivel kept his gaze on Shannon. "No."

"You're sure?" she asked.

"He left."

Shannon was curious. "*Who* left?"

Esquivel shook his head, as if confused. "I, ah ... Riley. When you came in, I just ... I heard a voice, and I just ... I thought he was back. And I'd fucking had enough, man. I'd had enough ..."

While Shannon considered what he was saying, she started to pat down Esquivel, check him for weapons. "Do you have anything on you that's going to hurt me? Knives, razors, needles, anything like that?"

"No."

He reeked of alcohol and sweat. She found his wallet in his back pocket. In his right front pocket, two unopened condoms. A gum wrapper. There was a faded stamp on top of his left hand, as if from a nightclub. An indiscernible pink blob.

"What happened, Mr. Esquivel? Who was in your apartment? Riley? Who is that?"

But Esquivel's head dropped to his chest. "He said he was a cop ..."

"He said he was a *cop*?"

She didn't realized Esquivel was crying until she saw the tears hit the floor.

He said, "I don't understand what's happening ..."

That makes two of us.

THEY GOT Esquivel calmed and drinking some water on his couch. The place was partly wrecked. A lamp on the floor, an upended potted plant with spewed dirt. The comfy chair that matched the couch sat askew.

Esquivel sniffed back tears and mucous. "He came in and started asking questions," he said about this person – this mystery guest he claimed had been there not long ago. "But he didn't seem to believe my answers. Kept asking me the same things. Then he started getting physical."

Esquivel had an accent – she supposed it was Peruvian – but it was light. His English was good. He was wiry but muscular, caramel skinned, young.

"When?" Bufort asked. "What time did all this happen? When was he here?"

"It was just a little after I got home. Like, fifteen minutes."

"Fifteen minutes after *what*?"

"I think I came in around 2:00 a.m."

"Okay. And how did *he* get in?"

"I don't know. You mean the building? It's not like we have security. The concierge is just for show. Anyone can come in. He just knocked on my door."

"Why'd you let him in?"

Esquivel looked slightly annoyed now. "Because he said he was a *cop*. He knocked; I asked who it was. He said he was Detective Riley with NYPD."

Shannon and Bufort exchanged looks. They were unaware of a detective NYPD had assigned to the case. The local precinct had sent a car to this location to respond to the missing persons report, but that was it.

Bufort said, "And you believed him? A guy shows up at 2:00 a.m. and says he's a cop?"

"I had missed calls from the police. I had a message."

"A couple of messages," Bufort clarified. And he pointed a finger between himself and Shannon. "*We* called you, too."

As they spoke, Shannon took pictures with her phone and wandered the apartment. Her hip hurt a little from Mateo's tackle; it felt good to walk it off. The place was a two-bedroom. Stainless steel appliances in the kitchen, hardwood plank flooring throughout, floor-to-ceiling windows in the living room with more stunning views, these on the Hudson River and New Jersey beyond.

"It was late," Esquivel said. "I was out with people. I didn't see my messages until I came home. I listened to one, and it was about Kristie. That the cops were looking for her. And then someone knocks on my door saying they were with NYPD. So? I opened up."

"Have a drink of the water, Mr. Esquivel," Bufort said. "Just stay relaxed right there. Let's see if we can clear this up." He glanced at Shannon, who gave him a slight nod. *Call them.*

She continued to explore the place as Bufort called

NYPD. Empty liquor bottles populated the kitchen that adjoined the living room. A smartphone sat on the marble-top counter.

"Hi," Bufort said into his phone. "Special Agent Charlie Bufort with the New York field office of the FBI, Squad C-23. You guys got a Detective Riley over there?" He paused. "Okay, how about at any of the other precincts? Could you check for me?"

As Bufort waited, Shannon moved in, getting closer to Esquivel, who leaned forward, elbows on his knees. He hung his head as if ashamed, sad, tired, or all of the above.

"Mr. Esquivel," she said, "can you tell me what this man looked like?"

"I don't know. White guy. Had a Yankees hat on. Older guy. Maybe sixty, seventy, I don't know."

"Seventy?"

"I don't know. Maybe."

"What sort of questions was he asking?"

"He asked where Kristie was."

"That's it?"

Now Esquivel looked up. His eyes were red. "I didn't know what he was talking about. I said goodbye to Kristie around six thirty when she left for the train to DC."

"She left on foot?"

"Yeah. She always walks."

"Alone?"

"Yeah, alone."

Bufort broke in. "There's a couple of Detective Rileys. One is a woman. They're patching me through to the second, up in the Bronx."

Shannon asked Esquivel, "He seemed to know for sure she was gone? And he thought you would know where she'd be?"

"Yeah. He thought I knew. Or he was ... hoping."

"Do you?"

He regarded her with those dark, bloodshot eyes again. Eyes that conveyed his self-pity more than anything. "I didn't know anything. I still don't know. I'm waiting for someone to tell me something. Is Kristie okay? Is she really missing?"

Bufort spoke again, loud enough into the phone so they could easily overhear. "Detective Riley? Hi, Charlie Bufort with the FBI. Listen, I've got a funny situation. There's a case being handled by Midtown North. And it sounds like you're way up in the Bronx. Any chance you're helping out, maybe filling in for someone?" Bufort listened. "Uh-huh. Uh-huh. Okay. And again, I know this is unusual – but you weren't over at the Silver Towers last night, were you?" More listening. "Okay, gotcha. Last question – what do you look like?" A smile spread across Bufort's face. "Good for you, man. I thank you."

He put away the phone. "Guy says he's Denzel Washington in his prime." Bufort's smile faltered a bit as he said, "And no, he wasn't here last night. It sounds like the person who busted you up wasn't NYPD." His eyes ticked to Shannon. "I'm having doubts he was a cop at all."

5

The agents switched roles, with Bufort roaming the house, Shannon focused on Fain's boyfriend. "Mr. Esquivel, has anyone else tried to call you? Or text you?"

He nodded. "Kristie's roommate in DC. Her name is Rachel."

"Did you respond to her?"

He looked slightly ashamed. "No."

Shannon went to the smartphone in the kitchen, picked it up. "Do you mind if I look through your phone?"

"Battery is almost dead. But be my guest."

She searched the text app until she found them: messages from Rachel Lockhart. The first one had come in at 10:42 the previous evening.

Hey Mateo. Kristie didn't get off the train. I can't reach her. Is she still in NY with you?

There was a missed call from Lockhart at 11:38. Another text followed.

I've called the police. Please respond and let me know if she's there and okay.

Mateo didn't reply until just after 2:00 a.m.

Don't know. Sure she's fine.

"You don't seem too concerned," Shannon said.

"I mean, I thought maybe ..." He sighed, gesturing with his hands, which he then dropped into his lap. "Rachel is a drama queen. She's got a thing for Kristie, if you ask me. Wishes they were more than friends. I figured she was worried just to stir things up, like she usually does."

Bufort spoke up as he examined a painting hung on the wall. "What did you think the answer was, though? When Rachel brought it up, where did you think Kristie was?"

Esquivel swiveled his head to look. "I don't know, man. Out with somebody else? Or her work – she works all kinds of crazy hours for Nickerson. Maybe she got picked up by his chief of staff. Whatever his name is. Sutter. Or Cutter. Maybe he picked her up from the train and whisked her off somewhere, and she forgot to tell Rachel."

Bufort pointed at the painting, a collection of colorful dashes, almost like bacterium, patterned in a variety of directions. "You do this?"

"No, man. That's Basquiat. I don't hang any of my own work in here ... Are you saying Kristie is definitely missing?"

Shannon left the phone and returned to the living room. "Yes. We are."

Esquivel switched looks between the agents. "Okay, but ... the FBI doesn't just get involved because someone missed a train. You're not telling me something."

Maybe Fain's boyfriend wasn't as airheaded as he seemed. And it was interesting that Lockhart hadn't said anything to him about her worrying texts from Fain. Maybe because she thought he was the reason for her disappearance.

"Why didn't you call the police back, Mateo?"

"Honestly? I was a little drunk last night. I wasn't really thinking straight. The whole thing seemed ... I don't know."

"What? What did it seem?"

"That maybe Kristie was trying to get attention or something."

"You think she was trying to get your attention? You seem to think everyone wants attention. Rachel, Kristie ..."

He shrugged. "It's an attention-seeking world."

Shannon pulled the same warrant from her pocket and set it on the glass coffee table between her and Esquivel. "This is a search warrant. Put your attention on that. We're going to need to have a look at everything here in your apartment. Okay? Anything we can find that helps tell us what might've happened. If we have to take something, I'll leave you with a receipt. You'll get everything back."

"There's not much. She didn't keep much here, I mean."

"But before that happens, Agent Bufort and I need to have a talk. Can you sit there and remain calm?"

Esquivel gave her a barely perceptible nod. "Sure."

———

SHANNON LED Bufort into one of the two bedrooms. This one didn't seem to be the sleeping quarters. No bed, but a desk, shelves, a filing cabinet – a home office. Also: stacks of fresh canvases, already mounted and primed, it looked like, and wrapped in plastic. A closet full of art supplies – paints and palettes and easels. Shannon pulled the door partway closed, but kept it open enough to keep an eye on their host.

Bufort said, "Maybe he beat himself up, make it look good."

"I don't think so." She glanced at Esquivel. "How do you want to handle this?"

"I think he's right – she doesn't seem to have much here. Him either. There's not any pictures, just the weird art. It's like they're barely home."

"I'm still going to call it in," Shannon said. "Get a team to do the search."

"Yeah, of course."

"You go ahead and check cameras. If there was a man who came in, we'll get a look at him. And we can see when Fain left. I'll wait until the team gets here; then I'll be down."

"Right on." He held up his fist, and she popped it with her knuckles.

"Get out of here."

Bufort grinned, a boyish expression with his fall of blond hair. But when he turned to leave the room, Shannon lingered, struck with a peculiar sensation.

Hard to say what; maybe something had triggered old thoughts, unsurfaced memories. Maybe it was having just been tackled to the ground by a confused young man. But standing there alone in the room with all the canvases and paints, the feeling persisted.

Something was coming. Something that was going to get very difficult, very dark.

And she didn't know how she was going to stop it.

6

"Here's our guy," Bufort said, and hit the space bar on the computer. The lobby video rolled forward. A man walked past wearing a black windbreaker and a New York Yankees cap. He was a good fifteen yards from the camera and never stopped at the concierge desk.

"That's it?" Shannon asked.

"That's it."

"What about at the elevators? There's a camera there."

Bufort showed her. Shannon stared at the image of an empty lobby as Bufort pointed out the running clock at the bottom of the screen. "This is the same time. Nothing."

"Wait, back it up."

Bufort did.

"There he is," Shannon said, pointing. "See? He just appears there for a moment, peers around the corner, like he's getting a look. Like he sees the camera, maybe."

"And he takes the stairs all the way to the thirty-fifth floor?"

"Not necessarily. He could have just gone up one flight, taken the elevator from there." She turned to Brianna, who was standing nearby. "Do you have cameras at the elevators on each floor?"

Brianna shook her head.

"Okay," Bufort said, "and here's last night."

Elevator lobby and main lobby cameras all showed Kristie Fain leaving at 6:33 p.m. She was wearing comfortable clothes – travel clothes, Shannon thought. Sneakers, yoga pants, a T-shirt, and a sweatshirt tied at her waist. She pulled a small suitcase on wheels. They watched her walk through the lobby and push out the front doors. The final camera, exterior, showed her turn down Eleventh Avenue. Then she was gone.

SHANNON AND BUFORT stood in the lobby moments later, speaking quietly and out of earshot from Brianna.

"How did he get in?" Shannon asked.

"There's no concierge at night. The doors lock at 8:00 p.m. He probably waited for someone to come in or out."

They returned to the concierge office and watched the video from a point prior to "Detective Riley's" entry. Another man walked through the lobby, headed out, seconds before. Riley grabbed the door before it shut. He seemed to interact with the resident a moment, showed the guest something, then the guest continued on. Riley entered the building.

"Bingo," Bufort said.

The image wasn't close or clear enough, but it seemed likely Riley had explained he was a cop. Maybe what he'd shown was a badge. Shannon had Brianna join them and asked if she knew the guest. She thought she did, and Shannon took down the contact information. They'd talk to him, get a description of the stranger from him, too.

But first, she had a few last questions for Mateo Esquivel.

As the forensic team worked their way slowly through the
apartment, Mateo Esquivel stood in the kitchen, drinking a
Red Bull. His eyes kept getting heavier; he was going to crash
soon, Shannon thought, caffeine or no. She studied his quasi-
hip-hop outfit, replete with gold bracelet and chain. The
blood on his white tank top, the stamp on his hand.

"Where did you go last night?"

Esquivel sipped his beverage. "Out."

"With whom?"

"Few friends."

"Where's the stamp from?"

"We went to a club."

She waited. "That's it? Then home?"

He nodded. "Yeah."

"That's how you dress for a club?"

He stared a moment, as if determining something about
her. Then he gazed down at his appearance, pulled at the
fabric of his shirt, let it snap back. "It was hot last night. Even
hotter in the club. Like a hundred and ten in there."

Her hunch – plus the condoms – told her he was unfaith-
ful. Fain was out the door, and he was living his double life.
She took another look at the pink blob stamp.

"Which club?"

"Rumpus Room. In the Bowery."

She'd heard of it. Pricey drinks, hipster atmosphere, good
dance music. "How long were you home before the man
came to the door?"

"Fifteen minutes, maybe."

"What were you doing?"

"Nothing. Getting ready for bed. Watching TV."

Still drinking, in other words. Maybe more. "Are my
people going to find any drugs in this apartment?"

She could see it in his face. He had something here. Maybe painkillers? Heroin?

She moved closer and lowered her voice. "Listen to me, Mateo. Right now things don't look very good for you. Your girlfriend is missing, and you were the last person to see her alive. When you finally responded to her roommate in DC, you were casual. Then you didn't answer repeated calls from the police."

Esquivel set down his can. "I opened up when I thought the police were here."

"Did he show you a badge?"

"He did, actually."

It squared with the video footage, the thing the interloper had showed to the resident, to reassure him. She asked, "What did it look like?"

Esquivel said he'd only gotten a quick glimpse, but he described a police badge pretty accurately. He hadn't noticed whether it said NYPD. "When he asked about Kristie, I told him she was in DC."

"But hadn't the texts from Rachel come in earlier? 10:42? And her missed call around 11:30?"

"Yeah, but I didn't look at them until later. Like, two. When I got home."

"Just before Riley showed up."

"Exactly."

"But you didn't think to tell him her roommate was worried about her."

"No. I didn't, okay? He was aggressive. He started pushing me. 'Come on. Where you hiding her?' And I was like, what? I asked him to leave. That's when he grabbed me, pulled my hair. He shoved me against the wall, pulled my arm up behind my back. Then he started asking about Kristie's job."

"What about it?"

"Last week, she had a thing in town. A big dinner."

"A meeting, you mean? Or what?"

Esquivel had to think about it. "A fundraiser."

"And the man asked about it?"

"Yeah."

Shannon wrote it in her phone. *Fundraiser for Nickerson.* "Tell me about it."

"I don't know. That's the thing. You know, it was just a work thing for her. She's been doing a lot of them. It's election year or whatever."

"Where was it?"

"Just a few blocks over. A hotel in Midtown."

Shannon wrote that down, too. Then she stood, wincing a bit at the pain still in her hip. "I need you to be specific, Mateo. What exactly did Riley ask?"

"He asked if she said anything to me about it."

"If she said anything – what does that mean? Like what? If it had been a nice night? What?"

He suddenly scrunched up his face and pressed palms to his temples like he'd developed a bad headache. Grimacing, he shook his head back and forth. "I don't know. You sound like him. She didn't say anything to me except that she was going, okay?"

"And afterwards?"

"I can't remember. I had a show that night. A gallery show. We didn't really see each other much during the day. Just texting. When I came home that night, it was late; she was already here. Sleeping. It was just a little before midnight."

Shannon stacked it all up: Four nights ago, Fain had attended a fundraising dinner for Senator Nickerson. Last night, she'd possibly gone missing. Never made it to DC, anyway. A man claiming to be a cop stopped by the residence she shared with her boyfriend, roughed him up pretty bad, scared him, wanted to know where Fain was. When Esquivel didn't know, the man asked about the fundraiser.

Esquivel was mumbling now. "'Tell the truth,' he kept saying. 'You know where she is. You're hiding her.' I finally told him to fuck off. And he hit me, and that's the last thing I remember."

Shannon figured the combination of the blow to the head and all the alcohol he seemed to have consumed – it continued to stink from his pores – accounted for how bewildered he'd seemed when she and Bufort had shown up.

"Next thing I remember was the phone ringing. I got up, took a leak; then I heard voices in the hallway. I heard someone say 'Hey,' right outside the door. I just wasn't thinking. I didn't want to go through that again ..."

And that was why he'd tackled her. He'd been knocked out for a few hours; then, still inebriated and disoriented, he'd thought it was the mystery man returning, and attacked.

Shannon opened the internet browser on her phone. "What's the name of the hotel where the fundraiser was?"

"The Takano."

"Can you spell that?"

She plugged it into the browser, had a look. A nice place with an Asian aesthetic. Luxurious, but understated.

Bufort, who'd been working the apartment with the forensic team, walked into the kitchen. Shannon showed him the image on her phone. "That's where we're going next."

7

She took Eleventh Avenue one block south to Fortieth, then east, cutting across Midtown.

"No wonder we can't afford the city," Bufort said from the passenger seat. "I checked – a two-bedroom apartment in the Silver Towers goes for $6,500 a month."

He fell silent after that, the sounds of the city rushing around them. Horns honking, engines revving, the warble of an ambulance in the near distance.

Bufort was looking at her. "You're quiet. What are you thinking?"

Partly, that she'd been a bit too harsh with Esquivel. He might've been a narcissist, might've not, but everyone had a story. He'd been beaten up by someone claiming to be a cop. She'd been okay with him, but a couple of times felt herself toeing the edge.

"Ames?"

"Just thinking about something he said. That Riley kept asking where he'd hidden her."

"Where *he'd* hidden her? Esquivel?"

"Riley seemed to presume she was deliberately missing.

Not abducted, but hiding. Listen – while we're driving, let's call Nickerson's chief of staff. Esquivel mentioned him. He made allusions to Fain's busy schedule. We need that schedule. We need to know where she's been, where she was going to be."

Bufort started poking at his phone, getting the information. "Keith Cutter," he said. "Nickerson's chief of staff. Here's the number for the office."

"Ask him about the fundraiser, but get everything she has going on. Her whole itinerary."

"I gotcha, I gotcha." He gave her a look. "Something happen up there?"

"No."

He opened his mouth to say more when his attention was drawn back to the phone; he was connecting with someone. "Hi. Special Agent Charlie Bufort, FBI. Can I speak to your ... Oh. Okay, great. Thank you." Bufort pulled the phone away from his ear and said to Shannon, "They expected our call."

There seemed to be a lot of that going around.

Bufort put it on speaker, and then Cutter came on.

"Special Agent Bufort, thanks for calling. How can I help?" He sounded in his forties, with a clear voice, used to telling people what to do.

"Hi, thanks for taking the call. Also with us is Special Agent Shannon Ames. Mr. Cutter, from what I understand, you were informed about this pretty early on?"

"Hello, Agent Ames. Yeah, we got the call very early."

"When was that?"

"Ah, right about 5:00 a.m. One of our staff assistants picked it up, then called me at home. I called the DOJ right away."

"Thanks for your quick action. Mr. Cutter, what can you tell us about Kristin? Anything been going on lately?

Anything with work, anything you might've noticed about her personal life?"

"Kristie is just a hard, hard worker. You may know she's our projects and grants coordinator."

"That means she seeks federal funding for state and district projects?"

"Correct. And she's a hustler. Always on the ball, always with good ideas, good follow-through. We couldn't ask for anyone better. But as far as what you're asking, any trouble I can think of, certainly not at work, or I'd know about it. Other than that, I can't really comment on her personal life. I make it a point to have an open door to all of my staff, and they know they can come talk to me about anything. But Kristie either just had a real solid situation going on, or she chose not to bring it to work, not to talk about it with me. In short, she's an ideal staffer and seemed to have no problems."

Shannon cut in. "Mr. Cutter, this event last week in Manhattan – was this one of her events?"

"At the Takano? No. That was a general fundraiser for Senator Nickerson's reelection campaign."

There was silence for a moment; then Cutter's voice came through the car speakers again. "Is there something about the fundraiser that's of interest?"

Shannon answered, "We're looking at Fain's schedule. Everything she had going on recently. We're hoping you can help us with that."

"Absolutely. I can get that up to you right away. And let me know anything else you might need from us, from Senator Nickerson." He paused again. "Is there anything you can tell me right now? I've gotta say, we're all pretty preoccupied with this. I mean, it's a great crew, they could work through a hurricane, but Kristie is ... she's beloved here."

Bufort said, "At the moment, we're trying to get the lay of the land. We're contacting family and friends, putting together this recent history." He glanced at Shannon, who made a face like, *Yeah, good enough.*

"Of course. Well, if you need to come down to DC to the office, I'll show you around myself."

"Thanks very much, Mr. Cutter. We'll be in touch." Bufort ended the call and put his phone away. They reached Park Avenue and arrived at the Takano moments later by pulling up to a green awning, where they parked the Impala and displayed their IDs for the bellman. Within minutes, they were shown the way to the hotel manager.

"THE FUNDRAISER WAS A TOTAL SUCCESS," the manager said after they made introductions.

He was Japanese, wearing a black button-down shirt and black pants, no tie. His name was Takeshi.

"That's good to hear," Shannon said. "We'd like to be able to have a look around if that's okay. See where the fundraiser took place, hear about what went on. And any video you have from that night, we'd like to ..."

But Takeshi was shaking his head. His close-cropped black hair had an almost bluish sheen. "We've had a ransomware attack over the weekend. We were hacked."

It took Shannon aback. "Have you reported it?"

"Of course we have. We called the local authorities right away. They sent someone here to look at the system. Huge chunks of our data have been encrypted. We can't access it. We're expecting a monetary demand to lift the encryption."

"What's been encrypted? Guest data?"

"No, no guest data. Some employee data. But mostly systems. Our heating and water. And our surveillance, which is why I can't show you any video."

"Your surveillance data is encrypted?"

He nodded. "All cameras. Everything recorded going back a week."

"Going back ... to the fundraising dinner for Joel Nickerson."

Takeshi's expression was hard to read. "Yes."

Shannon traded looks with Bufort. She told Takeshi, "I'd still like to see where the fundraiser was held. Get a sense of the layout."

"Of course."

"Did you have many guests staying in the hotel who were here for the fundraiser?"

He answered as he gave them the tour. The Takano was small but seemed spacious. Beautifully lit, spartanly furnished, typical of Japanese culture. A rooftop dining room and bar served as the venue for Nickerson's fundraiser. Takeshi recounted approximately a hundred and fifty guests. Not exactly intimate, but close. People with deep pockets and a fondness for Nickerson's brand of politics. Around two dozen rooms had been rented to guests attending the fundraiser. The rest had come only for the dinner, the speeches, then left. The whole thing had taken place between 7:00 and 11:00 p.m., though the rooftop bar had continued to serve guests until 1:00 a.m.

"And it had been open to regular guests throughout the night," Takeshi said.

"So people were coming and going. It wasn't an exclusive event."

"That's right. The dining room was only for the fundraiser. The bar and rooftop were open to anyone."

He showed them the locations of most cameras. Several were wedged in the ceiling between the dining room and the bar. One perched outside the door to the rooftop, with another behind the bar. More cameras populated the elevators, the hallways, and the downstairs lobby. Takeshi returned there with the agents, and Shannon thanked him for the tour. "We're going to need a list of fundraiser attendees."

"You'll need to get that from the senator," Takeshi said. "We didn't keep a list of Nickerson's guests."

"Of course." She was admittedly poorly versed in the world of senators and fundraisers and chic New York hotels. The way this case was shaping up, she'd need to learn.

"I'll call him again," Bufort said, meaning Cutter. He swiped at his phone screen and stepped away.

Shannon asked Takeshi, "I know you said it was successful, but did anything happen at the fundraiser that came to your attention? Anything unusual at all, even if it seemed good?"

"It was a busy night, but my staff handled it all with characteristic grace. There was nothing, no complaints; everyone had a wonderful time. I'm sure the senator found many willing donors."

Shannon showed Takeshi a picture of Fain on her phone. "Do you remember seeing her at all?"

"I wasn't here for the fundraiser – I was at home with my family."

"Sure. If I send this to you, you can distribute it to your staff? Ask them if anyone remembers her, remembers anything that stands out from Thursday night? This is Kristie Fain. She's the reason we're here."

"Ah." He looked closely at the picture, his face betraying nothing, then handed it back. "I didn't ask because it's not traditional. You don't question the purpose of your guests, no matter who they are."

"I'm sorry about your problem with the hack. We'll check into it once we're back at the office, and speak to who's in charge of the investigation."

Takeshi bowed. Shannon bowed back and handed him a business card. "If you can think of anything else."

"If I can think of anything else, or my staff has any pertinent recollections, I'll be in touch."

Shannon was listening, but her attention had been snagged. A man had entered the hotel from the street and was standing just inside the door, at the edge of the lobby. He wore a black windbreaker and a New York Yankees ball cap. His face was dark in the dim lighting, the bright backlight of the street through the glass fronting the hotel, but she could tell he was looking at her.

Then he turned around and left.

"Hey," Shannon said. Her voice was low at first, but as she started trotting toward the door, she grew louder. "Hey! FBI – stop!"

She pushed through the revolving glass door and out onto the street. She was just in time to see the man round the corner from Park Avenue to Forty-First Street. He was walking but taking big strides. Shannon started running.

The man went up a block on Park and then took a left. By the time she reached the corner, he was running too – and a good fifty yards in front of her.

She was in shape, but an injury from her first case felt aggravated by Esquivel's tackle that morning. The running turned painful, yet she kept up as the man crossed the next street. By the time she got there, the traffic light was changing, the DON'T WALK sign flashing. She pushed harder, leaping from the curb, her lower back and left glute aching. A horn blared. The taxi starting off at the green light slammed on its brakes as she crossed in front of it. In the next lane, air brakes on a city bus let off a hiss as the driver stopped to avoid hitting her. The driver blared her horn, too.

"Sorry! Sorry!" Shannon yelled. She finished sprint-limping across to the other side.

The man was ahead of her, weaving through pedestrians. He darted between cars, then bolted to the other side of the street. Shannon followed, again narrowly avoiding a vehicle – this time, a white delivery truck – as it swerved.

"Dammit," she said under her breath. "Dammit, dammit, dammit." The words came with the pumping of her arms. Her lungs were working hard, but that was okay. It was her leg, her back. The sense of sharp blades grinding together, mincing her muscle to shreds. She'd been catching up to the guy, but no more.

She just couldn't keep going.

Her body was forcing her to stop. She slowed from a run to a jog, limping along, and then to a grudging walk.

"No," she breathed. "No, come on ..."

Footsteps behind her. Bufort was catching up, his face red, his eyes wide. He stared at her with concern, beginning to slow as he reached her.

"No!" she shouted. "I'm okay – go for it!"

He surged ahead. Shannon kept walking, watching as Bufort ran past some surprised onlookers. Then she lost him over the distance. The man, too, was out of her sight.

She limped on, using the time to get on the phone with NYPD. She called for a canvassing of the area, and gave a description of the stranger. She'd only glimpsed him briefly, but he'd seemed a little older than her or Bufort. Fifties, maybe. Sixties, more likely – but not the "seventy" Esquivel had guessed at. She relayed what he was wearing, where exactly she'd last seen him. The police would issue a BOLO – be on the lookout.

When she caught up with Bufort a few minutes later, he'd gone three more blocks to the west. He was making his way up Sixth Avenue toward Shannon. Raised blood flushed his skin, lines of consternation creased his brow as he looked in store windows.

This part of Midtown was all business, with none of the flash of Times Square a couple of blocks farther east. A Chick-fil-A occupied one corner of the nearest intersection. On the southwest corner, a sign reading "Bead Center" hung on a nondescript building. Other buildings housed multiple shops without obvious insignia.

Bufort reached her. "I had him," he said, still catching his breath. "I was right behind him; then I lost him in a group of people. Fucking group of tourists. I get through to the other side of them, and he's gone." Bufort eyed the shops. "He's here somewhere. Just stepped into one of these places."

"Or maybe he was parked?"

Bufort shook his head. "I didn't see a car." He looked her up and down. "What's going on with you? You okay?"

"I'm fine."

He wanted to ask more, but when she saw an NYPD car slowly cruising, she waved her arms to flag it down. The patrol car pulled up to the curb, double parked. Bufort stayed on the sidewalk, continuing north, peering in windows. Shannon explained the situation to the officers as another NYPD car pulled up.

The cops spread out. Shannon limped along, checking every building, office, shop, along with the rest of them. Some pedestrians were interested, gawking, but most continued on with their lives. It was New York. At West Thirty-Seventh was a grouping of small buildings – the Herald Square District Shopping Court. Vendors sold bags and household knick-knacks out of a series of shed-sized buildings, each no bigger than an average storage bin. Shannon stopped when she saw a man down at the end of the middle aisle between the shops. He'd been standing there, in front of a graffiti-covered wall at the far end, and then had stepped out of sight.

She glanced around, made eye contact with two NYPD officers in proximity, and signaled to them she'd seen something. The officers nodded. Based on her hand gestures, one moved down the northernmost aisle between shops; the other made his way down the southernmost.

Shannon went up the middle.

As she limped along, she brought her hand to her weapon. Of the few scattered pedestrians, one older woman was browsing at a scarf shop, saw Shannon coming, and Shannon pointed toward the street. The woman understood, headed that way.

The graffiti ahead wasn't graffiti at all – on the side of the building abutting the shopping court to the west, someone had spray-painted a "selfie station," replete with a big apple and "NYC" painted in the middle of it. The idea was, take your picture with the wall as a backdrop.

Shannon held her breath, steeling herself as she reached the end of the aisle between shop rows. Not wasting any time, she then stepped out into the gap between the rows and the wall. The man she'd seen stood there, looking at his phone. He looked up at Shannon, then noticed the NYPD officers closing in from either side.

The man was about the right age, the right build, wearing a similar jacket. But she knew, even before the NYPD officers nicely asked him some questions, and he showed them his phone – he was just another tourist, and he'd taken a picture with his phone to send to his wife back home in Ottawa, Canada.

8

"It was Riley," Bufort said to Shannon as they drove back to the federal building. "And we lost him." He sucked down the rest of his Snapple iced tea, then wiped his mouth with the back of his hand. "He's looking for Fain, right? How's he on to the hotel? What's up with this guy?"

"He knows her schedule. Or maybe he was there at the fundraiser." Shannon turned into the parking garage. She stopped for the guard at the security gate and showed her ID, then rolled into the darkness, seeking her spot. Her hip continued to pulse, but the worst had subsided. She probably needed to have it looked at. Ugh. An X-ray? MRI? In the middle of all of this?

Upstairs, Agent Reese had gotten the list of fundraiser invitees from Nickerson's chief of staff. She met Shannon and Bufort in Shannon's office, ready to deploy a small team of agents to start calling the guests and obtain statements.

"And get any pictures and video anybody has," Shannon said.

"Are we compelling people?" Reese asked.

"Ask them to volunteer it. If they don't want to, that'll be interesting to us. But this was a fundraiser. I bet there's lots of pictures. Pictures with the senator, videos of the speeches, maybe even people blowing off steam."

Reese was nodding. "I can start assembling a timeline."

Tyler knocked on the door. He looked both worried and excited as he walked in. "Let's talk about this manhunt in Midtown."

"Not much of a manhunt. There's too many places he could have gone, ways he could have gotten out of there. Multiple subway entrances, a cab at just the right time, even his own car – there are two parking garages in a three-block radius from where we lost him."

After the telling, Tyler was thoughtful. "And he's calling himself a detective."

"At least it was how he got into Silver Towers. Does the name 'Riley' ring a bell?"

"No. But Jim Galloway would like an update. I guess that's what I'm going to give him. That a man impersonating a cop seems to be investigating our missing person, beating up witnesses. And my two agents had him, then let him get away."

Bufort cleared his throat. "If I hadn't stopped for coffee. You know? And I got a little sidetracked listening to street musicians in a drum circle. Amazing what they can do with buckets and spoons."

Tyler ignored Bufort's sarcasm. Shannon said, "Sir, I'd like to go to DC. We've got the schedule coming, but I'd like to see Fain's office, speak to Cutter and the senator in person. And I'd go to her house, hopefully talk to Lockhart."

"What's happening with the apartment right here in town?"

"The team is still going through it. The place looked more like a vacation rental than a home."

Shannon's desk phone rang. The incoming call was from

the main desk. "Sorry – hold on a second, sir." She picked up the handset.

"Agent Ames? Call for you on line three. He said he's a resident at Silver Towers? Milos Dudycha."

"Thank you." She pressed the button to connect. "This is Special Agent Ames."

"Hi, I ah ... My name is Milos Dudycha." He spoke with a heavy Eastern-bloc accent, maybe Russian or Czech.

"Yes, thank you for calling."

"Brianna at front desk, she say you ask about me. About man I saw last night."

"I did, that's correct. Can you tell me anything about him?"

"I not remember much. He was police. He show badge; he say he need to get into building. I think, why he not call? But I let him in."

"I understand. That's a normal thing to do." She grabbed a pen from a mug on her desk and flipped over a piece of mail to write on. "Can you describe this man? How tall? Short?"

"It was very brief ..."

Dudycha went on to describe a man in his late fifties or sixties in a Yankees hat, wearing a black windbreaker. He didn't see any tattoos or scars and couldn't remember eye color. Shannon thanked the resident and hung up the phone. The badge was confirmed – flashed too quickly for detail – but, anyway, you could buy them off the internet. And they already had the physical description. It didn't exactly break open the case.

Reese had eased her way toward the door. Her eyes connected with Shannon, who gave her a nod. *Go ahead.*

Bufort and Tyler stayed, with Tyler exuding more and more tension. He noticed that Bufort had put his foot up on

Shannon's desk. Bufort saw him notice and dropped his foot. To Shannon, Tyler said, "Talk to me about this hotel."

She explained about the hack. "I think this is a pretty big deal. Riley is asking about the fundraiser, and then the video surveillance of the fundraiser becomes inaccessible. We want to keep a close eye on that investigation."

"That's Midtown South. Have you reached out to them?"

Bufort said, "I'm calling them right after this. Find out where they've gotten with it."

"Good." Tyler eyed Bufort as he left, then turned to Shannon. "I don't have a problem with you going to DC. We just need to be sharp. Okay, we have to be consummate professionals. This is a US senator."

"I understand, sir."

"I start hearing about my agents chasing suspects around Midtown, it gets me nervous."

"Why, sir?"

"Why? Because it's messy. I like knocking on doors with arrest warrants."

"Yes, sir. And as soon as we get Fain's phone data back, I'll zero in on that. Mateo says he wasn't sure about a regular route she walked to the train. There's a couple of ways she could have gone." Shannon went to the map on her wall and dragged her finger from Forty-First down Eleventh Avenue. "She could've taken any of these across, then gone down to Penn Station. She probably wouldn't have gone any farther south than Thirty-Third before she crossed. We could pull video from this whole area, but that's ten or fifteen blocks. The pings from her phone should get us a closer look; then we won't be wasting any time."

Tyler studied the map a moment.

"Sir? Can I ask something?"

"Mmm."

"You and Agent Bufort seemed to be having some difficulties. Is there anything I can do to help?"

Tyler turned around. His jaw flexed more a moment before he spoke. "Agent Bufort has had a lot of opportunities. We've been working together for six years. I brought him here, and I'd like to see him ... I don't know. Show me something."

"Yes, sir," she said when Tyler seemed finished.

He started out of the room. "Talk to me from DC."

9

The afternoon train made a handful of stops and would take three and a half hours to arrive in DC. But traveling to DC this way could help get Shannon into Fain's headspace. What was it like to live this kind of lifestyle? Shuttling back and forth between two major cities on the eastern seaboard, working for a US senator, part-time cohabitation with an artist boyfriend – did she like it? Was she living the dream? Or had the blush fallen off the bloom?

Rachel Lockhart had suggested trouble in paradise. But that was mostly because of the boyfriend, the arrogant son of a famous South American musician. Lockhart had even gone so far as to say she thought Mateo might hurt Fain. Because Fain had planned to leave him.

If anything, Mateo Esquivel had seemed defensive, more like a child who'd been both spoiled and neglected, not necessarily a woman-abusing killer. But appearances could be deceiving.

He was an abstract painter who used acrylics, oils, and mixed media. The work was bright, colorful, and gestural – a

"Peruvian Jackson Pollock," according to one critic. But Esquivel didn't seem the reclusive genius. He was a socialite, his Instagram filled with pictures of parties and gala events, many of which featured him solo. Fain showed up a few times, always pretty, always smiling, but with a slight distance. The intelligence in her bright eyes was unmistakable.

Did she love him? Had she been set to break it off with him? Or had something else happened? He was rich – at least, his family had money. In a photo on his father's website, a teenaged version of Mateo Esquivel was nearly cropped out of frame by the sheer number of people crowding the shot. Behind them, a gorgeous home with a lush garden.

She studied the picture of a skinny young Mateo nearly lost in the family photo. Had he done something to his girlfriend? Were the signs of a struggle in his apartment really those of a domestic dispute? Did he hurt Fain, maybe kill her, then use her phone to conjure the story of a disappearance?

The problem there: Shannon and Bufort had just chased someone matching the description of a man who'd claimed to be a detective and was seen entering the Silver Towers. A man who'd seemed interested in finding Fain. At least, who kept showing up places she'd been. In New York, anyway.

And now Shannon was traveling to DC, headed in the other direction.

A mistake?

Fain's contacts, her family and friends, along with her own social media accounts, could provide more context, maybe shed more light on things. Shannon focused on getting to know her better for the rest of the trip.

Kristin Elizabeth Fain had been born in Stamford, Connecticut, in 1995. She had two brothers and two sisters, all older. Shannon could identify with having a big family and being the youngest.

Fain's father had been an aerospace engineer – that was where the parity ended; Shannon's father was a farmer. Fain's mother held two degrees, but seemed to have settled in as a homemaker for most of her life. Trudy Fain had already logged three calls to the FBI that morning; once NYPD had told her the FBI was involved, she'd started calling and asking for updates.

Fain had graduated from Bard College with a degree in journalism, having minored in political science. She'd then spent two years traveling around the world and had been to India, Russia, and Peru, among other places. It was the trip to Peru where she'd met Mateo, though the two hadn't gotten together right away, just kept in touch. A couple of years later, she'd switched from journalism to politics. Working for Nickerson was her first job in the field.

Grant writers didn't make all that much – Fain was lucky if she cleared seventy grand a year. It was possible, though, that Mateo paid the bills in New York, leaving her to only have to pay for one place.

She was typically understated, her hair in ponytails, just a touch of mascara. The night of the fundraiser, she'd stunned in an understated black cocktail dress. Her skin glowed, and her shoulder-length auburn hair flowed. She was young, vital, smart and pretty. She seemed approachable, down to earth. The cliché was the girl next door.

AFTER SHANNON TOOK a cab to Capitol Hill, Nickerson's chief of staff met her on the other side of security. He was bluntly handsome, with a square chin and short, dark hair. He smiled politely and held out his hand, but his eyes conveyed the gravity of the situation. "Special Agent Ames, it's nice to meet you. Though I wish it were a different situation."

"Me too." She marveled at being inside the capitol building, another place she'd never been, as Cutter walked her to
the senate offices. She knew how it all worked – House of
Representatives on one side, Senate on the other – but it
was one thing to read about it, and another to visit in
person. The entire place felt like a witness to history.
Statues and paintings abounded. The decorative fresco
beneath the capitol dome – *The Apotheosis of Washington* –
shined down with preternatural light. Everything felt just
out of reach.

When Cutter led her into a space busy with staffers and
aides, they glanced up from their laptops and phones as
Shannon passed by.

Cutter then stopped in the middle of the room. "Everybody, this is Special Agent Shannon Ames with the FBI. She's
here to find out what she can about Kristie. We need to give
her anything she needs, when she needs it, okay?"

They nodded or murmured agreement, and one aide
offered an awkward wave.

Cutter took Shannon back to Nickerson's office next.

The senator stood and walked around his desk to greet
her. He was dressed smartly in a navy suit. He was older than
Cutter by ten years or so, his hair graying around the edges,
as was his slightly longer-than-regulation beard. There was a
bit of rugged everyman to him, and his brown eyes were both
kind and cunning.

"Agent Ames, thank you for coming. Please have a seat."

"Thanks for meeting with me." She took one of the two
leather chairs. Cutter sat in the one beside her.

Once everyone had squeaked themselves into a comfortable posture, Nickerson folded his hands and looked earnest.
"How can we help?"

"We can start with the basics. How's work been? For
Kristie. What has she been working on?"

The men looked at each other, as if deciding who would answer.

It was Cutter. "Well, like I said on the phone, Kristie is a hustler. Some of the projects she's working on include funding for an addition to a school, improvements to a veterans' park, a new homeless shelter. She was also handling a bit of our communication."

"You mean press?"

"She was still writing for a while after she went to work for us. Writing and getting published in the *Atlantic*, places like that. Impressive stuff, but ... she had to let that go."

"Why?"

"It was just taking too much of her time," Cutter said. "You know – Kristie is so valuable, but there's only so much of a person to go around. We asked her, and she agreed. Plus, you know, when you work for a senator, you have to watch ... you know ... it gets tricky, the opinions you express."

He left it there, and so did Shannon, deciding to revisit it later. "What else can you tell me? Anything particularly difficult that she's been working on? Any major challenges?"

The men watched each other. Cutter shook his head first. "I don't think so. Things have been pretty smooth lately."

Nickerson broke in. "Well, come on, it's Washington. Everything here has some edge, some controversy. Otherwise it doesn't sell papers."

Shannon let herself smile.

"I know," Nickerson said, switching to self-deprecation. "Another cynic."

"No, I wasn't thinking that. When was the last time either of you saw her?"

The men traded looks again. Was it her, or did Nickerson now look a bit stricken?

Cutter answered, "Last Thursday. At a fundraiser in New York. Kristie will often work out of her home in Manhattan, spend weekends up there. We expected her here this morning."

"What can you tell me about the fundraiser?"

Cutter shrugged casually, like, *No big deal.* "Ah, it was a good event. We raised a lot of money, seemed to make a lot of people happy."

She decided to show some of her cards. "Kristie's boyfriend, Mateo Esquivel, was attacked last night. A man who said he was New York Police came in and proceeded to ask questions, then to assault Mr. Esquivel. One of the questions he asked was whether Kristie had said anything to him about the fundraiser." Shannon pulled out her phone. "Mateo states that the man wanted to know 'If she told me about anything that had happened.'"

Shannon looked up from the note and watched the men. They each thought about it, and Cutter shook his head. "There was nothing that night. Nothing that I can think of. Like I said, it was a good night."

She decided to hold back on telling them about the man being at the hotel, the ensuing foot chase. She expected they'd hear about it, and was interested in how they'd react once they did.

She thanked them for now and had Cutter show her to Fain's desk in the main office, where she spent a few minutes sitting in Fain's chair, looking through the drawers. She'd need another warrant to access Fain's desktop computer. Was it her only device? Shannon doubted it. Fain surely had a personal laptop. And if they didn't find it at either of her residences, it was likely with her when she disappeared.

Shannon thought of the suitcase Fain had been pulling as she left the Silver Towers.

A framed five-by-seven photo sat propped on the desk. Fain, her mother and, it looked like, her two sisters, all of them entangled in a kind of group hug. Shannon could see the shared genes in the features of their faces. Fain looked especially like her mother.

What happened to you?

The young woman just looked back from the picture, smiling.

R achel Lockhart moved around with the unsettled energy of someone just arrived home. Riffling through her leather backpack, she pulled out a pack of cigarettes. "I know, I know. Nobody smokes anymore. Kristie doesn't. I hide these from her. She would *not* like it if I was smoking in the house. I don't even smoke when she's gone. Do you mind?"

Shannon, standing just inside the doorway, waved her hand.

Lockhart lit the cigarette with trembling hands. She was average height, possibly overweight. She exhaled smoke and guiltily waved it away. "Maybe she'll smell it and she'll show up," Lockhart said. A moment later, she was hunched forward, crying.

Shannon approached, looking for tissues. Seeing none, she put a hand on Lockhart's shoulder. Fain's roommate seemed to grow more self-conscious and quickly gathered herself, moving deeper into the galley-style kitchen. At the back of the narrow room was a hallway, likely feeding the bedrooms and bathroom. A small living room connected the kitchen to the front door.

"Do you want to go sit down?" Shannon asked. She gestured toward the living room.

Lockhart nodded. She opened the cupboard first and took down a glass, added some water to it, then tapped cigarette ash into it.

Once they were seated – Shannon took the futon and Lockhart the stuffed chair – Fain's roommate seemed to go easier. Maybe it was the nicotine fix. Shannon asked her about Fain, what she'd been working on, how things had been lately. When Lockhart brought up Mateo, Shannon shared that he'd been beaten up. She didn't mention by whom, wanting to see how Lockhart might fill in the blanks.

The woman dropped her cigarette in the glass; it extinguished with a small hiss. She touched her mouth. "You're kidding me. Like, how badly beaten up?"

"Not too bad. Just handled really roughly. Knocked around."

"Why? What did they want to know?"

"Where she was."

Lockhart got a light in her eyes, like something occurred to her.

"What?" Shannon asked.

But the roommate shook her head. "I don't know. That's bizarre, isn't it? Maybe it ... I don't know ..."

"No, go ahead."

"I was just thinking – Mateo's family has lots of money. And people know it. This could be for money. You're thinking of that, right?"

"It's definitely a consideration. But there's been no ransom demand. And then there's the man who showed up."

Lockhart thought about it. The sleuthing seemed to further relieve her funk. "Maybe because Mateo's family thinks *he* did it. They think he's run out of money, and his father won't give him more. So he kidnaps Kristie and acts like he doesn't know where she is."

"Is that true? That he's hurting financially? Has Kristie said anything about that?"

"I mean – no – but that doesn't mean it's not true. Lack of evidence isn't evidence of anything, right? So maybe this guy shows up, he's been hired by the family, because they don't trust Mateo. They think he's the one who did it."

What Lockhart was saying was pure speculation, but it wasn't a bad theory. There was also a variation: Mateo's family *suspected* that he'd committed the kidnap himself to extort money from his rich father, but *Fain had actually been kidnapped* by real kidnappers. Someone who knew Mateo was dating Fain snatched her, hoping for a big payday.

And either ransom had been demanded and Mateo omitted it, or perhaps the kidnappers were dealing exclusively with Mateo's father. Going right to the source. *Give us ten million or we kill your son's girlfriend.*

It was risky, though. Kidnapping was always risky. But when it was a girlfriend? Not a wife or other loved one? Even less plausible.

And again, it left out the hotel. The fundraiser. The hack.

"There's something else," Lockhart said.

"What?"

"After I called the police, saying she didn't come home, I couldn't sleep. I lay awake for ... I don't know how long. It seemed like the whole night. And at one point, I thought someone was outside the house."

"Did you see them?"

"I was in my bed. I didn't see anything, but I heard it. Just someone outside, prowling around."

"About what time was this? Do you know?"

"I checked my phone. It was way past midnight. Almost

one. At first I told myself it was a neighborhood cat. But it would walk, then stop, walk, then stop. Like someone was looking in the windows."

"Really."

Lockhart nodded.

"And no idea who it was?"

"No. Honestly, I tried to convince myself I'd been dreaming. It took forever to get back to sleep."

"I'll look into it."

She brought up the fundraiser next and asked if Fain had drawn attention to it in any way. Lockhart was dismissive. "It seemed like business as usual. She barely mentioned it. And from now until November, it will be campaign, campaign, campaign. It's a good thing the senate terms are six years. Otherwise I don't know how they'd get any work done."

"Does Kristie like working for Senator Nickerson, in general?"

"I think she does. I think, for the most part, she feels like she's doing good work. That's important to Kristie. It's not just a paycheck for her. She believes in it. She wants to help people." Lockhart started to get emotional again and laughed through her tears. "I know, everyone puts someone on a pedestal when something happens. 'Oh, they were so *this*' or 'they were so *that*.' 'What a kind-hearted person, what a saint.' Kristie wasn't a saint, but she was the most honest person I know, the most genuinely caring ... Oh my God, I'm talking about her like she's gone ..."

She fumbled for another cigarette and lit it. They talked a little more until Lockhart calmed, and then she showed Shannon to Kristie's room. There, Shannon browsed pictures and memorabilia from Fain's worldly travels, her stylish clothes, and plenty of books – Isabel Allende, Gabriel Garcia Marquez, and Ted Chiang for fiction. Biographies on women in politics. True crime.

Compared to the Silver Towers, this space felt much more lived in, the repository of her life lived so far. An unlocked trunk teemed with journals. Hard-covered composition notebooks burst with Fain's writing. Observations on current events, travelogues, and it looked like many rough drafts for her freelance articles. She'd been published in the *Atlantic*, on Vox, in the *Post*, and in the *New York Times*.

Shannon spent nearly an hour in the room, getting to know Fain better, then went back to Lockhart, remembering something. She found Fain's roommate on the phone, talking quietly. Lockhart ended the call as soon as she saw Shannon coming.

"Sorry to interrupt."

"No, no. It's nothing."

"Um, you said there'd been a package. Something that came for Kristie last Friday ..."

"Sure." Lockhart hopped up and led Shannon to a corner table stacked with mail. The package was from Zappos – just shoes. Shannon looked through the mail – junk and bills, no personal correspondence.

"Thank you, Rachel. Listen, we're doing everything we can. Okay? I'm going to find out what's going on with Kristie."

Lockhart's lip quivered as her eyes filled with tears. She suddenly hugged Shannon. She promised she'd be alright; it had been a harrowing day, having to jump through all of the usual work and school hoops, she said, not knowing what was going on with her roommate and friend.

"Get some rest," Shannon said.

Before leaving, she had a look around the outside of the home. There were no obvious signs of someone who'd been loitering there, but that didn't mean there hadn't been.

SHE TOOK a cab back across town to Union Station and caught the last train back to New York. It was mostly unoccupied. Shortly into the trip, once more cupped by the large, faux-leather seats, she called Bufort.

"Hey, I was just going to call you," he said. "Spoke to Midtown South about the Takano hack. They've got their computer people on it, and they told me they don't even think it's ransomware. I mean, the hotel data is definitely encrypted, but they're not seeing any way to *de*crypt it. Like, the hackers wanted it that way permanently. As far as where it came from, they said, you know, the digital path bounces all over the globe. They're not optimistic."

She told him about the meeting with Nickerson and Cutter. How there was a lot of wordless communication between them.

"Typical political chicanery?" Bufort asked. "Or something more?"

"I think they were holding something back."

"Like what? About the fundraiser?"

"I think so. But I have no idea what."

"So we've got something that went down there last Thursday. Bad enough that someone hacked the hotel's security system and took all the video footage so we can't see anything. But the hotel manager says everything was hunky-dory. All the guests we've talked to so far say everything was hunky-dory. The senator and his main dude say everything was—"

"Don't say it."

"What?"

"Hunky-dory."

"Fine. Be that way." Bufort instead filled her in on contact with Fain's family and friends, which amounted to a lot of worried people, but no insights or obvious leads. He was currently working his way through Fain's social media. "She's sharp, man. She's a smart lady."

"I've seen a couple of her articles, but plan to read more," Shannon said.

"She's not obvious, you know? She doesn't just play team sports, but seems to take it all on a case-by-case basis."

"That's supposedly Nickerson, too. The press call him a 'maverick.' She was still writing when she went to work for Nickerson, they said. Publishing things. They went out of their way not to tell me why they asked her to quit."

"Huh," Bufort said. "Interesting."

"Yeah, so ... Happy reading to us both."

She spent the rest of the trip devouring everything of Fain's she could find online. Her eyes grew heavy as midnight approached and New York neared.

Agents were expected to work fifty hours a week; most worked more. Everything ran on a basic workday of 8:15 a.m. to 5:00 p.m., but agents worked all hours outside of that, depending on caseload. This case was going to be around the clock, she could feel it. Sleep breaks and whatever food she could quickly inhale. Come to think of it, she'd skipped dinner, and her stomach was rumbling. Maybe the train had a snack car? She got up to start looking.

Prior to the Fain investigation, she'd been tying up several smaller cases to hand over to agents at her old squad in Brooklyn, plus taking some with her to Manhattan. Tyler'd been having her doing things like checking over his speeches and even weighing in on which plants to bring to his new office on the twenty-seventh floor of 26 Federal Plaza. All of that was on hold now. This was a big one, and Tyler wouldn't want anything else in her way.

Jackpot. She found the car with the goods – a full deli with cold-cut sandwiches and chips and soda. Perfect. She was back in her seat, getting her mouth around a turkey sub, when her phone vibrated with a call. Not Bufort, but Caldoza. By the time she finished chewing and cleaned off her fingers with a napkin, the phone stopped.

She waited to see if Caldoza would leave a voicemail, but he didn't. They'd been broken up for a while. She hoped everything was all right with him. She decided to return the call when her phone vibrated again. This one was Reese.

"Phone records came back," Reese said. "Fain was definitely headed to the train station. Pings show her movement; she took Thirty-Third Street as she crossed east to Penn Station."

Shannon remembered it: one lane, everything choked with construction. Okay. This was good.

"The pings stop," Reese said, "and then when they show up again, she's moving a lot faster."

"A lot faster? Which way?"

"North, out of the city, it looks like. But they disappear completely around 125th Street."

"Like someone smashed her phone or threw it in the river," Shannon said.

"Yeah," Reese said. "As they sped away with her."

11

DAY TWO: TUESDAY

S hannon let herself sleep for four hours, drank her coffee standing in the shower, fed her cat Jasper, and was back in Midtown Manhattan as the sun was coming up.

Most crosstown blocks in the city took three to five minutes to traverse; the 500 block of Thirty-Third Street was on the long end. The buildings cast deep shadows as she walked between Eleventh and Tenth Avenues. Men in hard hats gathered in clusters beside corrugated metal containers – the shipping industry called them "cans." The men watched Shannon and Bufort, who'd met her there, as they made their way up the block. Traffic came through: a delivery truck, then a small car, an SUV soon after.

"We need to close the street," Shannon said.

"Yup. On it." Bufort called NYPD from his cell.

While he made the request, Shannon kept moving, looking for any signs of foul play, checking for any cameras. There were dozens of speed cameras in Manhattan, and hundreds more red-light and live traffic cameras all over the city. She bet they were posted at both intersections along this route, and phoned Reese to see.

"Yes," Reese said, "I can tap into the cameras at both ends of the block."

"Do that – and what do you see along the street?"

"Ah, give me a second ... checking ..." A few moments and several clicks of her mouse later, Reese said, "Okay, we got Warner Media, KKR & Company, Soul Cycle ..."

"Which side?"

"All on the south side."

Shannon stopped walking. "I'm looking at a barrier that runs most of the block. Pipe and drape, everything closed off. It will be much better viewing on the north side of the street."

"Okay – that's going to be trickier. There's nothing but Milbank LLP. Legal services, which is back down the other way, corner of Eleventh."

"Understood." The construction men were still milling around. Shannon let a car go past, headed west along the one-way, then stepped off the curb. "I'll see what else I can find."

"But I'll pull everything and put it together for you. Including the south side. You never know."

"Agreed. Thanks, Jenna." Shannon ended the call and approached a group of four men, each in a hard hat and a hi-vis vest. The one not wearing sunglasses wore a red hat and seemed to be in charge. "Hi. Special Agent Ames with the FBI. What are the chances you guys have any surveillance cameras going?"

TEN MINUTES LATER, NYPD arrived and shut down the street. Uniformed police at both ends began to redirect pedestrians.

The road was one-way, from east to west, so vehicles were prevented from entering from the intersection at Tenth.

Kristie Fain's phone records showed that her pings – the regular contact a phone makes with towers in proximity – had abruptly changed somewhere along this block. Even with as many towers as there were in New York, and as good as the technology had gotten, Shannon was unable to pinpoint *exactly* where she had been at any given second. Instead, she had the following information: Pings, coming in roughly every minute, showed Fain's route – or the route of her phone – having left Silver Towers, traveled south on Eleventh Avenue until Thirty-Third, and then to have ventured at least partway down Thirty-Third.

Given the frequency of the pings and the distance traveled, the phone had been in motion at about four miles an hour. Walking speed. But then there was a change.

Roughly a quarter of the way in to the block, Fain's phone had connected to cell towers in this manner for the last time. Because the next ping, having occurred a minute later, was on Twelfth Avenue, also called the West Side Highway. And it was a quarter of a mile away. That speed was fifteen miles an hour. Driving speed.

Had she hailed a cab or an Uber? Maybe. She could have also arranged the ride some other way. Perhaps a family member or friend. Someone she was secretly seeing. Someone that Mateo didn't know about, that Lockhart didn't know about.

It was possible her text to Lockhart about being followed meant a vehicle that then picked her up, but if she was on this block when she sent that text – and it seemed that she had been – then she'd been walking in the opposite direction of traffic, so it didn't quite fit.

She could have been trying to get away from Mateo. From

his family. She might've wanted out of a life and arranged an escape. So as not to arouse Mateo's suspicion, she'd left like normal for the train, but had a prearranged ride meet her and whisk her away.

But why throw her phone away? She would still be very findable. And why not quit her job with the senator? Why not move out of her DC home? Mateo had the address.

And then there was the text about being followed. Was Mateo, knowing what she was up to, coming after her? It might have forced her to make certain improvisations.

Or it was just a theory with too many holes.

Shannon would dig into Fain's phone records as soon as she could – Galloway was working on getting her the access she needed. For now, she walked the street and drank the coffee Bufort had brought her. She imagined Fain walking to the train. Surely there'd been some other people around?

Her eyes studied the ground, a typical city sidewalk. Old gum, mysterious stains, words etched in when the concrete was soft.

And long black smudges.

Shannon slowed, then stopped. She took a sip of her coffee and squatted beside the mark. A good four feet long, like something dragged. Rubber? Maybe plastic.

She stood and got her bearings. She was halfway down the block, maybe less. When her phone buzzed in her pocket, it gave her a little jolt.

Reese was on the line. "I've got video from Eleventh Avenue."

Shannon waited.

"Fain is on it."

REESE SENT it through seconds later. Bufort made shade with
his body, and they huddled around Shannon's phone and hit
play. The traffic camera showed a group of people waiting to
cross Eleventh Avenue. The light changed, and they migrated
across as a loose group, about eight or nine people. Though it
was on her phone, and the traffic cam was not the highest
quality, Shannon was able to identify Fain. Mostly because of
that suitcase she was pulling. But she also recognized the
sweatshirt tied around her waist, the black yoga pants and
white tee.

"Hello," Bufort confirmed.

They watched as she passed beyond the range of the
traffic camera. Bufort started to say something else, but
Shannon kept watching. Eleven seconds passed, and then
another pedestrian stepped off the curb.

He wore loose-fitting clothes, a billowy tracksuit. His face
was concealed by a baseball hat and the high angle of the
camera.

"Hello again," Bufort said.

The man in the baseball hat must've just caught the tail
end of the light, because the cars were moving through at
speed the second he stepped out of sight.

"Riley?" Bufort asked.

"Could be, though he's really dressed in a different style,
and Riley has been in a Yankees hat." She put her phone
away. "Now let's see the rest of it," she said, meaning Fain's
trip down the block.

They went into the Limited Liability Partnership on the
corner, Milbank. It was still early, and the only one around
was an aging security guy. After credentials were shown and
the situation explained – time being of the essence – he took
them into a back room where a computer stored the
surveillance data – several cameras throughout the partner-

ship, including bathroom cameras. The agents didn't need those, but the one camera on the street showed the same scene – Fain crossing the avenue with a group of pedestrians. It only showed their feet, at the very top of the frame, since the camera was angled to pick up people as they entered the building.

The construction group had promised to provide their own video. They used trail cams, the kind hunters used to spot game in the woods, but in this case, the foreman wanted to catch anyone stealing from the job site. He wasn't happy to admit their existence to Shannon, and had done so only after stepping away from the crew.

Shannon and Bufort gathered in one of the giant cans the foreman used as an office. Once he got the video up and running on his laptop, he was politely asked to step out.

Three cameras had recorded the event in low-light mode. One had been mounted atop the pipe and drape bisecting the road. Greenish, human-shaped blobs made their way from Eleventh Avenue, moving toward the camera. The image was worse than the traffic cam, but when one of those blobs stopped suddenly and then seemed to squat down, Shannon figured it out: "That's Fain. She's got a problem with her suitcase and stops right there to check it out."

The other pedestrians passed her. After a few seconds, she continued on. The man following her was nearer.

Shannon leaned closer to the laptop. He was at a distance and in low-light photography. But something seemed off.

"Do you see that?"

Bufort agreed. "Yeah ... His face?"

"Something is way off."

"Yeah, it's not right. I mean the image is pixelated, so that's part of it ..."

Shannon removed the image card from the laptop and

put it in her pocket. Outside the can, the foreman said, "Yeah, take it. I don't need it."

"I'll get you a receipt for it. I just want to make sure it doesn't go anywhere. We don't know what it means yet."

"I understand."

Shannon and Bufort returned to the sidewalk, where she spent some more time studying the scrape mark. She considered again that if Fain was abducted, the vehicle would've come from Tenth Avenue, since Thirty-Third was a one-way. She called Reese, who had already procured the video. "I want to see what vehicles, if any, turned off of Tenth onto Thirty-Third right before the pings change – we've got it to the minute, so that might only be a few cars."

"I'll do that right now," Reese said.

"We'll get a better look at it back at the office. And I want to get into Fain's texts and calls from the phone company. So we're on our way." Shannon took a last sip of her coffee and threw it in a nearby trash can.

Before she hung up, Reese said, "Hey, I got something else. Just came in."

"What is it?"

"I used Facebook to ask if anyone had video of Thirty-Third Street, Sunday night around 6:45. I got a hit. A woman who's an artist documenting the construction in the city had a GoPro camera set up on the north side at the 585 building."

Shannon looked around for a street number. She started east and found it three buildings from the end of the block.

"She shot video from the second-floor window," Reese said. The agent took a breath. "I'm looking at it right now. I can see Fain on there. I can see the guy following her. I mean, he's right behind her." Reese sounded funny. Almost nervous – something she rarely was.

Shannon's pulse quickened.

Reese said, "Okay, just sent it to you. And Shannon,

there's a second man, too. He comes around the barricade in the street, the green fence there. And he's ... well, you'll see."

That feeling returned. The sense of something very wrong in the offing. Shannon thanked Reese and ended the call. Moments later, the video arrived in her inbox. She opened it and watched with Bufort.

A much clearer image. The artist had cleverly framed it to get the sunset behind the construction project, the bones of the scaffolding. But there was a wedge of the sidewalk in the lower right corner.

The agents watched the loose grouping of seven people pass through. They waited. Ten seconds later came Fain, looking over her shoulder.

First there was nothing there. But it was a brief nothing; the man in the cap was right behind her. He was closing the distance.

Before he caught up to her, another man appeared. Like Reese said, he stepped around the barricade in the middle of the street. This was where the barricade ended, and he was free to cross.

His face was wrong.

For one thing, his eyes were too large and too black. And his mouth seemed stretched too far into a grin.

Emotions from childhood came flooding back to her. Her mother talking about the end of the world, demons walking the earth. Shannon's terror that her father and brothers weren't safe, that *she* wasn't safe.

The demon-man stepped up onto the street as if to grab Fain. But if he did, it was out of frame. There was only a flash of her brown hair in the very lower right corner of the shot.

The other one, following Fain, instantly sped up. Before he disappeared out of the picture, he became clearer, too. Because once Fain was grabbed by the first man, it seemed, the following man no longer had to hide.

His head came up, revealing a face equally monstrous. Hideous.

Evil.

Shannon sucked in a breath, almost dropping the phone. Bufort grabbed it.

"Jesus," he said. "What the hell is going on?"

12

T hree of them. Looking at her.

They were mostly out of range, but for a moment she thought she heard them speaking something other than English.

Of course it's not English. They're not even human.

Though she seemed to have just awakened, Kristie realized she was sitting up. The gag in her mouth prevented her from speaking; the ligature binding her wrists and ankles to the chair kept her from moving.

She was groggy, her thoughts not quite able to come together. *Drugged.* They must've given her something. But who were they? *What* were they? It was on the tip of her tongue, a memory she knew was right there, hiding just around the corner, but she couldn't get to it. Her scrambled mind could only produce one answer: *demons.*

But demons didn't exist. These were human. Bodies the shapes of men. Muscular, lean. Two of them, anyway. The third man was bigger, heavier, with a gut. She could see it because he wore a white T-shirt that was too tight-fitting for his physique. He had a gut and thick, hairy forearms.

And he looked at her again, sending a bolt of fear from her neck to her tailbone. A pulse of raw energy.

His eyes were black. His mouth was black. The same black formed dark blades beneath his cheekbones.

And something else was wrong. His image was somehow further distorted, as if she were seeing him from underwater.

Her mind was so sluggish it took her time to realize that the three (*demons*) men were standing on the other side of glass. Still indoors, then? No. It was sunny out there, with motes dancing in the rays, fuzzy dots that looked like tiny insects. Trees in the background.

So they were standing beyond the glass doors leading to – what? A deck? At some place in the countryside?

One of them put a cigarette to his misshapen lips and took a drag. He exhaled smoke from his nostrils, just two holes in his face. His nose was black. He nodded and exhaled again out of his ruined nose and looked in at her.

At this time, the first man to have started watching her – the heavier set man with the black eyes and wide, grinning mouth – slid the door open. Sounds and smells rushed into the room as he stepped through: birds chirping, cigarette smoke mixed with freshly mown grass. Crickets, maybe, or frogs, as if from a nearby pond.

Then he closed it, cutting off the input.

"You're awake," he said.

English. At least, she thought it was English. Her mind still balked at taking the full measure of reality. As if she was in survival mode, protecting herself from feeling too much too soon. From admitting too much too soon. Lest she go into a shock from which she might not recover.

He stopped a few feet away, where he put his hands on his hips and cocked his head at her, just slightly. An inquisitive demon-clown.

"Do you have to go to the bathroom?"

It was an unexpected question. She thought about it. Surprisingly, she didn't have to. She shook her head to inform him. She realized she was trembling. All over, trembling. And when she made a sound – she hadn't planned to – it came out like a pleading mewl.

That noise, one she'd made herself, was the most terrifying thing of all.

"Hey," the demon-clown said. He came closer, as if to touch her, like he might comfort her. But he stopped just short. "Don't do that. Okay? Don't cry that way."

He had an accent. Usually, she was good at detecting accents, but maybe not this one. Maybe not now when her mind was running away in multiple directions.

Oh god ... Have to get out of here! Oh god I'm gonna die I don't wanna die–

Stop it. Relax. Think. You can figure this out.

It's a dream. I'm dreaming about being in hell ...

The demon-clown lowered down on his haunches, putting his nightmare face directly in line with hers. She wanted to look away but couldn't. She focused on his eyes. The burst capillaries threading the whites around his dark brown irises. So brown they were black.

And he smiled. A full smile, revealing teeth.

And at that, her mind rebooted. He closed his lips, drawing the curtain back over those crooked teeth, but she'd seen it – a simple thing that helped her to make sense of everything. All the information that came flooding in, filling her mind – it had all started with that one small realization.

Paint.

He was wearing face paint.

Just then, when he'd smiled, the lines in his cheek had cracked the face paint enough to reveal fissures of flesh-colored skin.

Paint. That was what it was. The men had painted faces.

Of course they did. They weren't masks, and they certainly weren't creatures from another world.

The men wore makeup that looked like demonic clowns, for God's sake. Black eyes and mouths and noses – each was a little different from the next. One of the men outside had black across his chin, like a damn chinstrap.

She almost started cackling. But, like the scream, that kind of raw emotion would only send her over the edge.

And, besides, what followed this observation about her captors wasn't funny at all. As her faculties at last returned, as facts and memories reclaimed residency in her head, Kristie understood something.

She knew who these men were. If they were wearing face paint – and it had the same crude similarities to the type worn by men she'd previously encountered – she knew who they had to be.

Which, the more she considered it, was worse than them being creatures from the Bible.

The stink of cigarettes rode his breath. "Listen, I'm going to say to you something, okay?"

His face didn't match his voice, which sounded almost kind. His face was a nightmare, like a Rorschach blot.

"I'm going to say to you that I like you. I think that we would be friends in real life. So I'm going to watch out for you, okay?"

Not knowing what else to do, she nodded.

"Good," he said. "First things first. I'm going to pull out that nasty gag. Okay? That way we can communicate. But now, listen. You can scream if you want to – it doesn't matter; there is no one around to hear you, I promise. But we will hear you. My friends there on the deck will hear you. And it just ... it won't be nice. Okay? So no screaming."

Again, she nodded.

"Good." And he touched her now, reaching out to her knee, giving it a squeeze. With his other hand, he pulled the linen napkin from her throat, soaked in her spit.

Kristie gagged and tried not to do worse – vomit – as the demon-man walked out of the room. She heard something like a trash can open and close, and then running water. The kitchen was there, at the front of the house, same side as the deck. The two men kept their backs to her, still smoking their cigarettes.

She thought about what he'd said. But more than making the men mad, she worried that to scream now, she might never stop. She had to stay calm, had to stay rational. If she just reasoned with them, explained things, it might be over soon.

The man returned to the room, wiping his hands on a towel. "Yuck. Yucky business. But no more gag. Okay?"

She coughed a couple of times before offering, hoarsely, "Thank you. I'm sorry."

He waved away her apology as he dropped the towel on the back of a nearby chair. Part of a nice living room set, she saw. Her chair was wooden, as if pulled from a dining room table. "All part of life," the man said. "People think everything is supposed to be so nice all of the time. But life is messy. It's dirty and it stinks."

He took a few final steps toward her, then stopped. He smiled again, but then his attention drifted. For a moment, he was just looking around the room, neither admiring it nor judging it, but just taking it in. Then he turned for the glass door.

"Well," he said before sliding it open, "if you do need to use the bathroom, or if you're hungry, let me know. Okay? I'll be your friend."

Kristie swallowed dryly. She nodded and realized she was

shaking again. The two men outside had turned around and faced in as the third stepped out to join them.

I'll be your friend ...

They all looked in at her.

And she knew who they were.

13

"TIK," said Bufort, pronouncing the acronym *tick*. "We think it stands for Time Keepers. They don't call themselves a militia, but the Southern Poverty Law Center does, and so do we. They're an antigovernment citizens' group, relatively new, spreading fast."

Shannon had shaken off the initial fear – a reaction, an irrational response owed to some childhood memories – and her logical, analytical self was back in control. "What's their objective?"

"They're opposed to the new world order, but with a twist – they blame everything in the government on private capture. Corporate interests."

Bufort had brought up the file on his screen. Shannon and Reese looked on as he flipped through digital images. In most pictures, TIK members wore black and white makeup. Like sinister clowns.

Shannon said, "I've never seen a citizens' group wear face paint."

Reese spoke up. "It's to thwart facial recognition. See how a lot of them have black around the mouth? It redefines the jawline. Most facial recognition technology identifies areas of contrast around the eyes, nose, and chin to compare with a database. The black paint redefines someone's key features, making it nearly impossible for them to be recognized."

Bufort took a still frame from the video captured by the artist on Thirty-Third Street and placed it beside the image of a young male in similar makeup. The styles were the same.

Reese continued, "They got it from a heavy metal group called Insane Clown Posse. The members of that group – and their fans – wear similar makeup."

"To evade detection?" Shannon was vaguely aware of the group Reese referenced. Maybe college – she might've known someone who was a fan.

Reese seemed more familiar. "I've never seen anything to indicate that the musical group, or their fans, wear the makeup for that reason. And there's no evidence that fans of the musical group are the same as TIK members. What they share in common is aesthetics only – TIK co-opted the face makeup."

Bufort jumped in. "TIK is new. Four, maybe five years going. Organizations like the Oath Keepers and Proud Boys have been around for a while. When I worked domestic terrorism, the Time Keepers had just shown up."

"Time Keepers – do we know what it means, precisely?"

"No. They're clandestine and very clever online, so there's not much. But what little has been turned up suggests they're keeping time, keeping score. Or it's a countdown to some future date. The only other information we have is that the average member seems to be younger than the average member of all other antigovernment groups. But again, that's without having a lot of data, a lot of known members."

Shannon reached past Bufort and clicked an arrow key to see more pictures. Most of the images came from CCTV. "How are they organized?"

"There's a chapter in several major US cities. New York, LA, Chicago. But it's a cell structure – you know the guys in your cell, that's it. And the organizers leave action up to the individual members. Even within a chapter. They're careful to maintain plausible deniability."

"So they're mostly anonymous, they're young, they distrust the government and dislike corporate power. Do I have all that?"

"That's sums it up, I guess. They pretty much hate everybody."

Shannon kept scrolling through, hoping for a plain face, a profile. "You said there's only a small list of known members – anyone we could talk to?"

"For that," Bufort said, "we're going to need a trip downstairs."

THEY TOOK one of the dedicated elevators that ran between the twenty-second and twenty-eighth floors down two flights. Agents from the antigovernment squad recognized Bufort and seemed happy to see him. The one in charge of TIK information was named Kilburn. After everyone shook hands, he took Shannon, Bufort and Reese into a private room. They ordered in lunch and ate while perusing profiles of the eighteen known members.

Like Bufort had said, the Time Keepers tended to be on the younger side. Instead of cops and construction workers, they held jobs in mostly tech, service-retail, and many worked remotely. One thirty-two-year-old named Thomas Galdi worked for Priceline. He'd been identified through his interactions on social media.

"But Galdi is the exception to the rule," Agent Kilburn said. "Most of these guys, if they're doing any sort of interacting online, they're using aliases, using VPNs, sneaking around on the dark web. There are very few public access points. A lot of your other antigovernment groups, they like being right out there in your face. And their members aren't so disciplined. We've been able to identify bad actors in several instances where they telegraphed their plans online, essentially. Which makes sense, when you think about it from their point of view – most of these groups don't want to hide. They feel they've got every right to be doing what they're doing, and they don't care who knows it."

Bufort said, "But in those cases, we're talking about protests and the occasional scuffle. TIK might've kidnapped a congressional aide."

"Yes, exactly. Which is also why they're going to be a lot quieter, a lot sneakier, if they're doing something like this. And that seems to fit their MO – the anti-recognition makeup, the general underground nature of the group. Any ideas as to their motive yet?"

The agents on the other end of the table exchanged looks. Bufort and Reese then deferred to Shannon. "We're working on it."

"Fair enough. Most of these guys don't get in trouble. They're quiet. But that doesn't mean they're not dangerous. TIK has its share of pasty white guys who work at Kinko's, but that's just the outer rings. You start moving inward, and you get to guys with a sharper edge. Criminal activities that fund and support the organization. There's plenty of cybercrimes – we think this group is skilled in ransomware attacks, for one thing. And they like to have plenty of muscle around to protect their space. Which brings us to Drexel Murphy."

Kilburn was using a flat-screen that mounted to the wall and connected wirelessly to his laptop. When he clicked a button on the keyboard, a new face took center stage.

"Murphy didn't get on our board because of social media,

like Galdi. He was arrested last week for assault and battery. This is the type of guy we think TIK uses as muscle. He's twenty-six, and he's got a bit of an anger management problem. He beat up a couple of guys at his local bar. Apparently, it was a political argument. Murphy nearly killed both of them. One of them is in a coma."

"Nice," Bufort said sardonically.

Shannon had put *TIK=ransomware* in her notes. She asked Kilburn where Murphy was being held.

"You think he's the one you want to talk to?"

She studied the young man's face. The bruise on his cheek. The pain and anger in his eyes.

She glanced at Bufort and Reese, who each nodded, as if to say, *Go for it.*

"He's at Rikers Island," Kilburn said. "So if you want to go talk to him, see if he's the chatty type, that's where you're headed."

IT WAS GETTING LATE, just past eight, when Bufort knocked on the door to her office. Bufort typically had two speeds – regular-hours relaxed and overtime relaxed – but tonight he moved with purpose, pointing at her laptop. "Check your email."

He'd sent her a file, and she opened it. Mostly screenshots from his own computer. He stood beside her as she looked it all over. "Kristie Fain," he said, "has interacted with TIK online. More than once, and mostly on Twitter. They said something about Nickerson, criticizing him, saying he didn't go far enough with his agenda. Some libertarian stuff. Fain stepped in and said that they had good ideas, but they went too far into conspiracy territory and Big Brother nonsense. So they basically accosted her, called her a failed journalist, called Nickerson spineless, all this stuff."

Something twitched in the back of Shannon's mind. Nickerson's chief of staff saying something about how they'd asked Fain to stop her freelance writing.

"She didn't back down," Bufort said. "She was polite, professional, but she basically called them a bunch of bratty kids in tinfoil hats." He circled around to stand beside Shannon and look at her screen. "Fain says, in essence, 'I don't want you on my side if you're going to act like this.'"

"On her side how?"

"Politically, I guess. Nickerson is not as unpredictable as some people act like he is. He's a centrist Democrat who leans libertarian, basically. And the Time Keepers are presumably libertarian. They don't like what Fain says about them, and they let her know. She stands her ground, pushes back. Then, here – read this quote – this is how it all winds up."

Shannon did: "*I'd be careful, Fain. Keep talking like that and something's gonna happen to you.*"

She looked up at Bufort, who met her gaze with wide eyes. "They fucking took her, Shannon. They didn't like what she had to say, and they made her disappear."

AND THAT WAS THE DAY. At 9:00 p.m., Shannon urged Bufort and Reese to head home, get some sleep. Tyler seemed satisfied with their progress. A domestic terror group who'd abducted a congressional aide was big news. But more importantly than the optics, it seemed they were getting closer to the truth and hopefully to saving Fain.

With luck, TIK just wanted to scare her. Teach her a lesson. Have a couple of guys in their demon clown makeup pluck her up off the street. A show of power. *We can take you any time we want. We own you. Don't ever humiliate us again.*

It didn't explain "Detective Riley," but then, maybe it didn't need to. He could have been anyone, a PI hired to search for Fain by someone in her family. No one had come forward with that, but maybe Shannon needed to start asking the people in Fain's life some hard questions.

She drove the Impala home. Tomorrow she would visit Drexel Murphy and see if she could make a deal with him. Riley was important, but not a priority. Their goals might even be one and the same.

When she pulled onto her street, she noticed a familiar car in front of her building: the sixth-generation Ford Mustang was painted black with shiny silver rims.

Instead of parking on the street like usual, Shannon turned into the half-circle driveway and pulled up in front of the Mustang, nose-to-nose. A moment later, its driver's side door opened, and out stepped a handsome man. Muscular, dressed in jeans and a white T-shirt, his brown leather shoulder holster holding his Glock 17. The only thing missing was his aviator sunglasses, but it was nighttime.

Shannon opened her door and stood opposite him. "Hi."

"Hey. How you doing?"

"I'm good." She tilted her head at him. "How come you didn't park?"

Caldoza shrugged, and his mouth turned down at the corners. "I didn't want to be presumptuous."

He had texted her earlier in the evening, asking if they could talk. She'd felt bad for missing his call the night before, and invited him to swing by when she got home. She'd then texted as she left Manhattan that she was on her way.

"Well," she said, "when I invite you over, it means we can talk in my apartment. We don't have to talk on the street."

He shrugged again and tried to hide a smile. "Okay. Well

..." When his eyes connected, she saw the seriousness of his intent. "Listen, Shan. I just want to say something."

"Is Rafe okay?"

Rafe was his young son from a previous marriage. She had her reasons for concern.

Caldoza waved them away. "He's totally fine. He's doing great. He's not what I'm here to talk about. Well, indirectly, he is. But I mean, it's about us."

She felt relieved about Rafe, but concerned with where the conversation was headed. Was this the best place for a relationship post-mortem? Standing in front of her building, cars idling nose-to-nose? "Listen, why don't you come up ..."

"I just wanted to say that I should have told you about him. When we first met. Not later. I waited too long, and it spooked you. That's why I've been calling you – to clear the air about that. It hasn't been right with me."

He was referring to the fact that she and Caldoza had dated for over a month before he'd mentioned having a son.

"I'd say I was just being cautious, just protecting him ... and I think that's partly true."

"It's okay. You don't have to."

"Just let me say it, all right? I know that we had other problems, too. Especially after what happened. But not telling you about Rafe right away meant that I wasn't sure about you. That's at least how you took it. And you should've taken it that way. It was stupid of me. Because I knew as soon as I told you that I'd messed up. I'd waited. And I never should have waited." He crossed between the two cars, coming toward her. "I was just scared. Because you're amazing. And I was an idiot for hesitating. And then for hiding behind the idea I was protecting my son. And I'm sorry."

He reached for her, and she took his hands. She had some trouble meeting his gaze; he picked up on it. Again, maybe this wasn't the best place or time for this discussion, but here they were. "I appreciate that."

He looked into her eyes. "And Rafe is fine. I know you're worried. But he really is."

"That's good. I'm very glad to hear it."

Caldoza sighed then and frowned a little. "You're seeing someone? That's cool ..."

"I'm not, actually. Listen, we can talk more. I just need to ..."

But he'd let go of her hands and was already backing away. The line of his mouth curled into a kind of sad smile. "It's okay. I just wanted to say that. You deserved to hear it."

"Luis ..." But she had nothing else to say.

"And good luck in New York. I never got a chance to tell you congratulations. You're gonna do great there, Shannon. I wouldn't be surprised if someday you take over the whole thing."

She could only watch as he offered another smile, then sank into the Mustang. The engine gurgling, he backed up a little, then rolled forward. The window tint concealed him as he passed. He drove to the edge of the driveway and out into the road. The gurgle turned into a clatter as he raced up to speed.

She listened to the engine until it faded completely.

Back in her car, she parked on the street. She waved to the night manager as she passed him in the lobby. Jasper greeted her at the door to her apartment, and she fed him, gave him fresh water, then pulled off her shoes.

Oh, that felt good. So good that she decided to keep going and changed into some sweatpants. Before cinching them tight, she spent a minute examining the bruise on her hip from hitting the table when Mateo Esquivel had tackled her. She went to the bathroom medicine cabinet and shook out a couple of ibuprofen. She needed to take time out and see someone about her hip and back.

Soon.

Sprawled out on the couch, she clicked on the TV and watched for a few minutes, letting thoughts of Caldoza go, letting her mind fuzz out. She'd planned to stay there for a little bit, but the mounting fatigue was too much, and she went to bed.

And dreamed of men with demon faces, and dark rooms, and Kristie Fain calling out from one of them. Calling out for Shannon to save her.

"Here comes the airplane, right into the hangar," Eddie said.

Zoe wasn't interested. The three-year-old stared past Eddie at the TV, where some family of kangaroos – if that was what they were supposed to be – acted like people with Australian accents. Two girls and their mom and dad, going on family adventures, having family problems. Zoe loved it. And the old airplane-into-the-hangar trick wasn't working.

Eddie set down the fork with the eggs on it. He rose from the kitchen table, grabbing the remote. "Okay," he said. "Apparently we can't watch TV and eat our breakfast at the same time."

"Grandpa, no!" Zoe started kicking her legs. She shook her head back and forth.

"Well? What is it gonna be? You gotta eat, kid."

Sunlight streamed through the bay windows of the dining nook. It was shaping up to be a nice day out there; a shame his daughter was missing it. She worked so late, slept half the day.

Eddie aimed the remote at the TV as he looked over his shoulder at his granddaughter. "So? What's it gonna be? Eat breakfast and have TV? Or TV goes off?"

"Eat!"

"All right." He sighed. "But no more funny stuff."

She kicked her legs some more and bounced up and down in her booster seat.

Tammy's little row house was a nice place. Not very big, but cozy. Expensive, though, this neighborhood. But Tammy refused to leave. She said that, since Zoe had been born there, saw her first sights and smelled her first smells there, it was where she belonged.

Pretty romantic for New Jersey, Eddie thought, but his daughter was damn smart. If she said that the things a kid experienced when they were first born were too important to leave, then she was probably right. Eddie had pretty much stayed in the same neighborhood he'd grown up in, too. And look how he'd turned out.

He set the remote back on the table and sat beside his granddaughter. Zoe deserved every chance at happiness she could get. The kid was never going to know her father. Joe was gone. She deserved to stay in the house where she was born. And to watch the show about the talking kangaroo family while she ate her breakfast. "All right," Eddie said. "Open up, kid. You're a big giant, and you're stomping around, and you come across this yellow school bus. Eat it up!"

It was enough to distract her from the TV show and pay attention to him. The thought of being a giant eating a school bus seemed to delight her. She opened her mouth, and he forked in the eggs.

There. One bite down, a few dozen more to go.

HE'D NEVER WANTED Tammy to marry a cop. Not because of the mortality rate – cops actually did pretty all right in that department; deaths in the line of duty were rare – but because being married to a cop was a hard life.

Tammy had a big heart, though. Plenty of room. As a kid, she'd always helped people. In third grade, she'd assisted the Moritz boy on and off the school bus every day. People hadn't really known much about autism back then, but the Moritz kid could fly into tantrums and bang his head. So Tammy always helped him, sat with him at lunch, this kid in a hockey helmet, and talked with him.

She'd gone into nursing school and had just passed her boards when she'd met Joe. He'd come into the emergency room to see about a little boy he'd pulled from an auto wreck. Tammy had been the emergency room nurse. The boy had survived, and Joe had visited him once more when the kid was close to full recovery. During that visit, Tammy had asked him out on a date.

They hadn't been together long. Just three years before she'd gotten pregnant with Zoe, and then not quite two years after that. When Joe died, it was a week before Zoe's first birthday. She was three now.

In the interim, Tammy hadn't dated. She hadn't even made the attempt. She said she was too busy.

"You mind if I watch something, kid?"

Zoe didn't respond. She was on the carpet with markers and crayons strewn about, drawing some squiggly-looking creatures that might've been meant to be human. Eddie drank his coffee and flipped through the channels, stopped when he got to the news. The press conference was being covered by NY1, but it was also on CBS, NBC, Fox, and CNN. Big stuff.

An NYPD officer in uniform stood at a podium of microphones, flanked by other officers in blue and one man in a gray suit. According to the chyron, he was *Gale Warren, Assistant Chief and Commanding Officer for Midtown North.* Warren and company were on the street, with a backdrop of Midtown shops, including one bright red awning advertising 99c KU FAMILY DISCOUNT.

"... the report, originally with Washington DC Metro Police," Warren said. "From there, it came to us, since Ms. Fain is also a Manhattan resident."

The chyron switched: *Senatorial Aide Kristin Fain Missing Since Sunday.*

Warren continued, "We opened an investigation and have asked for the FBI's assistance. We're asking that, at this time, if anyone has any information as to the whereabouts of Kristin Fain, to please call the tip line number on your screen."

Warren, who had a mumbling problem and spoke too fast, went on for another minute, then walked off without taking questions. The news anchors spent a minute more speculating about Fain's disappearance before throwing it to a highlight reel on Nickerson, her boss, the "maverick" senator from New York.

Recent footage showed Nickerson talking to the press outside the Capitol Building. He planned to vote no on the upcoming infrastructure bill on the floor before Congress. The bill included a provision to overhaul municipal surveillance in the country's largest cities. Crime was up everywhere, particularly shootings, and law enforcement needed better tools for catching crooks. But, along with most Republicans across the aisle, Nickerson thought it went too far. *"This is a slippery slope. Today it's a surveillance system to catch and deter criminals, but by tomorrow, it's a social credit system. I'm not interested in taking our policy cues from Communist China. This is the—"*

"Did she eat?"

Tammy was scuffing into the room, wearing her worn-out pink slippers and ratty toothpaste-colored bathrobe.

"Yeah," Eddie said, looking at Zoe as she drew marker on the back of her hand. "Sort of."

Tammy bent and took the marker away. "Honey, Mommy doesn't want you drawing marker on yourself."

"Mommy!" Zoe jumped and locked her arms around Tammy's neck.

Eddie got up from the chair and grabbed Zoe around the waist, hoping to take some of the weight off his daughter. "Here, I got her."

"It's okay." Tammy scooped up the girl, who clung to her mother like a little monkey. Under the ratty bathrobe, Tammy wore a white, tight-fitting tank top. She looked too thin. She leaned toward him and gave him a peck on the jaw. He bussed her cheek.

"Thanks, Dad," she said.

"I got coffee made," he said, hurrying ahead of her into the kitchen. "And the pan's all ready. I'll crack you a couple of eggs."

"Just the coffee's fine for now." She bent to put Zoe down, but the girl continued to cling. She'd been babbling, too, the whole time, asking Tammy if she wanted to see her do a headstand. "In a minute, honey. Draw me a picture."

"Okay ..." Zoe released her grip and went back to the markers and paper on the floor.

Tammy shuffled into the kitchen. Eddie sliced off a dollop of butter and dropped it in the pan, where it sizzled. "Not taking no for an answer."

"Dad, I'm not hungry. It's too early."

"It's almost eleven."

"I work the night shift. I get in at five in the morning. It's a miracle I'm even up."

"I know, I know."

She took a mug down and poured coffee from the decanter. Yawning, she stirred in milk and sugar. Eddie cracked two eggs. His strategy was simple: quiet determination. He might even try putting a couple of slices of bread in the toaster next.

When he glanced at Tammy, she was pausing mid-sip and staring at his hands. "What did you do to your knuckles?"

"Nothing. Just at the gym."

"At the gym?"

"Hitting the bag."

Tammy looked at him, disapproval in her gaze. Along with worry. You used gloves to hit a bag when you went to the gym; everybody knew that. It was a bald lie. He'd considered putting makeup on his hands, or at least coming up with a better story. But Tammy saw through everything. They were two people who'd lost their spouses – well, hers to street violence, his to divorce – and they knew each other's tricks.

"Dad," she said in a low voice, "what are you doing?"

"Just making eggs." He pushed the spatula around in the pan. Eggs cooked fast. You had to keep them moving. "That's all," he said.

Finally, gradually, Tammy took another sip of her coffee and released him from her stare. When he plated her up the eggs a minute later, she actually sat to eat them.

And when he set the meal in front of her, he quickly pulled his hand away so she didn't have to see the bruises again.

15

D rexel Murphy was tough, but Rikers Island Jail Complex dwarfed him. Made his tribal tattoos look trite, the menace in his eyes transparent, a poor concealment of fear. Rikers was an old jail, notoriously corrupt, physically crumbling. The complex was on an island, and it felt cavernous, the home to some mythological creature. It served as New York's county jail, where offenders came while awaiting court dates or serving short sentences. Bail reform had changed some of that, but not for Drexel Murphy.

"Let's talk about why you're here," Shannon said, having sat down on the other side of the thick glass and put the phone to her ear.

"Why am I here? I think we want to talk about why *you're* here. That's more interesting, I think."

There was a slight drawl to Murphy's speech. He was from the Midwest, some whistle-stop town called Barre, Kentucky.

"I'm here because I want to know about TIK." No point beating around the bush. She waited to see which tack Murphy would take.

"TIK? Are you saying TIK? I don't know what that is."

Feigned ignorance, then.

"TIK is short for Time Keepers. Does that make it clearer?"

"No, I don't know."

Shannon scootched a little closer in her chair. "Mr. Murphy, I'm going to be blunt with you, because, speaking of time, I don't have much. A woman is missing, and I think TIK might have her."

"I don't know nothing about them."

"The FBI has a list of their suspected members, and that list includes you."

"What?" He shook his head, now feigning incredulity. He was twenty-six, but the lines in his face made him appear older. He wore his hair short on the sides and long on top. Each time he acted like he didn't know TIK, he ran his hand through the longer hair, sweeping it back.

Shannon said, "Mr. Murphy, you're in here because of an assault charge. If it were some nonviolent crime, you might be sitting at home wearing an ankle monitor while you wait for court. But you nearly killed this man. The New York district attorney wants to prosecute you for attempted murder."

Murphy barked a laugh and shook his head. He scraped his hair back.

She went on: "Your public defender is going to try valiantly, I'm sure, but you have a previous aggravated assault conviction. At best, you're going to get assault in the first degree, which is a B felony. A B felony carries a sentence of at least five years, as much as twenty-five, and that all depends on the judge."

Murphy's eyes connected with her. For a moment, he dropped the act and looked plainly concerned. Then he swallowed and shook his head, swept back his hair again. "Nah. My lawyer said I'm gonna get probation."

"Maybe if it was a class D felony charge. But that's not what the DA is moving forward with. Mr. Murphy, the DA considers you a danger to society and wants you in state prison for as long as possible. The only way that outcome is any different, right now, is through me."

In truth, she'd studied Murphy's file and thought he was a danger to society, too. Until he had some mental health support to deal with his abusive childhood, public safety was a concern, and he ought to be off the streets. But a woman was missing and in trouble. So Shannon had met with Jim Galloway that morning and proposed the following: that they get the DA to reduce charges and let Murphy go with house arrest and mandatory counseling for a year in exchange for his cooperation. Galloway had called over to the DA's office, and it had been arranged.

She explained this to Murphy. "But I need you to admit your affiliation and give me some usable information. If you can do that, your future looks a lot brighter. You can get out of here, for one thing."

Murphy chewed his lip and considered it. She knew the prospect of leaving was highly attractive. Murphy might be tough, but everyone had their limits. Rikers had racked up nearly ten thousand assaults the previous year. The blood-stained walls echoed aggressive catcalls, the rats squeaked in the dark. "Let's just say I give you something. What if I'm wrong, or it doesn't turn out to help you?"

"Then we're right back where we started."

"That ain't very fair."

She lifted her shoulders and let them drop. "I can't give you the kind of help I can give you for nothing. If what you tell me isn't any good, if it's some wild-goose chase, then I don't have anything to give. I need a name and an address. I need to know who set up the kidnapping of Fain."

Murphy immediately shook his head. "I don't know nothing about a kidnapping."

"Then I need names. I need every TIK member you know, their names and addresses, phone numbers if you got them."

When his long hair fell in front of his eyes, he left it. "I don't know anybody important in the group. Just a couple of regular people."

"Tell me about them. Tell me how you got involved in TIK. Did someone recruit you?"

He sighed and finally pushed his hair back, and then he told her his story.

Murphy had left home at seventeen and wound up in New Jersey when he was nineteen, worked odd jobs, including driving a delivery truck and stacking shelves at a grocery store. But his attitude kept getting him in trouble. He'd walk off jobs in anger. He'd even come to blows with his employers – the aggravated assault was from the grocery store job; he'd thrown cans of soup at the store manager, hitting him in the face.

"The best job I had was working for Getty's," Murphy said, referring to an auto mechanic located in the Bronx. "Getty was this old fucker, bent sideways from his bad back, from leaning over car engines for fifty years." Murphy had moved out of New Jersey and into the city once he'd landed the job working on cars at Getty's. He liked cars, and he liked Wayland Getty. Getty liked to talk politics and was the only guy talking that made any sense, as far as Murphy was concerned.

"Getty was old school, you know – all our problems were from the breakdown of society. People leaving the church, women going to work, the government handing out free shit."

"And Getty ... he was a part of TIK?"

Murphy shook his head. "Getty had another guy working there, too. Paul Kruger. Kruger was into politics, too. I didn't always agree with him. Neither did Getty. But he was smart. And, yeah, he brought me to a meeting one night."

"Tell me about it."

Murphy sighed. "I thought it was going to be me and him and some guys drinking and smoking and bitching about everything. But we went to this pretty swank place in Harlem. I'm talking, like, the new yuppie Harlem. This building was wild – there was red carpet in the hallway and ... what do you call those things. The soldiers that stand there, just the armor ..."

"Suits of armor."

"Right. This place had all of that wild stuff. And the people inside were pretty normal, right? Like an AA meeting. Except they were wearing this face paint. They looked like crazy-ass clowns."

This was good. She was getting somewhere. "Did you have to wear it?"

"I did, yeah. Paul had paint, and we did it. I thought it was a little gay or something. But I agreed with a lot of what the guy there had to say."

"What guy?"

"The guy running the meeting."

"Do you have his name?"

"No."

"Can you describe him? Height, weight, eye color, the sound of his voice, lisp, anything? Did he have tattoos like you?"

"He wore a white shirt. Like a dress shirt. He was maybe thirty? Thirty-five? Average height. He had the makeup on."

"Did you get the sense he was in charge? That he ran the New York chapter?"

Murphy shrugged. "Not really. He didn't talk about chapters or nothing. He just talked about the country. Society, the future. All of that."

"What did he say?"

"He said the government had become a private, for-profit corporation. A corporate state, something like that. Basically, the politicians are just there to protect the money. That's what Paul would always say that would get Getty all riled up. Paul would say that the founding fathers were just rich assholes. That it's always been about rich assholes protecting themselves – their rights, their property. Their slaves. And that now, we're the slaves. The working class. And they want to control us and spy on us and keep us dumb, fat and happy while they take us for all we got."

Shannon asked, "How long were you with the group?"

"Well, that was four years ago. I was twenty-one, twenty-two. So, that long."

"How many of these meetings did you attend?"

"Half a dozen, maybe? They were once or twice a year. The rest of the time it was just me and Paul."

Murphy explained that they were given missions. Sometimes they had to pick up a package and take it from point A to B. Once, they'd driven a truck, and Murphy was sure it was full of stolen goods. But most of what TIK did was online, and he wasn't much of a computer user.

"Like what? What did TIK do online?"

"I don't know. They might've been into hacking and shit like that."

"Ransomware?"

"I don't know."

"How about Riley? Have you ever met anyone named Riley, or heard the name mentioned?"

He shook his head. "Nah. Don't think so."

"Think hard."

"No. No one with a name like that."

She and Murphy talked a little bit more, but he seemed to have reached the limit of his useful information. Meetings were always in different places, he said, different apartments, and at random times. He had no idea of the names of the higher-ups in the group. Or who was in charge of the New York chapter, whether it was the guy from the gentrified Harlem neighborhood or not.

He struck her as someone who had the usual government angst, but chance had brought him to Paul Kruger and then TIK.

"Where's Paul now?"

Murphy shook his head. "No idea. For real. Getty had surgery on his back – his lower lumbar got fused or something – and eventually he had to sell the shop. Paul and I had to find jobs. We kept in touch for a while, but then I lost track of him."

"Have you seen anyone since Paul wearing the face paint?"

"No. No one."

Murphy said the last time he'd attended a TIK meeting was over a year before. He'd drifted away from it, or it from him. But not from politics. "You try to go out and have a drink and someone is talking shit at the bar."

He was surely referring to the assault that had landed him here.

"Yeah," Shannon said. "It's a problem. We all have to get ourselves under control."

Murphy nodded. He ran his hand through his hair and stared into the distance a moment. "I'll tell you one thing, though, man – TIK members like to party."

It sparked her curiosity. "You mean drugs?"

"Yeah, that. And I mean, like, raves and all that. Stuff a little country boy like me had always heard about. Clubs, raves. Lotta late nights."

Another twitch in the back of her mind. An image: the faded club stamp on Mateo's hand.

"Did you go out to some of these raves?"

"Oh yeah, definitely. I always thought, you know, I pictured, like, the Village People. But it's the real deal. Crazy scenes. Fuckin' intense."

"Can you tell me some of the places you'd go to?"

He started rattling off names of clubs or locations – old warehouses, large basements, giant empty houses in the deep suburbs. None rang a bell. What was the one Mateo had gone to? She'd have to check her notes.

"What about the guy from the meeting? The one in the white shirt? Did you ever see him out at any of these clubs?"

"No. Not personally. But I heard of a couple he sometimes went to. Real underground places."

"Can you write them down?"

He nodded. "That I can do. And then I get out of here, right?"

"I'll work on it."

16

They'd start with a citywide search for people in Time Keepers makeup. And they'd watch the clubs. In particular, the four clubs Murphy had named. It wasn't a perfect lead, but it was something.

It had been a long morning; getting in and out of Rikers involved lots of security. Shannon was glad to see the complex recede in her mirrors as she crossed the bridge back to Queens.

Astoria Heights had a place with good sandwiches, so she sat in the Impala for a few minutes, eating, trying to shake the chill that had invaded her bones. The August day was hot and humid, but the jail had left her cold. The feeling of being watched lingered. Inmates and guards dissecting her with their eyes.

She switched on her analytical mind. Jails were fascinating – they housed the failings of a society. Some people were born missing vital chemicals in the brain. Many more had been damaged by adverse childhood experiences, their humanity buried under layers of trauma. But we didn't yet know how to deal with that, not in the criminal justice sense, except to lock up the damaged person when they lashed out. It was necessary to keep the public safe, but it was only one piece of the equation. The rest we were still figuring out. If we ever would.

And in the meantime, there the inmates sat.

Finished eating, she balled up her wrapper and set it on the empty seat beside her. Thinking a moment about TIK and nightclubs, she called Mateo Esquivel. Thankfully, he'd learned to answer the police at this point.

"Mateo, how are you doing?"

"Considering my apartment is turned upside down? And everyone in Kristie's family has been calling me all day and telling me I'm responsible if anything happened to her? I'm good."

"I'm sorry about the mess in your apartment. Everything will get put back together. Mateo – you were at a club the night Kristie left for DC. You called it the Rumpus Room."

He hesitated. "Yeah ..."

"You ever go anywhere else?"

"Sure. I go wherever."

"Wherever?"

He hesitated. "What does going to clubs have to do with anything? Have you learned something about Kristie?"

"You'll be one of the first to know when we find her, I'm sure."

"You seem pretty confident."

She let that go, hoping he'd answer.

"Um, yeah, I've gone to Bembe, House of Yes, B66 ..."

She wrote them down. "Have you ever seen anyone at a club wearing face paint?"

"Doing *what*? Wearing paint on their faces?"

"Like the band – Insane Clown Posse."

"Insane Clown Posse? I've never heard of them."

"You're a musician. Your father is a musician. You never came across Insane Clown Posse?"

"No. Sorry."

"Okay, well, think about something elaborate, like a clown. Lots of white and black, geometric shapes sort of reshaping the face."

He was quiet for a while.

"Mateo?"

"What you're saying makes me think of Inti Raymi."

"Okay, and what's that?"

"It's Peruvian. It's a festival called the Celebration of the Sun. It goes back to the Incas. They celebrate on the shortest day of the year – June 21. It's the first day of the new year on the Inca calendar."

She wrote that down, too. "All right. Thank you."

"Your people were in my place for hours."

"That's their job."

"You're not going to find anything here to help you. I didn't have anything to do with Kristie disappearing."

Sensing the shift in tone, Shannon sat up a little straighter and chose her words carefully. "I believe you, Mateo."

"Maybe we were having trouble, but I'd never hurt her."

She could talk to him again if she needed to. "I appreciate your time. I'll be in touch."

She ended the call. It had crossed her mind to mention TIK, but if he had an affiliation, he might say something to other TIK members. She hadn't worried about that with Drexel Murphy; it was much harder for him to talk from jail, plus she thought he was genuinely isolated and had only connected to TIK through Paul Kruger.

She used her phone to get a little more background on the Peruvian festival. Peruvians wore masks at Inti Raymi, or white balaclavas that looked almost like Guy Fawkes, and extravagant costumes. The folklore was fascinating, but not very much like TIK, when it came right down to it.

Still, coincidences were rare and shouldn't be easily dismissed. She passed it to Reese in a quick email, then put the Impala in drive and headed towards Manhattan.

A COUPLE of desks had been put together in the common area of the twenty-sixth floor. Three people in suits, two men and one woman, were waiting as a staff member hooked up phones. Shannon made eye contact with each of them and smiled politely as she walked through to her office.

Mark Tyler knocked on her door moments later. "You saw our guests?"

"Yes, sir."

"The DOJ has a group of attorneys solely dedicated to cases involving high-level elected officials, and when one of their aides goes missing, they get the call. Everything you do here has been, and will continue to be, under a microscope."

"Understood."

He almost said *Counting on you, Ames* – she could feel it in the air. But Tyler just gave her a quick nod and left.

THE TIP LINE had been flooded with calls, filtered down to a few given priority. Shannon went through them, lingering over a call from a woman who said she thought she'd seen Fain stopped at her suitcase somewhere around Eleventh Avenue. The agent on the call had asked good follow-up questions, but the woman didn't recall seeing anyone or anything out of the ordinary after that, and could remember the make and model of no particular vehicles that may have passed her along the street.

Next, the subpoena of Fain's cell phone carrier had produced records of her recent calls and texts. Shannon and Bufort spent the afternoon poring over the data. So far, everything checked out. Calls to Fain's mother and sister seemed innocuous; nothing hinting at distress or previewing disaster. Nothing, even, related to her relationship with Mateo, other than a brief conversation with her mother, with Fain explaining, "Mateo? Oh, he's good. You know him. Busy with his projects ..."

But that was only her personal life. Work-related correspondence was another matter. Since Fain worked for a US senator, any calls dealing with work had been flagged. The DOJ attorneys needed to gain further court approval before the material could be made available for the investigation. Even then, every text, every email would be screened. The lawyers would redact any information they deemed sensitive. A tedious process, antithetical to the speed necessary in a missing persons case. But there you had it.

In the meantime, the lawyers were busy checking the statements Reese had obtained from fundraiser attendees. Shannon watched them a moment. A horseshoe of brown hair ringed the head of one lawyer who wore his white pressed shirt with the sleeves rolled perfectly. The woman was a redhead, hair scraped back into a tight French braid. She seemed the friendliest, but that wasn't saying much. The second man looked almost identical to the first, but with more hair. They could be brothers, but weren't. All together, they fit the stereotype of uptight government lawyers. But then, Shannon had always had a soft spot for uptight government lawyers.

When she ordered in dinner at 6:00 p.m., she asked them what they wanted to eat. Each politely declined and worked steadily until they were finished evaluating every statement. When they turned them over, Shannon and Bufort dove in. Reading for just over an hour, they concluded that no one had reported anything out of the ordinary. Each of the attendees, interviewed over the phone that day by Reese and other agents in the squad, recollected a fun evening, the typical fare. A night that began with cocktails, then evolved into a leisurely dinner punctuated by speeches, followed by another bout of cocktails, these imbibed at the rooftop bar. Only a few people even knew who Kristin Fain was, or remembered her. Those who did claimed she'd been cheerful and upbeat.

Nothing the attendees had to say seemed to shed any new light on the fundraiser. It was going on 8:00 p.m., and it felt to Shannon like they'd hit a wall. Bufort headed to the kitchen for an iced tea, and she popped into Reese's office.

"Hey."

"Hi. I checked into Inti Raymi."

"Okay, great." Shannon dropped into the empty chair next to Reese. "Anything interesting?"

Reese pointed her to a series of colorful images of a festive parade. "Some of the celebrators wearing makeup are Ashaninka, a large South American indigenous group. They have a history of bloody internal conflict in Peru. Right now, their communal reserve is under threat by a proposed dam. Completion of the dam could displace some thousands of the Ashaninka people."

Shannon studied the pictures. "So maybe Fain's kidnapping is some kind of political protest?"

"I checked to see if Mateo's father is in some way involved in the government's hydroelectric projects. Maybe a celebrity spokesperson. But he's not. There's really no way to connect the Ashaninka to this. Or the festival, really. The makeup doesn't match."

"I thought the same thing." Shannon sighed and sat back, gently twisting in the swivel chair. "What else? Bufort and I went through all the fundraiser statements ..."

"Yeah, nothing earth-shattering there. But, here – let me show you the pictures and video from the fundraiser."

"Great." She straightened up to watch. "Any shots of our beloved Detective Riley?"

"I've got no one who fits the description of Riley from the fundraiser night. Or, depending on how you look at it, I've got more than fifty. Because the most popular demographic at the Nickerson fundraiser is easily a sixty-something white man."

Reese had combed through hundreds of candid cell phone pictures provided by guests of the Thursday night fundraiser, and watched several hours' worth of cell phone video, including video from various "Marco Polos" – an app that people used to send short video messages back and forth.

She had grouped the images into files and opened one. "I'm separating out everything that has Fain in it, and in chronological order. So, in addition to the statements, we're starting to have a real picture of the night, a timeline of events."

The first thing Shannon noticed – it was hard not to: Fain looked beautiful. In an elegant black dress, straight hair brushing her shoulders, she was understated, letting her natural beauty shine through. She smiled in every picture she knew was being taken. Even when she appeared in the background, accidentally captured in the shot, Fain appeared relaxed, at ease, having a good time. Just like the guests had thought.

Reese had been grouping Nickerson's photos as well – of which there were many more. He alternately posed with guests or was caught in conversation, drink in hand. Plus videos and pictures of the speech he gave in the midst of the meal.

Shannon's mind drifted as she watched, thinking about culture. About the Ashaninka and the idea that Fain was a political captive. She worked for a US senator, after all …

Were the Ashaninka equipped to hack the Takano Hotel and steal system data? Why, for that matter, was anyone interested in wiping out that data? It looked so much like an ordinary evening, a successful, yet unremarkable event. A computer specialist team with NYPD were working the hack, but so far without results. Was it possibly a coincidence? Shannon doubted it.

So what was the point? What was there to hide?

Looking through the images, she lingered over one of the cell phone pics in the Nickerson group. A man and a woman were taking a selfie, foreground, while Nickerson crossed the lobby behind them. She remembered it: the statue of the giant black cat in the center of the room.

"Hang on … wait – that's Nickerson?"

The figure in the background was facing away from the camera, just a quarter of his profile.

Reese looked. "I'd say so. I grouped the image with the others."

Shannon studied the image closely. "I guess it looks like him."

"Same suit, same height, weight, hair color. He's headed for the stairs. Why? You don't think it's him?"

"Maybe it is."

"That jacket he's wearing is an Italian cashmere Sutton suit jacket in navy. Looks to me like a tailored fit. See that? That's a traditional notch lapel. I bet there's full Bemberg lining and a classic Sutton two-button closure."

Agent Reese knew clothes. Hands down, she was the best-dressed in the squad, anyway. "Is that rare?" Shannon asked. "Very expensive?"

"That jacket probably costs $1,200. The pants, maybe $800. I guess it depends on the standards. For a senator? Not that expensive."

Shannon thought about it. Something was off about the man in the photo; she couldn't let it go. "Can we get this moment from any other angle? Around this time? What's the closest you have?"

Reese showed Shannon the images by time. They looked at three images taken just before the one in question, and then three images taken just after it. None showed the man.

"All right," Shannon said, resigned.

"Wait. I only added this one photo from this guy. CEO of Metzer Pharmaceuticals. But he took two or three." Reese found the relevant images and pulled them up. Indeed, the CEO had taken three quick photos in a row. Each barely a second apart, it was enough to show a slightly different angle of the man's face in the background. More profile.

Shannon examined it closely, feeling her skin prick with goosebumps. She was right. "See right there? The nose is different. The cheekbone. This guy's younger, too."

Reese was looking. "I agree."

They didn't know what to make of it. Reese flipped through other photos that were clearly of Nickerson, pointing out the features of the suit, the cut of his hair. It was baffling.

Just that one photo with someone who looked like Nickerson, but with those slight differences that both she and Reese agreed were there.

Huh.

MAYBE SHE AND Reese were seeing things. Like Reese pointed out, he was the right height, the right hair color. All this shit with the weird face paint had her extra critical of faces, maybe. Skewing her judgment.

Causing her to obsess for no good reason ...

Back at her desk, she made a phone call. It was now going on 9:00 p.m., but oh well.

Keith Cutter, Nickerson's chief of staff, seemed happy to hear from her. "Agent Ames, I hope this is good news?"

"Not yet, I'm sorry. But we're doing everything we can."

"I'm sure you are."

"Am I bothering you at home, Mr. Cutter?"

"I'm still at the office. I'm here until ten or eleven some nights. I'm out most of the day – it's only after dinner that I can get any work done."

"I hear you."

"What can I do for you?"

"Well, a question. Do you ever use body doubles for Senator Nickerson?"

Cutter paused. "We have, yes. It's rare, but we've done it. Why?"

She hesitated too, weighing her options, then decided. "Did you use a body double at the fundraiser at the Takano last week?"

"No." This time his answer was quick. "Why?"

Again she considered explaining, but if they hadn't used a double, would they have invited the double anyway? It made no sense. It had to be someone who looked like Nickerson by chance. And who also had the same taste in two-thousand-dollar suits. "We're going through all of the images we can find of the fundraiser, and need to clarify some of them. To be sure we know who we're seeing."

"You still just looking at Fain's schedule?" There was a

dryness to his tone – he knew she was keeping things from him.

"I'm sorry, Mr. Cutter. It's an active investigation. I have to ask questions that I can't always give you the context for."

"No, I understand ... I also understand the DOJ has sent you some lawyers?"

"That's true."

"Are they behaving?"

"They're very polite."

She continued to converse with Cutter, found him easy to talk to. She said what she could say, no more. He added a few details about the fundraiser – Fain had left around eleven thirty, he said. She'd seemed in good spirits the whole night, though he'd barely had a chance to talk to her. They'd sat at two neighboring tables – Fain with other staff members, Cutter with his wife – but they might as well have been at different events.

Everything he said checked out with what others had reported, including Mateo, who'd said Fain had returned home shortly before midnight.

Cutter was dying to know why Shannon was so interested in the fundraiser, but she kept her confidences, and he stayed professional. After five minutes, they said their goodbyes.

When the DOJ lawyer knocked on her door – the balder man – it was to inform her that he and his colleagues were turning in for the night.

"Thanks. See you in the morning."

"You too." When his cheeks stretched back toward his ears, she realized he was attempting to smile. Then he left.

Bufort, arriving, watched the lawyer walk away. "That man is a sex machine," Bufort said. "I can tell." He slowed as he approached Shannon's desk, observing her with an almost catlike caution. "What's up? We ready to get out of here?"

"Yeah," she said slowly.

"What is it?"

She didn't know. That bad feeling lingered, but her thoughts were blurring together. She gave a slight shake of her head, felt her mind clearing a bit. "Nothing." She stood up, felt her hip give a little as she walked, then held out her arm for Bufort to take. "Let's go, big guy."

17

L ower Manhattan. Tribeca. Just west of Chinatown. Eddie didn't spend much time here, not anymore, but he knew the area: city hall, the 2nd District US Court of Appeals, the Federal District Courthouse, the Metropolitan Correction Center, all within walking distance. It was a neighborhood of law enforcement, the power of government hidden behind reflective glass and steel columns. Muted. Watching.

He'd parked on Thomas Street next to the fancy sandwich shop Pret a Manger to do some watching of his own. The rearview mirror reflected the entrance to the Jacob Javits Federal Building.

26 Federal Plaza.

The New York office of the FBI.

Of the fifty-six field offices in the United States, New York was its own animal. If it wasn't the biggest, it acted like it. When you pictured stuffy agents all looking like they came from Iowa, that wasn't New York. In New York you had wise-cracking city guys, slick Italians from Brooklyn, thick-skinned Irish from Woodlawn and Pelham Bay.

He'd been watching since 5:00 p.m., when some of the agents had started trickling out, done for the day. He'd been watching at 6, when the greater majority had left, some going south on Broadway, likely toward the subway station at city hall. Others rounded the corner onto Duane Street and entered through security to a parking lot, where agents with vehicles left for home.

Just before 9:00 p.m., Eddie saw the blond man exit the building. The one who'd been at the hotel, the one to chase him through Midtown until Eddie finally lost him by dropping down into the subway at Herald Square. He'd had to wait three hours before daring to go back for his car, but it had been worth it.

Right behind the blond man came the woman. The girl, really. Using his small binoculars, Eddie sized her up. Young, barely thirtysomething. Fit, but not overly muscular or athletic. He detected a slight hitch in her giddyup, a limp stemming from her right hip. Maybe that was why she'd been unable to catch him.

Just before they reached the street, the two agents stopped. They spoke a little, and she smiled, and he smiled. Did they like each other? Were they fucking? No – he didn't think so – but something was there. You got used to noticing; cops of all stripes were always jumping into bed together. It was how *his* marriage had ended, anyway.

The male agent then turned and headed north up Broadway. Either he lived close, Eddie figured, or he took the subway to the train and then the train home. Probably not Iowa, though this guy looked the type.

She went the other way, going south on Broadway until turning down Duane Street. She had a car, then! Good news; he wouldn't have to stash his again. Eddie quickly put away the binoculars and started the engine.

He was so excited he almost clipped a pedestrian who

was jaywalking across Thomas Street. The guy gave Eddie a dirty look; Eddie smiled and raised a hand and ducked a little, out of instinct, like he could hide his face. He drove quickly to the end of the block, made a right on Church. This was a gamble, but he didn't know any other way. He'd been watching the agents as they came out, measuring the time it took for them to get into their vehicle – if they were driving one – and leave. Just under two minutes was the average.

Goddamn all this construction. Every side street was cut down to one lane. There were concrete dividers everywhere, green cloths up to shield pedestrians. New York was always such a mess. Development never stopped.

He took Church to Worth Street, made another right. He was circling the block. Watching the clock on the dashboard as he went, too – almost two minutes had passed when he made the right onto Broadway. Now he was going south again, passing the FBI building on his left.

He quickly pulled over on the opposite side of the street, near a fast-food joint. *Dunkin Open During Construction!* People walked beneath the scaffolding, mostly suits, with a few tourists and oddballs thrown in. Eddie kept his eyes on the security gate just ahead and to the left. He hoped he didn't have to sit long. He felt too exposed here, too obvious. But that was just the jitters; it had been a while since he'd done any of this sort of thing. It was easy to forget the basic rules – like how, especially in New York, no one was paying attention to you.

On the other hand, tailing a fed was no joke. He could wind up doing a little time if he wasn't careful. He could even lose Zoe, lose Tammy. Maybe this whole thing was a bad idea ...

The cute agent rolled up to the security gate in a dark Chevy Impala. Government plates. They called them "BuCars."

Eddie could see her through the glass. Same brown hair, same youthful face. The gate arm lifted, and she rolled out and turned onto Broadway.

He followed her.

SHANNON KICKED off her shoes and stripped out of her shirt as she walked to the bathroom. Jasper greeted her with a plaintive mewl, then watched from his spot on the back of her living room chair as she finished undressing and turned on the shower.

Her mind felt crowded again. Too many things jostling together. The hidden significance of the Nickerson fundraiser. The man who'd beaten up Mateo Esquivel and run from the Takano. Mateo's nightlife, the testimony of Drexel Murphy. Not to mention the presence of the DOJ lawyers in her office.

Everyone was looking to her for leadership. Bufort, Reese. In recent months she'd been questioning whether she was even a good fit for the Bureau. Since her career began, she'd taken two lives in the line of duty, neither of which she seemed able to get over. She'd seen the therapist she was supposed to see for six months.

Now she was in charge of a team of agents for one of the biggest Bureau offices in the country. How was she doing? Holding her own? Or piss-poor awful? She had no sense of it.

What she *did* know: It had been forty-eight hours since Kristie Fain was reported missing. Every day in a missing person investigation meant the odds dropped considerably. Two days gone was a milestone. It didn't bode well.

She stepped into the shower, determined to right her mood. At least, to let the water beat down on her until she felt marginally better. Enough to maybe make a small snack – dinner felt like a day ago – and climb into bed.

Two minutes into the shower, her phone rang.

Damn.

She started to get out, then decided to let the voicemail pick up. But she couldn't do that. She was a lead investigator. People were counting on her. She hadn't even soaped up yet.

Shannon shut off the water and threw back the curtain. Her phone was still in her pants, halfway between here and the front door. Dripping, wrapping herself in a towel, she fished it out before it went to voicemail. It was Patterson, one of the agents put on the TIK leader detail, searching for places he might turn up.

"Hey," she said.

"Hey. I got a possible location. We're on a club in Long Island. Place called Save the Robots. Seems like a big night, lots of people coming in and out. And quite a few of them are in the face paint."

"Have you checked it out?"

"Holguin was in for a quick look, but he doesn't look like a clubber, and we didn't want to tip anyone off. Here's the thing – we've got people crawling the city. No other sightings of face paint. This is where they are."

HALF AN HOUR LATER, she was on her way to a suburb on the south shore of Long Island. She could have sent in other agents, but she wanted to do this herself. She wanted a look at this group. And maybe someone higher up in the chain of command was with them.

Patterson was parked in the lot of a Path Mark grocery store next to a smaller building with a big sign for BEST DEAL LIQUOR WAREHOUSE. Shannon got into the car with him and another agent, Holguin. Patterson was big and slow moving; Holguin was more lissome. Patterson had shaggy black hair; Holguin's buzz cut was gray around his ears and temples. Neither of them looked like club-goers.

The air smelled like seawater. The ocean was across the street, the Atlantic somewhere beyond the massive, mostly dark industrial building. The only part lit was the sticky red light from the street-level entrance. Muffled, beat-heavy music emanated from the same door. "It was a grist mill," Patterson said, looking. "Been converted into a nightclub. The millennials love this kind of thing. They either want to live in these old buildings or party in them."

Maybe, Shannon thought. Next door, blocks of townhouses sat on the water, brand new, raised on stilts, with banners claiming FURNISHED MODELS OPEN DAILY. Someone was snapping up those new homes, too. East Rockaway was once a shipping and trading center; now it was expensive housing and nightclubs. You couldn't stop the march of progress.

Patterson said, "Like I told you on the phone, we've been here since ten. Around eleven thirty, we started seeing the people with the paint on their faces."

Holguin showed Shannon pictures he'd taken with a digital camera and telephoto lens. Young men, mostly, but a few women, their faces white and black. Big, dark eyes for some of them; bleached, pointed chins.

"All right," Shannon said. "So what do we do?"

The agents in the front seat looked at her. "It's your show," Patterson said. "You tell us."

MORE AGENTS ARRIVED. Shannon had two of them run an errand for her; they'd need to find an all-night drugstore to accomplish it. By the time Bufort got there, the other agents had returned, their mission successful. Bufort looked at the contents of the plastic bag they'd brought back from the drugstore, then looked at Shannon with a flat expression. "No way."

"Yeah."

"It's just a nightclub." He'd joined them in Patterson's BuCar. He faced Patterson. "You've seen regular people coming and going, right?"

"Yeah, sure."

"I mean, it's not all clowns in there, right?"

"No. I'd say it's about half."

Shannon said to Bufort, "We have agents posted up all over the city. This is the spot where people are showing up wearing TIK makeup. If we go in looking like this, we're not going to get very far. I want to see and know everything I can. That's why I asked you to dress casual."

Bufort looked down at himself, as if considering whether the blue jeans and gray T-shirt fit the occasion. "Yeah, I'm the picture of neo-punk ..."

Shannon gestured to Patterson. "Can I get your jacket?"

The agent removed his blazer and handed it over. Shannon had Bufort put it on. "There. That's how they do it. Jeans, T-shirt, blazer."

"That's how they did it a few *decades* ago ..."

Shannon ignored him and opened the compact mirror she'd bought. The makeup wasn't top quality, but novelty – greasy face paint. But it worked. It took ten minutes to do a decent job. Bufort had finally acquiesced and smeared it on himself, too, mumbling curses as he did.

For her outfit, she'd chosen ripped jeans and combat boots, a personal favorite. Her T-shirt read "Throat Punch Donor" – it was a garment left over from one of her undercover jobs. TIK didn't seem particularly fashionable or interested in some sort of stylish statement. Their brand was their face paint, so Shannon concentrated her efforts there, helping Bufort when she was finished applying her own.

He avoided eye contact with her as she shaped the black paint below his mouth, creating a new jawline. Patterson and Holguin were grinning in their seats, whispering and occasionally tittering.

"I hate you guys," Bufort said.

EDDIE WATCHED the two agents cross the street toward the club.

"Holy shit," he muttered. "She's got some balls, this one …"

After the agents reached the other side, they stood in the queue at the entrance. It had been moving pretty swiftly so far. What was building up was the presence of agents in the Path Mark parking lot. Six of them, by the latest count. Eddie was glad he'd made the decision to stake out her apartment. But when she'd left it an hour ago, he had no idea he'd end up here, fifteen miles from Manhattan in goddamn East Rockaway. But the fact that he was – and that this agent chick was going to such lengths – meant they could be onto something.

The way the feds were descending on this place made him wonder – maybe Fain was in there? He remembered that the boyfriend, Mateo, said he'd been out to a club. Even had a stamp on his hand. Maybe he was a party to it after all. The people in that club could be working with him, and they had Fain in there right now. It looked like the kind of place you could hide someone – an old mill, a place that once ground cereal grain into flour and middlings, now with plenty of big rooms and dark spaces for hiding a kidnap victim.

God, wouldn't that be something.

But what was with the face paint? Was it some kind of party, some sort of cult thing? If so, he wasn't sure the cover was going to work for the feds; they looked like yuppies trying to sneak into a square dance.

Eddie decided he wanted to get a closer look. To have a front-row seat when this thing inevitably went all to hell.

18

T humping music. Blue laser lights crisscrossing the darkness. Everything else was shadows, grinning demons in the gloom.

A bar cornered the first room. The only liquor was vodka in a dozen brands. Bufort ordered for them while Shannon looked around. She was no expert on New York City nightlife, nor was this technically New York City. But the name – Save the Robots – she'd done quick research on it after Patterson's call. There was some attempt here to recreate another place called "Robots," a club that had once operated out of a basement in the East Village. Serving only vodka was a hallmark. As was the simple, grungy décor and the almost listless attempt at anything "clubby" – the wands of blue light like someone's afterthought of how a club should look if it was called "Robots": vaguely futuristic. Meanwhile, a few of the patrons wore leather with lots of hanging metal, like the punk rockers and skinheads of 1980s New York. They stood around tables and talked over the loud electronica music or gathered in small clusters. One skinny man juggled glow-in-the-dark sticks, off in a corner by himself.

This room was something of an antechamber for the main space. Bufort paid for the drinks and led them into the next room, where a DJ in a corner booth cranked out bass-heavy music. A thick crowd jumped to the beat, and the dance floor shook the room. A balcony circled it from above, with more tables packed tightly together. Shannon found the stairs and headed up, squeezing through the patrons who clogged the way. Bufort, tall and broad-shouldered, was barely able to follow.

Off the balcony, a room behind a glass partition might've been an operating booth when the building was a mill; now it was a second bar. And this one seemed to be catering exclusively to men and women in clownish face paint.

Shannon caught Bufort's eye and signaled to him. He saw it; he knew she was headed there.

Another bouncer guarded the entrance where a couple of young women waited for admittance. Shannon watched as the bouncer pulled a device from his back pocket. The women stepped closer, and the bouncer shined an ultraviolet light on their foreheads. The light illuminated an image inked on their forehead resembling a heraldic lion. He waved them through.

Shit. While the bouncer on the street had only checked IDs for age, this one sought a mark for entry. Shannon retreated, but bumped into Bufort. He was confused; he hadn't seen it.

"Hey! You two coming in?"

Shannon turned back around. "No, thanks – we're all right."

The bouncer came closer, eyeing her up and down. The crowd surged behind her and Bufort, blocking their escape. He shined the ultraviolet light on her forehead, then checked Bufort next. When he spoke into a walkie-talkie, it was too low to hear. But then he raised his voice to them: "Don't go anywhere."

Shannon said, "That's all right – we want to dance."

But it was too late. And she knew it even before she saw the other man in face paint shoving his way through the crowd toward them. Or the one who came out of the door to the private bar, eyes black and mouth white.

"I told you!" He was young, angry, spit flying from his white-painted lips. "I fucking told you we needed someone outside, some kind of security."

The second man was dubious. "We don't own the fucking club."

The thundering music kept most people from noticing. A couple of patrons glanced over, but what they saw didn't seem to be enough to worry them – a man and woman getting patted down. The rest jumped on the dance floor below.

It was enough to worry Shannon, though. Not because they would find weapons – she and Bufort had left their firearms outside. But the gun digging into her kidneys. The guy carrying it had been the one to grab her, while the private-bar bouncer had moved beside Bufort. Bufort could have the bouncer down on his face if he wanted, eating the floor, but Bufort had seen the gun. The last thing they wanted were casualties, and the armed guy was a live wire.

"Listen." Shannon tried to keep her voice level, but loud enough to be heard. "Let's just talk. If we can–"

"Shut the fuck up." The aggressive one dug the gun in deeper as his arm slipped around her neck. Drawing her close, he spoke in her ear. "And don't get any fucking ideas. I can see you getting ideas."

"We gonna take them downstairs?" The bouncer was still holding Bufort. He had Bufort's arm pinned behind his back, but seemed to guess Bufort was tougher than he looked.

Three more men came out from the private bar. Judging by their movements, their physiques, they were all late twenties, early thirties.

Surrounded, Shannon considered announcing herself as law enforcement. But would it change things for better or worse? Most people had a healthy fear of harming government officials, but TIK could be impulsive. Aggressive. Like the one holding her.

And if they were keeping Fain, this could lead to her.

"Yeah," he said. "Let's take them downstairs."

He shoved Shannon forward, and another member grabbed her, so that there were now two handling her, three on Bufort. The odds kept changing for the worse.

THE MUSIC WAS QUIETER, a muffled thudding overhead. The Time Keepers led Shannon and Bufort down a long hallway run with pipes: the underbelly of the old grist mill. The metal door at the end of it appeared to weigh a ton. Some kind of subterranean storage chamber in there. No telling what it was now.

The sweat and heat of the club had dehydrated her, and the adrenaline was jacking her up. She made a decision: "Okay, listen to me – we're federal agents."

The man behind her kept the gun at the small of her back, his hand in a vise grip on her arm. A second Time Keeper had a grip on the other. "Hold her," the first man said. He started riffling through her pockets. "Got any ID on you? Here we go: Shannon Ames. From Rego Park. Looks like your license expires in a year, Shannon, but that's about it."

"We didn't bring credentials, in case we got searched."

The bouncer from the private bar pulled Bufort's wallet. "Charles M. Bufort. *Sounds* like a fucking fed, anyway."

The aggressive member with the gun moved around in front of them. He wore black, tapered pants and a white, ripped V-neck. His leather bracelets clung tight to his wrist as he gestured with the gun. "All right, so what are FBI agents doing here? Who are you looking for?"

"You're surrounded by more agents outside," Bufort said.

"Bullshit."

"You need to let us go," Shannon said. "Right now."

"You won't tell me what you're doing here? You won't tell me what you want?" He leapt at Shannon, grabbed her by the back of her hair and shoved the gun up under her chin. She cried out at first, startled, then kept her tongue. "I could kill you right now, bitch."

The ice in his voice terrified her more than anything.

"Goddammit," Bufort said. "Let's ease up, guys."

But Shannon could hear the worry in her partner's voice – these were young men, angry at the world, pissed off at everybody. The one in the ripped V-neck could kill her in cold blood, just like he said. He felt safe in his anonymity, safe in the numbers of his fellow members. This was his turf.

"I think you're out of your league," he said to Shannon. "That's what I think. If you're FBI, you made a bad call to come in here."

A compartment slid open in the big door behind him, revealing a pair of eyes staring out. The eyes flicked from person to person; then the compartment shut. A second later, the door opened with a metal squeal. The man standing in the doorway wore a white button-down shirt. Black diamonds framed his eyes, his mouth smeared into a black grin.

"All right," he said. "That's enough."

The aggressive Time Keeper gave him a frustrated look, then stepped out of the way. He moved back behind Shannon.

The man with the black-diamond eyes first stared at her, then passed his gaze to Bufort, then back to her, as if assessing who was in charge.

"Federal agents?" he finally asked.

Shannon answered, "With the New York field office. Half a dozen more agents outside."

The man considered this. "Well, all right then. Would you like to come in and sit down?"

MOMENTS LATER, Shannon and Bufort entered, the guards keeping close. The room was cavernous, multiple stories, dim with lamplight. Old couches and chairs formed several sitting areas; faded tapestries sagged against the walls; sweat and smoke filled the damp air. Shannon and Bufort were directed to sit on a small couch opposite the man in the white shirt, who took a large chair with stuffing bursting from the seams.

"So. Your names are Shannon Ames and Charles Bufort?" He had their IDs in hand. "My name is La Jeunesse. You can call me William."

Surely assuming it was a fake name, Bufort said, "You're French?"

"It means 'the youth.' My great-grandfather was French, yes. But like most of us, I'm a mutt. What was it that writer said? We're losing our identity as ethnic whites. Now you're no longer Italian American or Irish American – you're just some white guy from New Jersey." La Jeunesse studied them both, as if assessing whether they'd engage him in the banter. When they didn't, he went on anyway.

"So obviously this is very ad hoc, whatever you're doing."

They didn't reply.

La Jeunesse pointed to his forehead. "If you'd been watching this place for longer, or watching us, I would've thought you'd know to wear the mark of the beast. No?" He looked between them. "Surely you know the mark of the beast?"

"I know what it is," Shannon said.

He regarded her. "Ames – that's French, too. Or maybe it's Latin. Everything goes back to Latin." He pulled out his phone and poked the screen. Surrounding Shannon and Bufort were the four Time Keepers who'd brought them downstairs. The aggressive one still had the gun. He watched her as La Jeunesse read from his phone. "I was right; *Amicus*. It means 'friend.'" He lifted his eyes to her. "So, friend, how can I help you?"

"We're looking for Kristie Fain."

It took him a moment. "That's the missing woman from Washington? I saw the press conference on YouTube. Not very informative, though. My guess is she's someone important, if you're involved. Something to do with the White House, maybe? But then again, you're so unprepared."

"She's an aide to Senator Joel Nickerson."

La Jeunesse's gaze shifted to the other members in their face paint, then he refocused on her. "And you think she's *here*? At this club?"

Shannon and the team hadn't anticipated a direct hit tonight – maybe they'd find someone who knew more than Drexel Murphy and was willing to talk. Getting La Jeunesse was a stroke of luck. But she decided to proceed with blunt tactics. "We think you might have her."

He looked stricken. His eyes widened, and his mouth turned down at the corners. Now he was a sad clown. "And why would you think that?"

She had the quote from Twitter memorized. "*'I'd be careful, Fain. Keep talking like that and something's gonna happen to you.'*"

Shannon watched as the realization sank in. "That was dealt with," he said finally.

"What does that mean?"

The TIK leader seemed to get lost in thought; then he abruptly stood. He went behind the overstuffed chair and leaned on it. "So let me get this straight. You – and your companion here, and whoever else is here, around, outside, sitting in cars with large antennae ... you think I took this person?"

"We do."

"Because of a tweet."

"And other evidence."

He narrowed his eyes, assessing. "Fine, so you have other evidence. But why? Why would we take her?"

Bufort spoke up. "Because she humiliated you. Your group. She called you paranoid. And I know there are no mirrors in here – but have you had a look at yourselves lately?"

La Jeunesse grinned, his teeth contrasting brightly against his wide black mouth. "I like you. You look like a very large volleyball player. But I think you're missing a big contradiction, Agent Charlie." He moved into the chair again, leaned toward Bufort, then pointed at his own face. "We wear this as a symbol. We're not going to be followed, tracked, and studied every second of every day. And before you try to give me your 'gotcha' moment by saying we can be followed by our phones ..." He shook his finger back and forth. "We all use burner phones that can't be tracked. We use untraceable search engines and virtual private networks. We do things I shouldn't say to the FBI."

"Like ransomware attacks?" Shannon asked.

His gaze locked on her. "Who *isn't* doing ransomware attacks these days? There's even websites where you can train to do it yourself."

"Is that what happened? You trained yourself to hack the Takano?"

"The what? Is that a hotel in the city? We haven't hacked any hotel. And you're both still missing the point."

"That you're ideologically allied with Nickerson," Shannon said quickly. "That he planned to vote no on the upcoming infrastructure bill. Is that the point?"

La Jeunesse looked at her approvingly.

She continued, "The bill increases public surveillance in certain major cities, including DC and New York. And you'd be against that."

"That's exactly right. Why would I want to hurt someone on Nickerson's staff? We want him focused and ready to vote. Not distracted and pulling his hair out because of his missing aide."

"Maybe you want to be sure he votes the way you want," Shannon said.

"Or maybe you just don't like Fain," Bufort jumped in. "Not only did she shut you down on Twitter, apparently she wrote an article about you in the *Post*. Scathing, I heard."

"It was the *Atlantic*," La Jeunesse corrected.

"Right," Bufort said, glancing at Ames. He'd known the correct publication, but had been testing La Jeunesse.

The TIK leader shook his head slowly, as if sad. "You hear what you're saying? I mean, Nickerson is a Democrat who plans to break with party on this. He could be getting pressure from other Democrats to vote yes along with them. Or from Republicans to vote no. Why does TIK even have to factor in? Oh, right – the evidence you won't tell me about."

Shannon thought of their faces on the video. Made up just like the men in this room. Grabbing Fain off the sidewalk. Disappearing with her.

She had more questions for La Jeunesse, but was interrupted by the door. Two of the Time Keepers trotted over to intercept someone there – a woman in the requisite face paint who spoke urgently, drowned out by the music coming through the ceiling. A member jogged back over to La Jeunesse. "There's more agents inside. They're coming down."

Shannon glanced at her watch. Had it been an hour already? Patterson was supposed to check in, but the Time Keepers had their phones; Shannon had been unable to communicate with the team outside.

The member with the pistol seemed to relish this news, happy to have a reason to get violent. He hurried to a table in the corner and yanked away the cloth, revealing a duffel bag stuffed beneath that he slid out and unzipped. Shannon watched as he tossed guns to other members.

"I knew it," he said as he armed them. He glared at Shannon next. "You fuckers are gonna *pay*."

"Stop. You don't have to do this …"

But it was too late.

19

A Time Keeper in leather pants looked through the view port in the door, his gun pointed at the ceiling. "They're coming down the hall!" He stepped back and aimed.

"They're coming because we didn't check in," Shannon said.

"Shut up." The one in the ripped V-neck pushed past her and joined the other at the door. "This is it, guys." He took aim, too.

In the midst of things, Shannon noticed La Jeunesse had moved toward a small bar in the back corner of the room. A second later, he slipped behind one of the tapestries.

Another door.

It made sense; even an old grist mill had fire codes to follow. La Jeunesse had escaped from a mandatory second exit. Bufort saw it too. So did the two Time Keepers who'd remained near the agents.

"William left!" one of them called to the other members.

The aggressive Time Keeper in the ripped V-neck turned away from the main door, his eyes searching the room.

Confirming La Jeunesse's absence, he seemed to make a critical calculation. "Grab them!"

A member gripped her neck and forced her to her knees. Four on two, armed against unarmed; she wasn't taking any chances.

"They're right here!" said the Time Keeper in leather pants.

Shannon heard the pounding on the big metal door. A muffled voice: "*FBI, open up!*"

Patterson.

"Fuck you!" The one in the ripped shirt hopped around like he was going to explode with adrenaline. "Back away! Get out of here, or we're going to start shooting! We've got two of yours right here!"

The Time Keeper holding Shannon squeezed, keeping her in place. She felt the hard tip of the gun barrel against her scalp.

Bufort met her gaze. He was in the same situation. On his knees, a gun to his skull. His eyes shone with emotion. Hard fear. Anger.

The aggressive TIK member kept bargaining, shouting for the FBI to leave the club. Leave the area entirely. "Get out of here right now, or I start shooting motherfuckers! I fucking mean it!"

The agents on the other side of the door fell silent. Ripped shirt wasn't sure what to make of it. Everyone stared at the door. No one saw when the tapestry shook against the back wall. Or when Agent Holguin eased out from behind it, both hands on his gun. "Nobody move."

He aimed it at the Time Keeper holding Shannon, and she felt the barrel slide away. With his attention diverted, she scrambled to her feet, took him in a choke hold and knocked the gun from his grip.

Bufort made similar moves, but ended his maneuver with

a punch. And then another. The TIK member hit back, and the two men were trading blows.

Ripped shirt didn't like what was happening and started shouting again, louder.

A gun went off.

Shannon let go of the Time Keeper she was holding and dropped down onto her stomach to avoid getting shot. When she did, the Time Keeper crawled away, toward his loose weapon. Shannon leapt to her hands and knees and hurried in that same direction, cutting him off by heading behind the couch where she'd been sitting. She just beat him to the gun. He pounced on her as she grabbed it. Behind her, out of her sight, Bufort continued to struggle with the other member. As she wrestled for control of the weapon, Shannon saw Ripped V-neck standing in the middle of the room, his gun aimed at Holguin. The one in leather pants was holding the door to the hallway. Agents on the other side were pushing it open, and he was trying to stop them.

Chaos.

Ripped V-neck, his eyes wide, spit flying from his lips, told Holguin to drop his gun. Holguin shouted that he do the same. Shannon struggled to control the weapon of her captor while he tried to mash her into the ground. She was losing her grip on it; it was slipping away ...

"Back off!" Shannon wasn't sure she was heard above the din. "My people! Stand *down!*"

She let go of the pistol. The pressure on her eased up, just a little, as the Time Keeper stopped struggling for it. Then his weight moved off her altogether.

The agents at the front of the room stopped trying to barge in. Leather pants was able to get the door closed again. Shannon slowly stood, arms in the air. Bufort was getting up beside her.

She faced Holguin. "Put it down," she said.

The agent hesitated, then did as ordered. He holstered his weapon and raised his hands.

Ripped V-neck kept his gun pointed from the center of the room. "Good," he said. "Good. Now–"

"Listen to me," Shannon said quickly. "I'm going to be very clear. Walk away right now, and we won't pursue."

"Shannon ..." Bufort held his tongue after she gave him a searing look.

Ripped V-neck was no more than a kid, really, breathing rapidly, wearing his demon-clown makeup. His hipster clothes, leather bracelets and turquoise ring.

"Everybody just walk away," Shannon said. "You're not going to get a good deal like this again. Within minutes, this whole area will be swarming with cops. This is it, right now – this is your chance. Walk away."

Nobody moved. Finally, after looking at Shannon across the distance, right into her eyes, he made a small nod to himself and lowered the gun. Not entirely, but brought it to his hip and aimed from there. "All right," he said. "Let's go." He raised his voice at Shannon and Bufort. "I know your names. You don't know mine. Remember that."

The Time Keeper in leather pants opened the door. Shannon could see Patterson on the other side, plus two agents behind him. They all had their hands up, weapons holstered. The members gave them a wide berth and passed them down the hallway and slipped out of sight. The other two left from the door behind the tapestry. It was over.

AN AGENT NAMED Drenning had stayed behind in the parking lot when Patterson and Holguin had gone in. He'd been the first to speak to NYPD when they'd arrived. Apparently, a club-goer had seen someone with a gun and called local law enforcement. Bufort was talking with the sergeant in charge now, over by the liquor store. The eastern sky was just beginning to brighten. At any minute, the media was likely to arrive.

Shannon wiped the makeup clean from her face, using the Impala's side mirror to see. She noticed Drenning hovering close and asked, "Anything?"

"Nothing. Twenty, thirty cops and agents have been going through the mill for forty-five minutes. She's not in there."

"How many people got out before we started stopping them?"

"Probably two-thirds, something close to that. You think she would have escaped with the crowd? Why? If anything, wouldn't the Time Keepers have taken her?"

"Well, we got every license plate, right? And I have visual descriptions. A name – La Jeunesse. I think we just about doubled the amount of information we had on the Time Keepers in one evening."

Drenning looked off at the industrial building surrounded by cops. "Yeah." Then he said, "Oh, wanted to tell you, I saw someone outside. Before the mass exodus. One guy."

Shannon stood up, dabbed her face with a paper towel. "What was he doing?"

"Just hanging around, like he was scoping the place. I thought maybe he was taking a piss at one point, then I spotted him coming back into the Path Mark lot. He was parked way over there." Drenning pointed to a shadowy corner. "Mid-sixties, gray hair. Wore a black zip-up windbreaker, white sneakers. He took off before NYPD showed up."

"Did you make his vehicle? Get his reg?"

"I did, yeah. Later-model Ford. Blue. New Jersey plates."

Her interest piqued, she thought about it. It sounded like Riley. But how was he onto the club? "That's good work."

Drenning seemed pleased. Then he scowled as he studied her face. "Here," he said. "You missed a spot."

She handed him the paper towel, and he wiped along her hairline. Bufort, still with the sergeant, looked over. He shook his head. *What a mess.*

LEMON-YELLOW DAWN THICKENED into deep blue daylight. Not a cloud in the sky. Shannon knew she should be getting some sleep, but the search for Fain had yet to conclude, and information was still coming in on the Time Keepers who'd fled the scene. Ripped V-neck was Brad Myers, twenty-four, from Mount Vernon. Leather pants might've been Alex Dobrovsky, twenty-eight, from Queens. La Jeunesse was not an alias in any database. He'd managed to slip out just before Holguin had come in using that same back door.

But it was Drenning's report of a rubbernecker who fit the rough description of "Detective Riley" that had her tantalized. She waited in her office for the license information to come back.

As soon as her desk phone rang, she picked it up. "Ames."

"I've got that reg for you," said a voice.

"Go ahead."

"Edward F. Caprice. Male, age sixty-eight. Eyes blue, hair gray. Lives in Kearny, New Jersey."

"Thank you very much." She put the phone down and used her computer to run a check on Mr. Caprice and quickly found that he was a former police detective out of Newark.

That made sense of the badge he carried, as well as his cover story.

He was also divorced and had a daughter who was an RN. She lived in Jersey, too.

Interesting.

Caprice wasn't on social media, but he appeared in a few places online, each of these from his time on active duty as a detective in the robbery-homicide division. Cases that made headlines.

Like the one in which he'd been almost shot to death in a courthouse. A perp had broken free of the corrections officers and gotten hold of a gun. Caprice was spared thanks to an intervening civilian.

Shannon stared at that civilian's picture in the paper.

"Hi there, Senator Nickerson."

20

Tyler was furious. "You take off in the middle of the night to a club in Long Island. You go in – wearing *face paint* – end up talking with a TIK *leader*, and then you let everybody go! Jesus Christ, Ames. *None* of this went through the DOJ. *None* of it produced anything except a lot of overtime pay."

"That's not true, sir. We've added a lot to the Time Keepers file. Not that I think they're responsible. To be perfectly honest, sir, I don't."

"And so now you want a trip back to DC? You want to drive down there."

"I don't think Nickerson told me everything."

"You're saying he's lying?"

"Well, by omission."

"You think he has something to do with this?"

It was two hours since she'd learned Caprice's identity and found his link to Nickerson. The office had slowly come to life as agents arrived for the day. Tyler showed up looking like he hadn't slept – and he probably hadn't, not after hearing about the events in East Rockaway. But he had yet to let her explain.

She told him about Edward Caprice, about his connection to the senator.

Tyler slowly sat down in his chair, like he felt dizzy.

Shannon said, "I think Nickerson is looking for Fain, sir. That's who Caprice is, a private hire. Maybe just a friend doing a favor. And it tracks with what we know. He fits the description of the man who assaulted Mateo Esquivel, and the man who ran from us at the Takano."

"But why? Why would Nickerson hire someone? He's got Washington PD, NYPD – he's got the DOJ and the FBI working on this. This doesn't look good for him." Tyler felt silent and stared into space. He seemed to be recalculating his feeling for the whole thing. He'd wanted to do a good job in the eyes of a US senator who influenced the FBI spending budget. But Tyler was a man of self-preservation; he would distance himself from Nickerson the second it soured, if it did.

"He might've hired someone just for extra help," Shannon said. "He's worried about Fain, and he has this relationship with Caprice ..."

Tyler focused on her. "A man who goes around beating up witnesses? Running from the FBI?" He shook his head. "No. This is something else. Have you called him? Nickerson?"

"He's either very busy or not answering. I'm getting the runaround. But if Nickerson hired Caprice – and it's too huge a coincidence otherwise – then not only did he keep that from us, but it means he knew about Fain's disappearance before Washington PD called them."

"How?"

"Nickerson's chief of staff said WPD notified him at 5:00 a.m. Monday morning. But Mateo Esquivel was assaulted by

Riley – who is most likely Caprice – at 2:00 a.m. Three hours before."

Tyler thought for a moment. Then he picked up the phone and called Jim Galloway.

The AUSA arrived in under twenty minutes: He had glittering dark eyes, a hard cut to his jaw. Understatement defined his gray suit and burgundy tie. "Good morning." After shaking Tyler's hand, then her hand – his grip was as smooth as his voice – he folded himself into one of the chairs at Tyler's desk. "So – do you have the affidavit setting forth the probable cause to arrest Nickerson?"

Shannon glanced at Tyler. "I just want to talk to him. An arrest might not be necessary."

Tyler added, "But we need to be prepared. It's looking like he had prior knowledge of Fain's disappearance. And he acted on it."

"*If* you can prove he hired Caprice," Galloway said.

Tyler nodded.

Galloway considered it and looked at Shannon. "You think he might tell you?"

"I don't know. I'm going to try, to see if I can get him to clear it up."

Galloway nodded. "I'll prepare a complaint charging the appropriate federal violations. We'll have a warrant to accompany the complaint signed by a federal judge. I think you should contact your Washington field office–"

"I won't give the arrest to another office," she said. "If it comes to that."

Galloway, his mouth open mid-sentence, slowly smiled as he looked at her. "I understand. Of course not. I'm just suggesting you have them ready for your arrival."

"Thank you."

"My pleasure. And I'll be happy to contact the AUSA in

DC, as well as the DOJ, just to keep them apprised. They're watching this like a hawk, you understand."

She nodded.

Galloway got that look in his eye again, like he found the whole thing fascinating. His mouth opened to speak, but Tyler interrupted. "What do you think, Jim?"

"Well, I wonder – is it premature? What about taking a run at Caprice first?"

Shannon answered, "If he's working for Nickerson, then he'll talk to Nickerson as soon as we talk to him. Right now, he doesn't know he's made. So Nickerson doesn't know we're interested. That's the way I'd like to approach him, with his guard down."

Both men watched her, listening. She read what she thought was in their eyes: that this whole thing could be one of the biggest scandals in national history. And that was saying a lot.

In DC, she first went to Capitol Hill and checked Nickerson's office, but he was still out. She tried his cell phone again, but it went straight to voicemail. Cutter's, too.

She left and drove the city in her BuCar, and its outskirts, passing the house where Fain lived with Lockhart, thinking about Lockhart's description of someone outside on the night Fain disappeared. That couldn't have been Riley, too? He wasn't able to be in DC just before 1:00 a.m. lurking outside Lockhart's home and in New York assaulting Esquivel just over an hour later.

Maybe he was working with someone?

Maybe he was a Time Keeper? It would explain how he knew the club. But like she'd told Tyler, their involvement seemed less and less likely.

She went to a coffee shop, where she spent the next twenty minutes catching up with Bufort on the phone, trying to iron out some of these kinks, when an incoming call interrupted her.

"It's them," she told Bufort.

"Give 'em hell."

Cutter was apologetic. "Agent Ames, my staff told me you were here, and I see your missed calls. I'm so sorry. The senator and I have been in meetings all morning. Phones off, no distractions, that kind of thing. But we're here now. What can I do for you?"

"I've got something I'd like you and the senator to see."

<hr />

ONCE BACK IN Nickerson's office, Shannon opened the laptop she'd brought. She glanced at the two men before playing the video.

"You ready?"

Nickerson looked intrigued, but worried. "Ready," he said.

Cutter was more stoic. "Okay."

Shannon hit play. On-screen, Kristie Fain crossed Eleventh Avenue with a group of pedestrians. The shot switched to a different camera as she continued down the street, pulling her suitcase.

"Jesus, there she is," Nickerson said. "This is from Sunday night?"

"Yes. This video is compiled from cameras along Thirty-Third Street. It shows her movements between 6:43 and 6:47 p.m. We believe she's on her way to board the seven o'clock train."

They watched as the suitcase stopped working, and as Fain knelt to deal with it, then kept going. Shannon pointed out the man behind her.

Nickerson's hand floated to his mouth, like he knew what was coming next.

The man on the video gradually caught up. He wore a baseball hat low over his face, but it was clear there was something off about him. His face, when observable, was a blur of geometric shapes.

They watched as the second man, a ghostly figure captured on the low-light video taken by the construction foreman, crossed the street toward Fain. And then, thanks to the video provided by the artist who'd been recording the sunset, they watched the two men converge on Fain. To grab her and hold her still as the van screeched up to the curb. How they threw her – and her suitcase – inside and sped off.

After Shannon pressed stop, Nickerson sat back, looking pale. Sickened. Cutter had the look of a man considering a problem to be solved; he wandered away from the desk, arms crossed, fingers brushing his lips.

Nickerson stayed slumped in his seat, staring into space. Then he bent forward and put his head in his hands. "Oh God ..."

"Why would they take her?" Shannon asked. She looked from Nickerson to Cutter. "Because of a dispute on Twitter? Because of the way she wrote about them in the *Atlantic*?"

Cutter slowly shook his head; he had no answer.

Nickerson, snuffling back emotion, said, "Kristie is in danger."

It was an odd statement. Clearly, Fain was in danger. But Nickerson seemed to mean something else. "What are you saying?"

The senator stuttered, "I thought maybe ... When she disappeared, I thought ... But clearly she's in trouble. She's in trouble, and they could hurt her."

Shannon checked Cutter for a reaction. Nickerson's chief

of staff had stopped looking lost and gained an emotion: worry, perhaps over what Nickerson was about to say.

Shannon began to feel light-headed, like someone had pumped laughing gas into the room. Her pulse quickened as she asked her next question. "Senator Nickerson, did you have something to do with Kristie Fain's disappearance?"

His eyes slowly came up, and he looked at Shannon for a long time. "To answer that, I have something to show *you*."

She both heard and felt the reaction from Cutter this time: a disapproving exhalation. It sounded like the sound someone makes when the jig is up.

Her insides contracted. She stayed zeroed in on Nickerson as the senator pulled out his phone. He made a couple of motions and then pushed it across his desk to her.

21

A camera angled down from the corner of an elevator. Roughly three-quarters of the space was in view, the remaining quarter hidden. The back wall consisted of three long panels, silver and gray, a pattern like ridges of sand in a desert. Two panels adorned each of the side walls. Shannon knew what she was looking at – or could at least guess. This was an elevator at the Takano Hotel.

A man stepped into view. Nickerson.

A moment after, a woman followed. She was also familiar – Shannon had seen enough photos of the fundraiser to recognize the black dress, the wavy fall of auburn hair. Even though the woman's back was to the camera, her face only partly in profile, it looked like Kristie Fain.

Nickerson said something to her in the elevator, but only his lips moved.

Shannon leaned closer. "Is there volume?"

"No," Nickerson said.

Shannon stayed riveted to the small screen. The Nickerson in the elevator pressed a button. The image vibrated slightly; the elevator was moving. He said something else to

Fain – Shannon again saw his lips move but couldn't read them.

He laughed. He shook his head. His body language was revealing. The way he was standing close to her.

When he reached out and grabbed Fain's waist, Shannon wasn't surprised.

He leaned toward her. She seemed hesitant and dipped her head back.

Nickerson said something else, then his face disappeared as he leaned in to kiss her. At least, that was the impression. One hand on her waist, the other on her back, pulling her to him.

When Fain pushed him off, Nickerson was momentarily idle. His face, imperfectly resolved on the small screen, seemed to convey both sadness and determination.

Then he moved in on her again, this time more forcibly.

It pushed Fain partly out of frame. Shannon could still see her shoulder, some of her hair. Her reflection in the elevator panels was murky and indistinct. Mainly she could see Nickerson shoving himself against her, pinning her arm as he continued to kiss and grope her. Judging from their hazy reflection, it looked like he reached between her legs.

Shannon exhaled a held breath, her heart starting to knock. Seeing a woman in distress was itself distressing. And this was a major piece of the puzzle unfolding before her eyes.

On top of that was the prospect of arresting a US senator. What it was going to mean, the media circus that would ensue ...

She managed to drag her eyes away from the video and look at Nickerson beside her. He watched with that same stricken look he'd had after witnessing Fain's abduction. Was he feeling remorse? Was that why he was confessing? Why did he seem so shocked by Fain's abduction? Or maybe he just didn't like to see something he himself had set in motion.

She had a hard time not judging him, and forced herself to finish watching the video through to the end.

The struggle continued, with Nickerson kissing and fondling Fain. His face was visible intermittently as he came up for air or she pushed him back. His hair was messed up by the encounter.

And then the elevator seemed to stop – to reach its floor – and Fain shoved him back one final time before leaving the car in a hurry.

On the video, Nickerson stood there a moment, breathing heavily, and wiped his mouth. He might've flicked a look at the camera, might've not – hard to say with the small screen – but then he stepped out of the elevator and out of sight.

The video ended.

Shannon took a cleansing breath as she wondered where to begin.

Maybe it wasn't that hard to decide.

"Senator, you have the right to remain silent."

22

"That's not me," Nickerson said.

His statement was so out of line with her perception, for a moment Shannon was mute with incomprehension.

"It's not me on the video." He stared at her with sorrow, anger, and resignation all mixing in his eyes. "I didn't do this."

Her pulse was pounding in her head. He was denying it? After just showing her the evidence? The pivot made her head spin. "Senator, I just watched video of you assaulting Kristie Fain. I'm going to need you to come with me." She moved toward him with her handcuffs.

"I know it *looks* like me."

"It looks *exactly* like you."

"But it's not me."

She let out an exasperated breath and felt herself at a momentary loss.

Cutter, standing near, spoke up. "It's a deepfake. It's very possible now, the technology getting better all the time. They take someone's face – usually someone famous – and put it on someone else. A body double."

"I know what a deepfake is." Irritability was creeping in, covering her profound unease. "But that's a very convenient thing to say right now, after I just watched you assault your aide." She studied Nickerson. "Why didn't you show me this before? When did you get this?"

He glanced at Cutter before answering, "Sunday night."

"You've had this for three *days*?"

"Yes."

"Why? Why not come to us?"

"I panicked. I didn't know what to make of it."

She shook her head, feeling the resistance. Like a living thing, a gravity inside her, pulling her toward the conclusion: *he's lying.* It was hard not to trust her senses. Her primary sense. She'd just seen him sexually assault Kristie Fain at the Takano Hotel. Not misconduct, not harassment, *assault.*

But – Eddie Caprice.

If he hired Caprice, it now made more sense as to why. To keep things quiet while Caprice dug for answers.

While he searched for Fain.

Shannon kept shaking her head, micro-movements, back and forth as she waged this internal debate. She'd just watched Nickerson do this horrible thing. She'd seen it plain as day.

But she'd seen it because *he* showed it to her.

She blurted her question: "Senator – did you hire someone to look for her?"

Nickerson didn't answer, but his eyes affirmed it.

"You sent someone to the Silver Towers."

He finally nodded. "An ex-cop. A friend of mine. I knew he'd keep it completely quiet. I told him I'd pay him, but he wouldn't take the money. He said he'd check her place. And I asked him to visit the Takano."

"Why?"

"I wanted the original video from the hotel elevator. The real video."

Shannon remembered. "But they were hacked."

Cutter interjected, "Exactly. But that video – the original video – if we'd been able to get it, would show what really happened in the elevator. Who that really was."

"Isn't that another convenience? The video proving that this is a fake is stolen?"

"Why would we arrange that? The original video would be proof of what we're telling you. What you won't believe because of what you saw." He pointed at Nickerson's phone. "*That's* the video that's been altered. They mapped his face onto whoever that is."

She thought of the man she'd seen in the photos gathered by Reese, the one who looked like Nickerson, but wasn't. She closed her eyes a moment. "So who are you saying did this?"

"We have no idea."

It flashed through her mind, and she opened her eyes: "Do you think this is the Time Keepers?"

Nickerson answered, "I considered it. We both did. But then I got something else." He leaned across the desk and switched his phone to the text app. He scrolled until he found what he was looking for. "This message came in last night. Late. Two in the morning."

Shannon read it.

Vote yes Monday or the video goes public.

IT TOOK her a few moments to process. Once she did, she thought of La Jeunesse saying that TIK wanted Nickerson where he was supposed to be on Monday, voting no. That their interests were aligned.

Politics, after all.

So who wanted him to vote the other way?

Whoever it was, they were playing for keeps. If she was to believe Nickerson, then not only had the criminals faked him in a video assaulting someone supposed to be Kristie Fain, they'd had the real Fain abducted.

Shannon said, "And if this video ever gets out, it looks like you abducted her."

Nickerson's brown eyes were dark, haunted. "Yes. That's what it's supposed to look like – that I assaulted her at the Takano, and then, three days later, I kidnapped her. So she wouldn't say anything."

After another few minutes with the senator, Shannon stepped out. From the hallway outside Nickerson's offices, she called Jim Galloway and told him.

"What do you want to do?" he asked.

Her voice sounded far away to her own ears. "I want to take him into custody."

"Because you think he's lying? About whether it's really him in the video?"

There were too many people around, coming and going, so she started outside.

"I want to arrest him for the same reason we prepared the complaint and the judge signed the warrant. He's withheld critical information from a federal investigation. We were ready to arrest him based on his connection to Edward Caprice. But I think we both knew that was shaky. We wanted to see what happened when I showed him Fain's abduction, when I gave him a push. Well, something happened. He showed me a video where he appears to sexually assault her. The fact that he's had it since Sunday and not shared it is grounds enough to arrest and charge him."

Her blunt statements seemed to quiet the assistant US attorney for a moment. "Shannon, I like you. I'm familiar with your reputation. You're not a hothead. You don't create animosity between yourself and the local authorities. You're deferential to your superiors. And you've been steadily moving up the chain."

"Why do I feel a warning coming? With due respect, sir, this morning you seemed for it. Even before I had a video that either incriminates him or at least proves he lied to us ..."

"From what I've been told, the best thing about the Bureau is that you are left to investigate as you see fit ... Within reason."

"I feel perfectly reasonable," she said.

"I might agree with you. But I can't say you're going to get the same feedback from anyone else."

"So you're worried about how others will perceive this?"

He hesitated. "No. I'm worried that everything right now is riding on you. All eyes are on you, Shannon."

Within the hour, she'd heard from Tyler, from FBI headquarters in Washington, and the DOJ itself. Galloway was right. At least, they were unanimous that her very next move was to notify Nickerson's attorney. Together with the senator, the attorney would arrange a time for Nickerson to turn himself in.

"That's how the director wants it," Tyler said. "Nickerson should not be arrested like a common thug. No perp walk, no six-o'clock news clip of him getting pushed into the back of a waiting police car."

It left her uneasy. Not because she wanted Nickerson humiliated, but because Fain was out there somewhere, and the clock was ticking. The sooner Shannon had Nickerson in a room, the sooner he was formally interviewed, the sooner Fain might be found. She couldn't wait for attorneys to negotiate a time and place for Nickerson's surrender. She wanted him questioned immediately, not days from now in an SAC's conference room.

She stood on the wide steps of the Capitol Building under a low, bruised sky and felt shaken, really. For the first time since she'd started this job, she didn't plan to follow orders.

She told as much to Bufort when she called him.

"So where is he?"

"Inside. In his office. With Cutter and all of his staff."

"Who are you going to get to help take this guy in? You're not going to find anyone willing to blatantly disobey the top brass. There are no Charlie Buforts in Washington, unfortunately."

She appreciated his humor – and loyalty – but she was in a serious mood. "It's not a legal requirement that I wait for him to contact his attorney and come in when he feels like it. These are extenuating circumstances."

"It's three o'clock. If you wait just a little bit longer, you'll miss the window for initial court appearance. He'll end up sitting overnight with some undesirable people in county jail. You know what I'm saying? Might get him softened up."

"He's already soft. He wants to plead his innocence. That would waste time, too."

She fell silent, her mind running ahead to next steps.

"You're a badass, Ames. You'll have the respect of every agent in the Bureau."

"Thanks." She didn't care.

Though minutes later, as she reentered the Capitol Building through the security checkpoint and walked past the offices of other senators, it seemed like word of her presence was spreading; doors opened and congressional staffers watched as she marched down to Nickerson's office.

When she went in and back to his private room, she found him sitting on the edge of his desk. His feet were off the floor a few inches. He was boyish, in that moment, and he looked up at her.

Cutter stood a short distance away, white sleeves rolled, arms folded.

Shannon held out her handcuffs to Nickerson. The senator watched her a moment, then nodded. He hopped down from the desk and put his arms out for her. She attached the first cuff to his wrist. "You have the right to remain silent," she told him for the second time.

23

They're not going to let you go.

Kristie fought against the fear. The sense of total helplessness.

They're not going to let you go, and you're never going to see anyone you love ever again–

Stop it, stop it, stop it–

But it was hard not to despair. To lose it. For one thing, she could see their faces now – the makeup was gone. Scraped away.

Why would they identify themselves? If they were going to let her go, they wouldn't.

Think about something else.

Fine. There *was* something else she could preoccupy her mind with, push some of that stark fear aside: she didn't think they were Time Keepers anymore.

Washing off the makeup wasn't necessarily the clue; obviously even the most stalwart activists cleaned up. It was the language they spoke. The foreign tongue they used in the other room, the heavy accents when they spoke English. Well, one of them – the other two didn't talk to her, but acted like she didn't exist. When they spoke to each other just within earshot, it sounded Arabic. And the one who dealt with her – she'd heard them call him Mahdi.

While TIK membership had some ethnic variation – it wasn't white and Christian, and some twenty-five countries claimed Arabic as an official language – she hadn't encountered any Arab-speaking Time Keepers in her investigations. And she'd dug pretty deep.

It was also the type of guns they carried. The weapons resembled .22 LRs, small pistols that packed a punch, like the Beretta 70. She knew about these weapons from another series of stories she'd done, back in college, about the Mossad. The deep state intelligence agency of Israel.

She remembered because she'd been confused. "LR" meant long rifle, yet the guns once preferred by the Mossad were compact, single-action semiautomatic pistols. Apparently, "long rifle" referred to the ammunition. Guns were confusing, but she remembered the description of these. *Lightweight design, light recoil.* And the pictures of the men handling them she'd used for her journalism project – she remembered what they'd looked like, too.

Like these. One with a thick black moustache, another's broad jaw unshaven, stubble that could sand wood. The third was a bit fairer haired and skinned, but still looked Mediterranean. Their mean age was probably forty-five. Time Keepers were younger, some as young as teenagers.

So who'd taken her? And why had they worn the same facial makeup as TIK – or, for that matter, fans of the Insane Clown Posse? Was it a coincidence?

In the absence of an answer, she considered her missing person status. By now, most certainly someone had made a report – it had been three days. Rachel, probably. But maybe Mateo if Rachel wasn't around – she was sleeping with a married professor and sometimes disappeared herself.

Who were the cops on the case? Washington PD, maybe New York. It could be FBI because of the two jurisdictions – she lived and worked in both places. Police would be talking to all her friends and family. Accessing her phone records ...

That won't tell you much.

No, there was nothing on her phone that would indicate she was about to get kidnapped, in broad daylight, in the middle of New York City.

She thought back to the man following her. The ball cap he wore. Her drag-along suitcase getting stuck. That damned pebble in the wheel. He'd caught up to her after that.

What if the wheel hadn't jammed? What if she'd still been walking amongst the other New Yorkers whom she'd crossed Eleventh Avenue with? Most certainly, the men would have figured out a way to separate her from the pack. They'd seemed confident, practiced in what they did.

Were they ex-flipping-*Mossad*? Was that whom she was dealing with?

She watched Mahdi out on the deck. She didn't know where the other two were – they'd been out there moments ago, then left, leaving the one man alone. Mahdi had the gun – the Beretta, if it was that – tucked into a waistband holster at his back. A little black Velcro holster. He dragged on his cigarette, gripping with the crook of his first two fingers, a kind of European way to do it.

You're making shit up in your head.

Maybe.

When she was a girl, she'd made up stories. Her home-town was small, under five thousand people, and not much happened. She'd crafted headlines for her own amusement. Her father had been the one to first suggest journalism.

She missed him. Gregg Fain had been brilliant and he'd been outgoing; someone who genuinely liked people. And he'd been a wonderful dad.

Why did they always take the good ones young?

Mahdi finished the cigarette. He dropped it into a coffee can and just stood a moment, seeming to gaze out at the pines and alders. The lake beyond – she could just see a slice of it, a breeze stippling the surface.

He slid aside the glass door and stepped in. At first he didn't meet her gaze, but studied his phone. He swiped, read something, then put it away. Finally, he looked at her. "How are you feeling?"

"I'm thirsty."

"Yeah? I'll go get you a Gatorade."

"Thank you."

"You bet." He walked off into the kitchen, where she heard him rummaging around for the drink.

You bet ...

Some of Mahdi's expressions reminded her of Mateo. *What are you – Avon calling?* Someone who'd learned the language in part from watching American television.

And they never offered her water, only Gatorade. She wondered why. Maybe they worried she would learn something if it tasted soft or hard – sulfuric or tannic?

You're overthinking. This is the problem with you. The answer to all of this is much simpler.

"Blue," he said, reappearing. "I got you a blue one. Blueberry Riptide.'" He twisted the top, the air making a little pop, and took a sip. "Ah. It is delicious." After drinking, he set it aside and came around behind her. He cut the zip ties on her hand.

She rubbed her wrists. *Now is the time. Say something.* "My wrists hurt from those things. And my legs are numb. I'm sitting in this chair all day."

"We give you bathroom breaks. You walk then." Now that she was hands-free, he gave her the drink.

She didn't care that he'd already sipped from the bottle.

She didn't even think he'd done it to upset her; he'd just wanted a taste. The liquid was lukewarm. Salty and sweet, but room temperature.

Whose house was this? Why didn't Mahdi use the refrigerator?

It doesn't matter. All that matters is that you've seen their faces. They'll never let you go now. They're going to kill you.

After drinking half, she returned the bottle, and he capped it. Scowling, he tilted his head at her. "You're shaking."

She tried to keep her voice even. "How long am I going to be here?"

"It depends."

"On ... what?"

"Partly, on you."

The panic was rising again. She felt herself cracking. "I'm doing everything I'm told. I've been sitting in this chair for three days. I'm *sleeping* in this chair. My neck and back hurt, my circulation is bad – look at my feet. They're swelling. How can you keep me like this? What are you doing? Why are you doing this?"

Mahdi shushed her, looking around as he patted the air. "Okay. Okay. You want me to walk you a bit?"

"What I want is to be let *go*. Or if you're not going to let me go, if you're going to hurt me, at least tell me why!"

"I can't do that. You need to be quiet now."

She'd been too terrified to speak for the first twenty-four hours. Now she was practically making demands, nearly screaming. "Then do something. Give me a bed to sleep in. I can't keep going like this. Sitting here day after day. I'm going to go crazy!"

"Okay – stop. Don't do that."

"What do I care? What do I have to lose? Can I at least

have a change of clothes? You have my suitcase, don't you? Where is it? Where are my *things*?"

He bent to eye level. So close she could feel his breath on her skin, see the flecks of blue and green in his otherwise dark brown eyes. "You have everything to lose, Ms. Fain. Your past, your present, your future. Don't be foolish."

For a moment, his words almost didn't register. Emotion roiled through her, blocking out rational thought. But she brought herself under control: if he was saying she had her life to lose, maybe there was still hope. Yes, he could be bluffing. But she didn't think so.

"Okay. Yes ... Please. I'll take a walk."

"Good." He sighed with relief. "Very good." He helped her to her feet. It was true; they felt like they were swelling with liquid. Her numb legs prickled as the blood returned.

Mahdi took her the same route as he did every time she wanted the bathroom: around behind the chair, through the living room and into the dark dining room with its chairs upturned on the table. After that, into the hallway that led to the bathroom. And, she assumed of the closed doors at either end, to two bedrooms.

Every trip she made down the hallway – at least, after recovering from the initial, unobservant shock of her situation – she'd noticed the nails in the walls, but the absence of pictures.

Once they reached the bathroom, Mahdi asked her if she had to go.

"No, thank you."

He hesitated, perhaps waiting to see if she was being modest.

"I really don't. I'm fine."

If anything, she longed for a bath or a shower. The men were bathing; she was pretty sure she'd heard splashing in the lake. She would take anything right now – a sponge and a bucket would be heaven.

Meals, at least, had been three times a day. Though with no one cooking and no one ordering takeout, they ate dry food: cereal for breakfast, peanut butter and jelly or bologna sandwiches for lunch, and fruit and cheese and crackers for dinner. The fruit – apples and bananas – were room temperature. Stashed somewhere on the premises was a cache of food, a seeming stockpile of abduction supplies. How much did they have? How long was it intended to last?

You're doing it again.

She counted the nails in the wall as she shuffled back down the hallway. Six nails. No pictures. She focused on that as Mahdi walked her back to the chair. "Again?"

"Yes, please."

It was hurting her feet, but her legs were still waking up. She didn't want sores, for one thing. And if there was a chance to run, she wanted her strength up.

"*Mahdi!*"

The voice startled her; she tensed. A moment later, she saw them standing in the open kitchen doorway. The one in front, with the coarse beard stubble, was staring. "What are you doing?"

"Just taking her to the bathroom."

The man's hard gaze switched to Kristie. "I didn't hear the toilet. The plumbing."

"Ah, maybe we forgot."

"Don't lie to me, Mahdi."

Mahdi put Kristie back in the chair. He reattached the zip ties around her wrists, and from her ankle to the large chair. "Okay, I help her to walk because her legs ..." He seemed to search for the words in English and then finished by explaining in Arabic.

The man retorted rapidly and angrily, a slew of verbiage indicating his clear disapproval.

Mahdi seemed sheepish, keeping his eyes lowered until the man stormed out of the room, back through the kitchen. Kristie heard a door slam.

The mustached man remained. Mahdi moved into the kitchen with him, glancing back at her before disappearing. His face had changed. What had been open in him was closed. If she'd had an ally there, he might be gone.

Kristie hung her head.

Don't ...

But she couldn't help it, and she cried.

24

The interview room at the Washington field office was walled in gray concrete, fifteen by fifteen, with one large section of one-way glass for observing.

Dark rinds of fatigue underscored Nickerson's eyes. He'd been missing sleep, no doubt, fixated on his predicament. His hands still locked together in front, he leaned forward against the table across from Shannon, as if propping himself up.

The door cracked open, and an agent came in holding a canned soft drink. The agent was named Matheson, from the Washington office. Shannon had managed to bring in Nickerson alone, and he'd been processed through the WFO, but having an additional agent work with her on the questioning was nonnegotiable. And there was no mechanism by which she could transport Nickerson to New York. Nothing legal, anyway, that didn't violate his rights. It had to be here.

Nickerson lifted up out of his slouch and pulled back the tab on the can after Matheson set it in front of him. He drank for a few seconds while Shannon watched him. His mind seemed elsewhere.

Matheson, well built with a ruddy complexion, took his

seat and activated the recording device on the table, which resembled some high-end auto part more than an interview mic. "Okay, let's get started." He named himself and Shannon and the senator and noted the date and time.

"Senator Nickerson has waived his right to counsel. He has further not invoked his right to silence, though he's been Mirandized. Senator Nickerson has also consented to both a search of his office on Capitol Hill and his home in Falls Church, Virginia. And he has waived the Speech and Debate privilege afforded to members of Congress, which claims a congressperson cannot be prosecuted for information involving his or her legislative duties. Senator Nickerson, I appreciate you being so cooperative. We all do."

Perhaps Matheson referred to the agents observing from behind the glass. Tyler was hidden there with them, having flown in just moments before.

Nickerson said, "I want Kristie found as much as anyone else does."

"That's fine, yes. Right. Or – and I think we have to address this up front – you could want the appearance of that."

And so it began.

Nickerson faced the Washington agent. "Why else would I be here? I've said it's not me in the video, and we can't see if it's actually Kristie or not – her face is always turned away. Is it even really evidence? I could have fought this, I could have invoked the Speech and Debate privilege, but I didn't. I'm here. Without a lawyer."

"It looks like you in the video," Matheson said.

"Because it's a fake. A good one."

"Right. A 'deepfake.' We're working on that; we're checking it out. But if this technology has gotten so sophisticated, it might be a hard time proving it's not you. Wouldn't you agree?"

"I'm sure you have people who can detect that sort of thing. They're learning how to spot it at Facebook, at Twitter. They're making algorithms that can recognize it. I'm sure the FBI, the DOJ, has *something*."

"And why this fake, though, Senator? What's the motive?"

"To get me to vote yes."

"On the infrastructure bill. The one with the surveillance provision."

"Correct," Nickerson said, with grit in his voice. He was exerting effort to keep himself from yelling at Matheson.

The Washington agent leaned on the table. "I don't know if I have to tell you this, Senator, but law enforcement, people like me, are generally in favor of that provision."

"I'm aware. And in my opinion, you're in favor for the right reasons. But it's the wrong approach."

"Let me ask you, Senator Nickerson. Can you see how this looks? Someone trying to coerce you to vote yes ... well, *I'm* motivated for you to vote yes. How about me? Am I the one who set this all up?"

"Of course not."

Shannon spoke up for the first time. "Senator Nickerson, it's likely that an investigation will soon open looking into these extortion allegations. But that will be a separate case. Right now, I'm conducting a missing persons investigation. I want to find Kristie Fain."

He looked at her with less enmity than he regarded Matheson, but still seemed alienated, unconfident whose side the FBI was on. "They're obviously linked. My situation and hers."

"How do you think they might be linked?"

He seemed to assess whether she was manipulating him. She wasn't.

"I showed you the text indicating what I was supposed to do. To vote yes. What more do you need? It's a setup to coerce my vote. And Kristie is ... she's a part of it, clearly against her will. I didn't do this. And if she were here, she'd say the same."

"The implication there is that she's been abducted for her silence. Precisely so she *can't* corroborate that it's a fake."

"I would say that. Yes. Exactly."

Matheson interjected, "Can you see how that seems convenient?"

"Convenient? If you were in my position, you'd understand how that word is antithetical to everything I'm going through."

"I'm saying – and maybe I'm missing something – that your story is a perfect cover if the truth is that you had Kristie Fain abducted to keep her from talking about her sexual assault."

"That's *not* the truth," Nickerson emphasized. "*I'm* telling you the truth." He was getting worked up again.

Shannon intervened. "Senator, let's go back to the night of the fundraiser. Did you ever get in that elevator?"

He hesitated. "Yes."

"To do what?"

"To go to the bar on the roof, at one point. But I was with several people."

"Were you ever in it otherwise?"

Again, he seemed to pause. "I was. I went to the room."

Shannon made a note. "You had a room?"

"Sure. We expected the fundraiser to run late. There's lots of schmoozing, lots of glad-handing. My office booked several rooms for anyone who needed to stay."

"And did you? Stay?"

"No. I had my driver take me home. I went up to the room just to use the bathroom. Splash some water on my face. That sort of thing."

"And you were alone?"

"Yes. I was alone."

"Can you approximate what time this was?"

"I know exactly what time it was. Because I sent my wife a text while I was in the elevator. It was 11:33. You people have my phone. Check it. You'll see the text."

"Your wife wasn't with you that night ..."

"Correct. She wasn't. She was at home in Virginia. Our Falls Church home."

"Is that normal for her to stay back when you travel to the city?"

"I travel constantly; I'm a senator. She accompanies me on certain occasions. Yes, to answer, it's normal for her to stay home when I'm away. We have three kids, all grown, but two live in the DC area, and my wife spends time with them. We're a close family, and I'm a happily married man. So the look the two of you are giving me—" Nickerson pointed at the agents, then aimed his finger at the one-way mirror "–the thing everyone in there is thinking right now: Did I go upstairs with Kristie Fain? Did I get aggressive with her in the elevator? Did I *assault* her? It's absolutely untrue. Do you hear me?"

Nickerson's skin, getting red, stood out against his white button-down shirt open at the collar. His sleeves were rolled up, revealing bulging veins in his forearms. His blood pressure, Shannon thought, must be currently through the roof.

"Senator ..."

"What?" His eyes snapped to her.

"When *did* you see Kristie Fain that night?"

"I saw her half the night! She was sitting at the table next to mine. Right near me – I could lean back and say things to her and her to me. Kristie has been working with me for three years. She's one of my best people."

"Did you see her at the bar upstairs after the dinner?"

"Yes. But from afar. And she – I don't know – I think she

left some time after that. I went to my room – well, I went
back downstairs, first, to the lobby, to see some people off
who were leaving. That's when I went to my room to use the
bathroom and freshen up. When I returned to the rooftop
bar, she was gone."

Matheson asked, "How much did you have to drink that
night, Senator?"

"Oh, please. A glass of wine at dinner. A short whisky at
the bar before I went to my room, then another after. Three
drinks over four or five hours." He turned his gaze back to
Shannon.

"Did you change your clothes?" she wondered. "When
you went to your room?"

"I did, actually. I took off the suit jacket and changed my
shirt and left the suit jacket in the room. One of our New York
assistants, Jake, picked everything up for me afterward. You
can confirm it with him."

Matheson said, "Thank you. We will."

So far, Shannon thought, it all checked out. She knew the
interior of the Takano, the location of the elevators. She'd
actually already known that Nickerson's office had booked
rooms, and where they all were, and which one he'd used.
And the time he'd said he'd texted his wife while in the
elevator was just around the time Fain had left.

Matheson: "So who is in the elevator? Are they actors?
How do you think it works?"

Nickerson made a face. "Why don't you cut out the
routine?"

"I'm serious," Matheson said. "I want to know what you
think."

Nickerson sighed. "Yes. I think that actors have to be used.
You need someone in the physical space. The images are
manipulated, but these aren't digital people. Someone physi-

cally 'played' me, and someone 'played' Kristie. Then they put my face on the one playing me."

His words hung in the air. Shannon considered their implications and lingered over the thought of an actor hired to play the senator. Someone who might not have to resemble him facially, but had to be dressed the same.

Like the man she'd seen in the photos.

Would someone be willing to do that? To pretend to be a senator, step into an elevator and act out an assault? If so, would that person directly connect to the perpetrators? Was he one of them?

Outside the interview room, in an empty office the WFO had provided them, Shannon called Reese in New York.

"I want to know everything about this deepfake stuff. The best examples of it, how they're done. Maybe we even try to do one ourselves."

Reese sounded enthused. "I'm on it."

"And this guy, the one who looked like Nickerson – do we have any more pictures or video of him?"

"Just what we've seen. He doesn't show up again, that I found."

"If you could just check again, I'd appreciate it very much."

But Shannon thought Reese might've already seen all there was to see. This guy, this lookalike, whether he was heavily involved or an outside hire, he was supposed to be in and out. They weren't going to spot him at the dinner or the rooftop bar. Just in the hallway, on his way to the elevator to be Nickerson for those few crucial minutes. If it hadn't been for those few images, they might not have known he'd been there at all.

25

S ENATOR JOEL NICKERSON (D-NY) TAKEN INTO
FEDERAL CUSTODY
        The headline in the *Washington Post* was big and
loud.

Online, anyway. It had just happened a couple of hours
ago and hadn't made print quite yet. In the morning, it would
be on doorsteps and front lawns everywhere.

Eddie read the first few lines of the article on his iPad
while cramming a sandwich into his mouth.

*Disappearance of Kristin Fain ... congressional aide ... lives in
both Manhattan and DC ... last seen on Sunday ... Nickerson
claims he's the subject of an elaborate hoax ...*

The main picture showed Joel coming out of a Washington courthouse. He'd been turned over to the US
Marshals instead of going to jail. Behind the marshals, almost
out of view, was a young female agent who looked familiar.

"You ... You are something, huh?"

Finished his meal, Eddie walked the plate into the
kitchen, put it in the sink and ran the water. His small house
was hot. He left off the AC most of the summer to save

money. Not that he needed to be that thrifty, but why bother? The heat didn't bother him. Sweat didn't bother him.

But it wasn't good for the iPad his daughter had bought for him a few years back, so he wiped off his hands and blotted his neck and forehead with a paper towel before returning to the living room to finish reading the article.

He sat in his easy chair and set the iPad on his old TV tray. Beside it was his iPhone – also a gift from Tammy.

The phone jittered, rattling against the metal.

Eddie picked it up, studied the screen. The incoming number was blocked. Uh-oh. That wasn't good. He had a feeling who it might be. But why would he risk calling?

Eddie took it anyway. Life was short, and mostly he didn't give a shit. "Hello?"

A woman's voice told him he was being called by the US Marshals Office. The person who wished to speak to him was Joel Michael Nickerson.

"Yeah. Put him through."

There was a pause and a couple of clicks. Recorded call. *Sheesh.*

"Eddie?"

"Yeah. The marshals, huh?"

"I'm sorry, Eddie. The FBI interviewed me; then I had my first appearance in court and entered the marshals' custody. The judge didn't want me released."

Eddie grunted. Nickerson was an old friend, so the candor was apropos: "If you were going to talk to the Bureau and show them the video, why didn't you just walk into their office?"

"Because I didn't know I was going to."

"Until you got talking with this agent?"

Nickerson paused. "You know about her?"

"That's why you keep me around, right? To know about things?"

"She showed me pictures of Kristie being abducted." Emotion thickened the senator's voice. "I didn't know, Eddie. I didn't know ..."

"All right. I understand."

After a long period of silence and the click of recording, Nickerson said, "I'm sorry, Eddie. That I involved you in this."

"I haven't done anything," Eddie said quickly. "Nothing against the rules. I did what you asked. Nothing more."

It felt weird, like Nickerson might have a half-dozen agents sitting around, listening in on headphones. But why would he do that? What would he gain? Nothing. And what was there to pin on Eddie? Again, nothing. He'd banged around the boyfriend a bit, but the boyfriend had been drunk and belligerent. More importantly, Eddie had nothing to do with Fain's disappearance. They would know that. Ames, the sharp young agent, she would know that.

"I think she believes me," Nickerson said.

"That's good."

"She's gonna look into the deepfake." Nickerson paused. "*Fuck*, I wish we had that original video from the elevator. What do you think they did with it? I mean, maybe they held onto it. They could show me, use it as more collateral – 'See? We have the original footage. We'll release it and restore your reputation if you vote yes ...'"

Nickerson stopped talking, and Eddie heard the senator chuckling softly. It was a sad sound, a man at the end of his rope, unable to do anything but see the absurdity of his situation.

Eddie had the TV on, sound turned down. Senator Atwell, a Republican from South Carolina, was holding a press conference. Eddie read the chyron: *Atwell and other Senate Republicans Call Nickerson Arrest a "Witch Hunt."*

I'll bet they do, Eddie thought. Nickerson breaking from his Democrat Party aligned with GOP interests. Atwell and his buddies were against the new infrastructure bill. They wanted Nickerson in there voting no, the way he'd planned. As far as Eddie understood it, this can had already been kicked down the street for weeks, the voting delayed by fili-buster until a three-fifths majority put an end to it. It was firmly on the calendar for Monday morning. No more debate, no more clock to run out.

"Where's Cutter in all this?" Eddie asked.

"He's here. In DC. He's got to hold the fort down, now."

As if talking about Nickerson's chief of staff had the power to conjure him, Cutter appeared on-screen. "He's on TV now," Eddie said.

"Yeah, he was going to talk to the press with Atwell and some others," Nickerson said.

Eddie raised the volume in time to hear Cutter answering a question from a reporter about whether the FBI would release the video from the Takano elevator.

Eddie muttered, "Of course that's what they want to know. All they care about is selling papers ..."

On-screen, Cutter responded: "*I don't know. I don't see how that helps them find Kristie Fain, which is their primary obligation.*"

The reporter made a comment about the Freedom of Information Act, implying she or others might sue the FBI and the Washington Police Department. So they could see Senator Nickerson – or a digitally generated version of him – assault some woman in an elevator that was supposed to be Fain.

The vultures. Eddie muted the volume.

The media didn't care whether it was true or not. The video alone would draw attention, and attention made money.

"The world we live in now," Eddie said.

"I'm gonna get this sorted out." But Nickerson didn't hang

up. He breathed, and the line clicked as it recorded. He said: "Eddie, I don't back down when it comes to criminals."

Eddie sighed. "I know you don't, Joel. I know it."

A moment later, an automated voice notified him the call had ended. Eddie set his phone down. He slowly wiped a hand over his mouth and stared at the soundless TV. Nickerson wouldn't vote yes to keep the video under wraps, no.

But would he vote to save the young woman's life?

26

The fluorescent lights flickered overhead. Blackout drapes concealed views of the Potomac. The air smelled like coffee and carpet cleaner.

It was a meeting with the top brass, located in the Washington field office's main conference room. For Shannon, there were several new names and faces. Agent Matheson was there with the Washington SAC, Gary Hegedus. Seated across from them, a US Attorney from the Eastern District of Virginia, Christopher De Leon. Two chairs away, a prosecutor from the Department of Justice named Mary Stanz. And Mark Tyler, the new assistant director in charge of the New York Office, sat nearest to her.

Everyone at the table seemed happy Nickerson's head was about to roll. "The Senator will be back in court in two days," Hegedus said. "In the meantime, we'll see if he lawyers up. If not, the public defender will likely be Joanna Winthrop. She's good, but the defense doesn't have a leg to stand on. Not with that video, and with Fain still missing."

Shannon massaged her sore hip. She sighed when she did, but only half-consciously. When she looked up, the

people in the room were watching her. Either blatantly staring, or casting furtive looks as they checked their phones.

"Special Agent Ames?" It was Hegedus. "Do you have
anything else you'd like to add?"

She felt Tyler's eyes on her as she answered. "No, sir. I'm
sorry, I ah ... I'm just anxious to get back to work, and I'd like
to explore the deepfake possibility."

The air in the room seemed to tighten.

"We're all intrigued by the possibility. But, of course, it'll
take a lot at this point."

The AUSA present, De Leon, interjected. "We're not
saying it's impossible. But for Nickerson to evade this, the
evidence for a deepfake has to be incredibly compelling."

"Certainly. Yes, sir."

De Leon said, "And I would remind you, Special Agent
Ames, how you did a kind of end run around the order to
have Nickerson turn himself in."

"Sir, I felt that taking the senator into custody right away
was urgent. I felt that I was ... in a unique position to exercise
discretion. I had been in the room with the senator. I felt the
emotion of it, his desire to come forward. I worried that any
hesitation might change him, close him down. I executed a
legal and valid arrest warrant. I just did it how I saw fit."

She felt Tyler's judgment. Was he embarrassed? Furious?
Maybe. In the beginning, Tyler had seemed protective of
Nickerson – it was the senator's office who'd called him, after
all, asking for help. And Congress affected the FBI. The way
Bufort had put it: *Senators vote on DOJ appropriations.*

But now Tyler had changed his tune. He supported the
arrest of Nickerson, the questioning. So maybe he would give
her a break; she didn't know – she hadn't spoken to him
directly yet.

"You felt the emotion of it," De Leon said. "You rushed to
bring a sitting U.S senator into custody despite express orders

from your superiors. It's just interesting how you keep seeming to find your way to the center of attention."

"Sir?"

He was calling her a glory hunter, essentially. They felt Nickerson was guilty, but didn't like her swift action. Maybe because it undermined them. She didn't like thinking this way, but it rang true.

"What I did," she said quickly, "was because Kristie Fain is still missing. What I did was directly related to that. I'm not worried about who gets the credit."

DeLeon started to respond, but she hurried on. "I do understand that, until proven otherwise, it looks very much like Nickerson has sexually assaulted Kristie Fain in an elevator."

"Yes. It does."

She swallowed through the dryness in her throat, glancing at Tyler. "And I understand that Senator Nickerson has taken a seemingly anti-law-enforcement position on an upcoming bill. He's not a favorite here."

"Special Agent Ames, the FBI is not handling this matter in any way that has to do with politics. Is that what you're saying?"

"No, of course not. I'm only talking about this room. Where I feel like I'm in the minority."

"Well, I'm sorry for how you feel, Agent Ames. But yes, you're in the minority, I suppose. There are more compelling reasons to think this is a hoax to cover up a sexual assault than some elaborate plan to coerce a vote. Occam's razor." He added, "And saying that this video was faked is tantamount to saying the assault never happened. I, for one, am not taking that position at this time."

Tyler wouldn't meet her gaze.

God help me. She felt like the case was starting to swallow her up.

Hegedus said, "Is there anything else?"

They all waited, studying her.

"I need to get back to work," she said.

IN NEW YORK, Reese had continued to assemble images from the fundraiser and fit them into a timeline. She'd found more of the Nickerson lookalike in addition to the three cellphone images from the CEO of Metzer, including a video when he showed up for a couple of seconds in the background.

Shannon, beside her, was replaying it. "Do we know where he's going, here?"

Reese pulled up a map on-screen. She'd titled it *Doppelganger Route*. "Could be the bathrooms, the dining room, the hallway to the elevators – they're all back in that direction. Along with the gym and the pool." Reese had made an X and an arrow indicating his apparent direction. The lookalike had been in the lobby and was headed out.

The map also indicated every other location he'd been spotted: also in the lobby. "This is a group from upstate New York," Reese said. "They're down for the fundraiser, getting ready to leave for the night. They stop in the lobby to take pictures. Each takes a turn, and one shoots a quick video. Our doppelganger appears in the background in the video for just over two seconds."

Doppelganger ... but was he really? He seemed younger than Nickerson – quite a bit, really – but it was hard to be sure. He was always in the distance.

Reese said, "I've spoken with each member of this group and asked if any recalled seeing him. Only one did. She said she thought it was Nickerson."

Shannon leaned close. "Is this enough to pull facial recognition?"

"I grabbed what I could." Reese opened a file where she'd cropped, enlarged, and enhanced the images of the stranger's face. There was almost someone there to be identified, but it wasn't much. She looked to Shannon for instruction.

"Run it anyway. Run it against driver's licenses, professional licenses, and booking photos. Facebook, Snapchat, Instagram."

"You got it."

Shannon stayed there sitting beside Reese a moment, unspeaking. She nibbled at a fingernail. "Okay. How about the deepfake try? Any luck with that?"

Reese wheeled over to a second computer, and Shannon followed, pushing off with her heels.

"Didn't have much time for this, but I sent over the request to the people in video. I just told them to run an experiment. See if they could create a deepfake in a couple of hours." Reese paused as she brought up the video. "They did, with plenty of time to spare."

She hit play. Shannon watched as someone walked down a hallway, dressed like an agent. But as he came closer, Shannon realized he didn't look like an agent.

He looked like Tom Cruise.

"This was done right here in the building," Reese said.

Having walked down the hall, the agent stopped in front of the camera and slowly rotated, like a bizarre runway model. The face of Tom Cruise tracked almost perfectly – just a couple of jittery glitches. Once he was facing the camera again, the agent/Tom Cruise said, "Okay? Good?"

But it wasn't Tom Cruise's voice.

"That took the guys in video about ninety minutes to produce," Reese said. "They found free, available software online, downloaded it, and then dumped in a few thousand images of Tom Cruise. They could have done the voice, too – there's software that can mimic a voice once you feed it enough samples – but there was no one talking in the elevator scene, so I told them not to worry about it."

Shannon was listening, but distracted, watching the agent head back down the hallway. He had a slightly stiff walk, and he was lanky. Cruise, the actor, was shorter, stockier, and had a certain gait. This wasn't it.

Shannon's gaze wandered back to the other computer. The doppelganger's image was still up on the screen.

"Acting magazines," Shannon said.

"What?"

"What are they called? *Backstage*? Is that one of them? Where actors look for jobs."

Reese followed Shannon's line of sight. "You think someone advertised for this in *Backstage*? 'Looking for actor to play senator in sexual assault scam'?"

"No, the other way around. Can't actors advertise themselves? There must be a kind of classifieds like that. Websites, etcetera." She faced Reese.

"I'm sure."

Shannon stood up from the chair. "Here's what I'm thinking. Let's say you're putting this deepfake together. You need the person, the stand-in, to get into the elevator and go through the physical motions. Then you take that footage and map on Nickerson's face. So who is the person you get to go through the physical motions? Someone who's part of the operation?"

"Would be my guess."

"I don't know about you, but I'm a terrible actor." Shannon pointed at the computer where the agent playing Tom Cruise had just walked stiffly down the hallway. "Maybe not as bad as he was, but bad."

"You were undercover last fall. Did a pretty good job."

Reese was referring to a case in which Shannon had posed as a prostitute for two months. She'd used a fake name, gotten an apartment, and walked the streets. "That was a long-term project. I had time to get into it. This would have been more spur of the moment. And to me it seems that if you want to pull this off, want it to be convincing, you want someone who knows how to act."

She thought of Nickerson in the elevator. His body language had been convincing.

Maybe because it was true.

Was she going out on a limb for a senator who'd nearly raped and then kidnapped a woman?

For a moment, the shock of that question paralyzed her.

Reese said, "I think you're right. Why risk some random thug playing the role of Nickerson and have it look inauthentic? They have to play a scene and sell it, and it's a difficult scene. Plus, Nickerson has certain mannerisms."

"And there's the suit. You said that was pretty decent tailoring, right?"

"Not bad."

"Okay, so you'd need an actor who was the right height and weight. Someone who would fit into the suit. Was that a rare enough suit that we might be able to track recent sales, shipments?"

"It could be. I'll check."

Shannon touched the mouse, then asked, "May I?"

"Be my guest."

She navigated through the photos of the lookalike, watched the video, and looked at the map.

Reese said, "What are you thinking?"

After a moment, Shannon answered, "There's only the main entrance unless he came in through the kitchen."

"No. Definitely not. It's way back here. And he approaches the elevators from the other direction."

"Then he came in the front, and he walked back to the elevators. That's it. You can see here in this photo, he's kind of looking sideways at the upstate group. He doesn't want to be seen. He's got to get in, get out."

They considered it in silence.

Finally, Shannon asked, "What about Nickerson? He says he was in the elevator at a specific time, went to the room, texted his wife. We have the texts – he showed us – but we don't have his phone data yet. That may be a bridge too far. Anyway, what about corroborating data from the hotel? Or was that wiped out, too?"

Reese was already nodding her head. "Yes, part of the hack. Whenever someone enters a room, their key card registers in the system. If we had video of the floor, of Nickerson's room, and we had the key card data, we'd be able to put him there. But right now, we don't have that. Nor do we have any data that excludes him from being in the elevator at the time the video shows him being in the elevator. Which, as far as the video time stamp is concerned, could be as spurious as Nickerson's face."

"Ugh." Shannon leaned back and shook out her hair. "And NYPD has hit a brick wall as far as finding the hackers …"

"Yes."

While Shannon was staring up at the ceiling, Reese tapped the keys. "All right," the agent said after several seconds, "here you go. This is a database of actors in the five boroughs and surrounding regions of northern New Jersey and Westchester. And if there's anything an actor needs, it's a headshot."

Shannon stretched forward again, reinvigorated. "Where did this come from?"

"We're the FBI. We've been watching actors since the 1920s."

IT WASN'T TRUE, actually – Reese was making a rare joke. She was simply fast and had been able to collate several different social media platforms for actors, craigslist, and other sites where actors posted their résumés, all in a few keystrokes. What would take longer was looking through it. The system that ran the images of the lookalike against the database turned up zero results. But that didn't mean they weren't there – they just needed to be gone through by a human.

"And then we'll cross-reference with any suit deliveries we find," Reese said.

They settled in for a long evening.

BY THE TIME Shannon got home, it was going on one in the morning. She pulled her mail from the boxes in the lobby like usual and almost didn't notice the package addressed to her.

She wasn't expecting anything. And it was small. From somewhere in the Midwest.

Huh. She brought it upstairs.

27

DAY SIX: SATURDAY

The sunlight stabbing her eyes made no sense. When she'd first moved to Queens, Shannon had specifically opted for an apartment with a windowless bedroom. She'd be working late and sometimes need to sleep in. So where was it coming from?

It streamed through the blinds of her living room window. Instead of her bed, she was on the couch. In her clothes. With the package opened beside her, its contents sitting on the table. She'd been so tired last night that she hadn't even made it to the other room.

Sitting up, she rubbed her face and looked at the gorgeous necklace and wondered again where it came from. She thought it looked authentic – something you'd wear to a fancy, upscale event. It consisted of rose gold, diamonds, and amethyst. But she was no expert. The packaging called it a *Rose Dior Pre Catelan Necklace*, and by pricing it online, it seemed to cost over two thousand dollars.

Who would buy her such an expensive piece of jewelry? The only candidate seemed to be Caldoza. But a New York cop paying child support? It would have set him back. She'd texted him last night, but he had yet to respond.

Is this you, Luis?

Picking it up, it felt both fragile and solid to hold. She guessed it weighed a couple of ounces. The rose gold was the necklace. The diamonds glinted from within the golden leaf that adorned the top of the amethyst rose, which looked cut by hand.

She walked to the bathroom with it, clasping it around her neck, and admired it in the mirror. She removed her shirt – she needed a shower anyway – and lifted her long brown hair, as if wearing it up. She turned one way and then the other.

Beautiful.

AFTER HER SHOWER, she checked the phone. Still nothing from Caldoza. Either he was ignoring her, drawing this out for fun, or he was caught up in a case. Probably the last one.

What if it wasn't Caldoza? Was it arrogant to think Bufort might be behind this? Or even Jim Galloway? He looked at her in a certain way …

Forget it. That was ridiculous. She felt vain considering any of it, and put it out of her mind for now.

Even though it was Saturday, she planned to go into the office, but she first spent the morning working from home, reading up some more on Joel Nickerson. Most of the current political news revolved around the bill before Congress, the controversial infrastructure plan with the provision for adding cameras. It was available online to peruse, so she did.

Coming in at a whopping six hundred pages, the bill

intimidated. Did a congressperson even read it all? More likely, a given senator jammed the part in that he or she considered most important, then fought vehemently against anything included by the other side.

Except Nickerson, one of a handful of senators who broke from the party.

Nickerson was being hammered in the press for being against much-needed infrastructure funding. His critics complained that, for decades, America had been spending recklessly on wars and foreign projects while neglecting infrastructure and education – the bedrock of the nation. Nickerson countered that, while he wanted America to prioritize domestic needs, he couldn't go through with the bill when it had the surveillance provision.

"We want to be a strong country, a healthy country, and that comes when we continue to celebrate the sovereignty of each individual," he said on MSNBC. "I can't sign off on anything that delimits that sovereignty or impinges on our right to privacy." He added, "While I understand the need to make sacrifices for the greater good, I also have to agree with some of my colleagues across the aisle that it's a slippery slope. If you're not careful, freedom gets eroded, one wave at a time."

On Fox, Nickerson was less poetic, more scathing: "Well, China is a surveillance state. Nobody argues that. Cameras cover nearly every square inch of major cities, and it's paved the way for a social credit system. Everything you do there is being watched. Every move you make can count for you or against you. Do we want that? Do we want a social credit system? I know I don't, nor do my constituents."

In the *New York Times*, Nickerson went after the bill from a different angle. "Does increased surveillance help law enforcement? The data's not conclusive. Or have body cams helped reduce police overreach? Again, it's dubious. I'm here to protect my citizens. To act in *their* interest. This provision primarily benefits the private companies that would implement and run it. It's profit-driven legislation in *their* interest, and I can't abide by it."

Shannon wondered what private companies Nickerson might be referring to. She found a handful connected to the bill. Multiple tech firms that would potentially handle the hardware installation across the major cities designated for the municipal upgrade. Another was a shoo-in to be awarded the largest government contract of all, for software and algorithms that would run the almost entirely automated system. Plexus.

The name was familiar. A quick look online reminded her that Plexus owned several subsidiaries, including two major social media platforms.

The Plexus CEO was a thirty-four-year-old man named Brian McWilliams. Shannon went down the list from McWilliams, through the CFO and COO, noting the board members, the locations of their various offices. She read the company mission statement, "to enrich and expand humanity," et cetera, and dug a little deeper into McWilliams. He had an impressive CV, having attended Stanford, now splitting his time between New York, Silicon Valley, and Singapore. He'd founded Plexus at twenty-five. The company was valued at fifty billion dollars.

Shannon picked up her cup of coffee and took a sip – empty. Jasper was sitting on the back of the couch, watching her with sleepy eyes.

She checked her phone. No Caldoza.

"All signs are pointing to me getting my butt out the door," she said to Jasper. His tail swished once; then his eyes closed.

Ten minutes later she was in the Impala, driving out of Rego Park.

As soon as she reached the office, she called Nickerson. "I need you to think about anyone who might be pressuring you to vote a certain way."

The senator sounded tired, like he'd given up. "Look, my whole life is about being pressured. That's half the job, dealing with influence peddlers. I have to be true to the people who voted me into office. Their vote – what I ran on to get their vote – is all the influence I need."

Shannon studied the city from her office window. "You represent New York, though, Senator Nickerson. A blue state very much in favor of this bill ..."

"Aren't you from upstate?"

"Yes."

"Then you know it's a lot less blue up there. In some places, it's deep red."

She returned to her desk and sat. "I know this is a delicate subject. But I need to know if anyone has exerted pressure. For you to vote in a way that ensures they get this contract."

"And by anyone, you mean Plexus ..."

"I mean anyone."

"I haven't talked to any of the companies who would potentially gain from this. The government can't name contractors before a bill is passed. It's an assumption that Plexus would get the contract. They have their lobbyists, and I know a few of them, but that's it."

Her cell phone vibrated once against her leg – an incoming text. She ignored it.

Nickerson said, "I've had all kinds of people working on me. That's what I'm saying. My own party whip – it's her job, but she's been after me hard. My chief of staff, he's been trying to convince me for a long time. I've had Democratic senators calling me all hours of the day, every day, for weeks. And across the aisle, same thing."

His voice dropped in volume at the same time he grew emphatic. "Special Agent Ames, half the world now thinks I kidnapped or murdered Kristie Fain. After I sexually assaulted her. And they'll always think that. The harder I fight, the tighter the noose gets. There's no coming back from this."

As Shannon considered a response, she realized the clicks had stopped. So had the sound of Nickerson breathing. A recorded voice informed her the call had ended.

He'd hung up.

***

A FEW MINUTES LATER, she remembered the cell phone buzz. She took it out and read an alert from her bank, notifying her that the deposit had gone through.

Deposit?

Checking that the door to her office was closed – it was – she called her bank. They verified a transfer of $15,000. She nearly spit out her coffee. "From where?"

The bank employee told Shannon she would send over the relevant information. The routing number of the bank and the account number from the source. Shannon thanked the employee and opened her personal email, awaiting the information.

Her phone wiggled again, this time with a call.

She was relieved to talk to Caldoza. "Something's going on."

"Yeah?"

"Yeah – you got my text?"

"I did. And I'm almost disappointed to say it, but I didn't

buy you anything. Sounds like you've got a secret admirer."
Jealousy laced the otherwise playful humor in his voice.

"I don't think so."

"Okay. So what's it about?"

She almost told him about the bank transfer, but didn't.
The fewer people knew about this before she had an idea
what was happening, the better.

Instead she asked him about his son, making some
chitchat as she refreshed her browser window. Nothing yet.
"I'll talk to you soon, okay?"

"Yeah." His skeptical-cop self had taken over. "Be careful."

"I will." She hit refresh again. The bank had sent her an
email.

From Naomi, the bank manager:

Hi Shannon,
I'm sorry I've not been able to be more helpful. But I can't
seem to locate a routing number for this transaction. Or an
account number. Whatever the source of this deposit, at the
moment we're not sure yet. We'll keep looking into it.

28

Galloway showed up at the door. He'd been arriving each day for in-person updates, briefings that included Tyler, Reese, Bufort, and were audited by the DOJ attorneys. But those happened at the end of the day. It was still morning.

"Hi," Galloway said. "Bad time?"

She set her bag and coffee on her desk, then stepped closer and shook his hand. "Not at all. Would you like to have a seat?"

"I won't keep you." He stayed standing, but moved away from the door and checked the view at her one window. "Nice spot."

"I like it."

He kept his dark eyes on the city a moment. "How are you doing?"

"I'm good."

He nodded, like this nonanswer summed up a lot. He walked to one of the chairs at her desk and sat down after all, then seemed to focus on the space in front of him. "I know you're under a lot of pressure."

"I'm used to it."

His gaze locked on her at last. "Are you?"

She gauged his motives and decided he was genuinely interested. Maybe even concerned. But as soon as she felt her guard coming down, she re-erected it. "No question, this is my biggest investigation yet, and with a lot of moving parts. But I'm feeling all right, if that's what you mean."

She wasn't the type to ask who'd been talking about her, but it crossed her mind – the meeting in DC, getting grilled by the AUSA there, De Leon. He'd likely spoken to Galloway about it.

Galloway watched her, then smiled. But the smile gave in to another considered look of concern. "Just remember, though, that I'm here to help you. All right?"

What was he after? It was beginning to unnerve her.

He said, "I trust you have things well in hand. And we're keeping the people calm and reassured who need it. But I don't need to tell you ... well ..."

"You don't need to tell me that it's been nearly a week. People are getting anxious. Is that it?"

"Sure, people are anxious. People are always anxious. What I mean is, I called down to Lima. I spoke to Gianmarco Esquivel."

She studied Galloway, trying to decide how to feel. "When?"

"Yesterday. They were very concerned – Gianmarco and his family. Listen, Tyler set it up. He asked me to have the talk. Like I said, I'm here to help."

"He doesn't think I'm doing enough with that line of enquiry. Do you feel the same way?"

"I have to admit, at first I thought the ransom theory might have legs. Even though we hadn't heard anything. I thought the Esquivel family might have been scared into being quiet. It's what happens in those situations. There aren't a lot of kidnappings for ransom in the US. They're far more common in South America. If it had originated down there, it could be playing out down there, outside of our jurisdiction."

"Except for the abduction itself."

"Right. I thought she could be being held somewhere while the kidnappers made their demands on the Esquivel family. But Tyler was on the call. So were the three DOJ lawyers. And nobody thought Gianmarco was scared into being quiet."

She thought she finally understood where Galloway was taking this. "Which suggests ..."

"Which suggests ... well, you know how it works. Investigation is a process of elimination. Eliminating the Esquivel family elevates the idea that Nickerson is telling the truth."

Shannon felt a wash of relief.

Galloway said, "Kristie Fain wasn't kidnapped for ransom. And she didn't disappear because she wanted to. I think you're right, Shannon – she was taken so that this vote extortion could play out."

HER RELIEF WAS SHORT-LIVED. While she'd considered telling Galloway about the mysterious bank deposit, she hadn't. Now, the guilt clung. She felt like she was about to get caught in something.

But what? She hadn't done anything wrong. There was obviously some mistake. Well, a mistake and an oddity. She'd received a package no one had admitted to sending. And the next day, a wildly unusual bank error.

She kept checking her account on her phone, but it was there: $15,000 that'd shown up unbidden.

No, it wasn't a bank error. Banks didn't randomly add

money to your account. Ever. And together with the random, expensive jewelry ...

The two together meant something. She just didn't know what.

29

S he had Bufort meet her at the address in New Jersey. They walked up to the door of a small house that said *Caprice* on the mailbox.

"You really think he's gonna be here?"

"No." Shannon found the doorbell and rang it. After it made a sickly chime somewhere inside the house, she knocked anyway, then stepped back and checked out the street. A tidy little working-class neighborhood, a suburb of Newark. According to the workup on Edward Francis Caprice, he'd lived here all his life. In fact, he'd bought the house from his mother after his father died. The effort had relieved her of her mortgage. When she'd passed a few years later, he'd briefly listed the house for sale, then moved in.

He'd been married for thirteen years, divorced. His wife had moved out west and remarried, had a new family. But they'd had a child together, Tamara, now thirty-four, with a three-year-old daughter of her own, Zoe. Tamara and Zoe lived nearby.

"Come on," Shannon said to Bufort. "It's fifteen miles from here."

THE ROW HOUSES were white with purple trim. Tamara Russo's looked like any other, but Shannon noted the late-model Ford parked in proximity. And the license plate was a match. He was here.

"Let's be careful," she warned Bufort, and checked her firearm before getting out. She fit the weapon back into the holster at the small of her back before she and Bufort exited the Impala and crossed the street.

EDDIE SAW THEM COMING. Zoe played on the floor. Breakfast had been over ten minutes ago, but he was still at the table, nursing a cup of coffee.

He was unarmed. With Zoe around, he wasn't taking chances. One of the worst things he'd seen as a cop for three decades was accidental shootings. Some guys would say he should always be carrying, and just keep the gun safe. But those guys didn't have a Zoe.

The agents both knocked and rang the buzzer. He could see them on the stoop. She looked confident, on the ball. The guy with her – tall, shaggy blond, like a surfer – looked a little dopey. But looks could be deceiving.

Ames turned her head and saw him through the window. She raised her hand.

"Hey, Zoe? Grandpa's gonna talk to some people, all right? You keep playing."

"Is it the mailman?"

"No, it's not the mailman. You keep playing with your blocks, honey. Watch your show. I'm just going to step out."

"Okay, Grandpa."

Eddie cracked the door. The agents each lifted a billfold. Picture IDs and shiny flat badges. "Mr. Caprice?"

"Yeah?"

"I'm Special Agent Ames, and this is Special Agent Bufort." They put the credentials away. "Can we have a word with you?"

"Sure," he said. He started to step out.

"May we come in?"

"Let's talk right here," he said.

SHANNON HAD a sense of this guy: he knew his rights, he knew how police thought, he knew procedure. Keeping them on the stoop was a measure of control. He wanted his own foot on the gas, no one else's.

"Sorry to just drop in on you, Mr. Caprice."

"I'm happy to talk, but it'll have to be quick. I'm watching my granddaughter."

"Oh – she's inside? We don't want to leave her there alone, sir."

"My daughter is in there, too. She's right on the couch, snoozing. She's a nurse, works nights. We're fine, but just the same, let's see if we can keep it brief. What's this about?"

And with a perfectly straight face, Shannon thought. He was impressively guileless.

"We're investigating the disappearance of Kristie Fain," she said.

"Ah, yeah. Okay. The senator's aide. The one who lives in New York."

"And Washington."

"Sure." Caprice looked between the agents. "So how can I help with this?"

It was their turn to exchange glances. Bufort was chewing

gum. He offered a little smile, but stayed silent, deferring to her.

"Sir, we know you were at a club in Long Island two nights ago. An agent saw you outside and read your plates when you left. Will you tell us why you were there?"

Caprice didn't answer, just held her eye. Not intimidating, but resting his gaze there, like he was patient. Waiting for the inevitable ultimatum.

She said, "I'll get right to the point. I know you've been asked by Senator Nickerson to help find Fain. You've been to the club, you've been to the Takano Hotel, and just before that, you visited Mateo Esquivel."

Caprice stayed silent. Shannon could hear TV voices coming through the door.

"Thank you for not denying it," Shannon said.

"Why would I?"

"Well – because we could arrest you."

"For what?"

"For running from us. That's one thing. We made it clear we were FBI; we asked you to stop."

He said nothing.

"Or for physically assaulting Mateo Esquivel."

Caprice kept quiet, then wrinkled his brow. "Why don't you tell me what you want? And then I'll know what I'm admitting to and what I'm not."

Bufort snorted a chuckle. Shannon ignored it and stayed on Caprice. "I want to know everything you do. You went to Mateo Esquivel because you knew he was Fain's boyfriend. You went to the hotel because Nickerson was hoping to get the original video. Is that about right?"

"I won't contradict you."

"And you followed me? Is that how you got onto the club?" Thinking the honesty might soften him, she added, "It was a lucky break, really, spotting you at the club. At the same time, while you've been keeping a low profile, you've been bold, too. Like you've got nothing to fear."

Again, Caprice made no response.

"I think you've been working for Nickerson and you've been investigating this on your own. Maybe you feel protected by him? Please, Mr. Caprice, this is about Kristie Fain. About finding her, helping her. We'll show our cards, you show yours. Okay?"

For what seemed like a long time, he stayed mute, his gaze now wandering the street. A loud motorcycle muffler blatted in the distance. Somewhere, a siren.

Caprice looked at her. "All right. Come on in."

30

Z oe was on the floor, contentedly drawing pictures and watching Netflix. Caprice's daughter, Tammy, was just in sight in an adjoining room, on the couch; she woke up when they came in. Caprice talked to her, made assurances as she gawked around him, trying to get a look at the agents, then he closed the door to the room and returned.

Shannon tried to reconcile this seemingly calm, collected father and grandfather with someone who'd beaten up Mateo Esquivel. Someone with the bruises on his knuckles to prove it. As a cop, Caprice's record was as close to spotless as it got. No citations for excessive force, no scandals, not a whiff of corruption. Maybe it was just a compartmentalization thing. He was able to close part of himself off and get the job done.

He led them to a round table in the bay window at the front of the house and offered them coffee. Both agents politely declined. He poured himself a cup, mixed in cream and sugar, stirred it with a teaspoon, put the teaspoon in the sink.

Sitting down, he said, "I still get little cravings. For cigarettes. Not every time I have coffee, but now."

"Why is that?"

"Anything to do with this sort of thing, I guess. I was on
the job for twenty-eight years. Being around other cops
makes me anxious."

Shannon considered the statement and Caprice's
demeanor. Not unkindly, she said, "It's very disarming, what
you're doing."

Caprice took a sip from the coffee mug and raised his
eyebrows at her.

She continued, "You invite us in, offer us coffee, freely
share some vulnerability – your addiction to cigarettes, your
nervousness around law enforcement. It's both intimate and
informational. You're telling us you have a long history being
with the police. You've seen and done a lot."

Caprice set down the mug. His eyes flicked to Bufort, back
to her. "I did all that, huh?"

"I'd like to know why you followed us."

He was quiet a moment. "If I did follow you, and I'm not
saying I did, I suppose it would be to see where it led. Like
you indicated just now, if I've been looking for Kristie Fain,
same as you, then we have mutual interests."

"And what have you found? Or – what *would* you have
found, hypothetically?"

"Hypothetically? Nothing definitive. Or I'd know where
she was."

Shannon and Bufort shared a look. Caprice liked
being coy.

Shannon said, "Can you describe your relationship to
Senator Nickerson?"

"We're friends."

"You met about ten years ago? There was an incident at a
courthouse, is that right?"

Caprice gave her a look, like he was thinking it all through, then nodded. "Before he was a big-time senator, before he was even in politics, ol' Joel was an assistant district attorney in Westchester County. A perp was making drug buys down here in Jersey and selling to his suburbanite friends in White Plains. The operation expanded, more people got involved, making the buys, selling, and it turned up the investigation into a multi-agency task force. I met Nickerson through the course of it."

"I didn't see that you were Vice Narcotics," Shannon said. "Your background shows you were robbery homicide."

"That's right. Nineteen years in robbery homicide, right up until I retired. I got involved because there was a murder. When the whole thing came down – when Nickerson and the task force were making their case, there was a related homicide. So when the time came in court, I had to show up, play my part. The guy who I collared, this tough son of a gun named Eric Chambers, he pulled free of the officers bringing him into court, got one of their service weapons. I was there, Nickerson was there – we're all in the hallway outside the courtroom, and Chambers gets the weapon. He's got his hands bound up, but he can still pull the trigger. And he does. He starts squeezing off rounds, and it's loud, as you can imagine, and everything is chaos. The officers are trying to get him back under their control, but Chambers is single-minded. He wants to kill me. Because I'm the guy who caught him for this murder, and if he's convicted, he's going to do life.

"There I am, and I've got a broken arm. This was from another case, but I'm not as quick on the draw. Chambers gets the jump on me, and I can see him targeting me, I can see down the barrel of the gun. I'm thinking, these are my final seconds, my last thoughts. I've got a wife and a young daughter, and they're going to be left without me.

"But then there's this assistant DA, and he bum-rushes Chambers. Slams right into him like a defensive end. Knocks him off balance. The gun goes off – I can feel the bullet tug the air a few inches from my face."

Caprice looked out the window a minute, as if sentimental. When his faded blue eyes came back, he said, "And that was it for me. This guy, Nickerson, I was going to owe him my life. Do anything he asked of me. Because that's how I'm built. That's how my mother raised me."

Shannon absorbed it. "So what happened then? You kept in touch here and there, or you became closer?"

"We were busy, we lived in different states, there's ten years between us ... but I never forgot it. You don't forget something like that. He did what a lot of people wouldn't do. And it stuck with me. And I followed his career; he switched from the DA's office to working criminal defense. Defending guys just like Chambers. Which I didn't judge – you've got to respect the law, and that means both sides. And then the next thing I know, he was running for state senator. And when he won, I called him up and congratulated him. I reminded him that if he ever needed anything, he should let me know. That was six years ago. And then, a week ago, I got the call."

When Caprice stopped there, Shannon picked it up. "What was he like on the phone? What did he say?"

"He'd been out to dinner with Roseanna, his wife. They'd just gotten back home, and he got a text. He told me it was a video showing him doing something he couldn't possibly have done."

"Did he send you the video?"

Caprice shook his head. "No. But he described it."

"What did he think was happening?"

"He thought maybe money, but he wasn't sure. At that point, he didn't know. He hadn't gotten the text yet. About voting." He looked between them. "You guys know about the text, right?"

"We do," Shannon said.

"Well, all he knew on Sunday was the video. He asked me if I would go to the Takano Hotel for their elevator video from that Thursday night."

Shannon felt the timing was off. "But you visited Mateo Esquivel first. Why?"

"Because Nickerson was calling Fain, trying to reach her. He sent someone to her place in DC and asked me to stop by her place in New York. She was supposed to be back, but he wasn't sure."

"Who did he send to her place in DC?"

"Cutter."

Shannon recalled Rachel Lockhart describing someone outside the house on the night Fain went missing. Nickerson had wanted to see if Fain was at her place in DC. Probably because he was hiding the video from everyone, including investigators.

But she was getting ahead of herself. "Why were you rough with Mateo Esquivel?"

"I didn't plan to. But he copped an attitude with me. And at that point, Nickerson didn't know what to think. He considered that Fain might be in on it. That this might be some extortion trap. Maybe she'd been paid off. So I played the heavy with Esquivel. I'm good at it."

The glint in his eye and set of his jaw confirmed his statement, as far as Shannon was concerned. She was rapidly getting the sense about Eddie Caprice – he might've gotten through his career in law enforcement unscathed, but because he was smart. He knew how to keep himself out of trouble. And he had this disarming, gentle-seeming side.

But he could be brutally violent.

"And then Nickerson contacted you again? To tell you about the text?"

"Called me in the middle of the night, must've been 3:00 a.m."

"What did you think?"

Caprice shrugged. "I thought – there's Washington for you."

"You think this kind of thing happens on a regular basis? Blackmail?"

"I think a lot of extortion schemes happen, yeah. I think this one's pretty blatant. But I wouldn't put it past anyone."

There was still something he wasn't saying.

"Mr. Caprice ..."

"Eddie. Mr. Caprice was my father. And I didn't care for him."

"Eddie, what I would really appreciate, what we both would – and I'm sure Joel would agree, he would want this – is full disclosure here. Anything you can tell us. Anything you've found. Even any hunches. If you could–"

Zoe, Eddie's granddaughter, interrupted. "Grandpa, look what I made." She had done some drawings with marker, several of them, each with figures almost impossible to discern as human beings. "That's Mum, and that's Dad. And that's Kimmy, and that's Riley. See?"

"They're beautiful, honey." He kissed her on her head.

Shannon was interested. "Riley?"

"It's a kid's show," Eddie explained. "It's a cartoon. They're a family of kangaroos in Australia."

He looked at Shannon, and she looked back.

Riley.

From a kids' show.

The door to the adjoining room opened. Eddie's widowed daughter tied a bathrobe around her waist, hair mussed and sleep darkening her eyes. She beckoned with and outstretched arm. "Come on, baby. Let's you and me go get cleaned up. We need to wash your hair."

"Noooo."

"Come on, let Grandpa talk to his friends."

Zoe gave each Shannon and Bufort a shy look. Bufort said, "I wish someone would wash *my* hair."

Zoe just stared at him. Shannon stifled a smile.

Eddie gave the girl another peck on the head and urged her gently toward her mother. "Go on, honey. I'll see you in a minute."

Zoe went to her mother, who started for the stairs.

Shannon said, "We won't keep him long. Sorry for the inconvenience. You have a lovely home."

Tammy looked back – coldly – and Shannon felt her good humor drain.

The woman walked upstairs with her daughter, out of view.

"She works long hours," Eddie said. "She's an ER nurse."

Shannon let a moment pass, everyone's mind surely on the same thing. "Eddie," she said, "I can't stress to you enough how important it is you share with us everything you've found."

Eddie watched her, then inhaled sharply. "I brought in another guy."

Bufort leaned in. "Another guy?"

"I want to help Joel, but I can't be in two places at once – as you can see, I've got obligations. So I called a buddy down there. His name's Tom Merkel. M-e-r-k-e-l. Tom was on the job over thirty years, now he just sits around waiting for something to happen. So I asked him a favor. I had him follow Joel's number-two guy there. Keith Cutter."

It sent a chill up Shannon's spine. "Why?"

Eddie studied his hands. "Look, when Joel came to me with this, the first question I had was *who*. Who did he think might be behind this? He didn't know. But he said Cutter suspected this group, the Time Keepers." He made quotes in the air and passed his gaze between the agents. "I thought that was fine. But I also wanted to look at Cutter."

"Why?"

"Cop gut, I guess. Almost thirty years on the job. You see a lot of guys taken advantage of by their own people. And the closer they are, the more dangerous. It's just how I think. So I did. I didn't tell Joel, but I had a little look at Cutter."

"That was early on, then."

"Right from the beginning. I called Tom Merkel that same Sunday night. And Tom's tailed him every night since."

"Did he find anything?" Shannon took out her phone, opened the Notes app.

"Well, first part of the week seemed normal. Cutter rolled around with Nickerson, meeting with politicians, having lunches, all that sort of thing. He also went off on his own, running errands. At one point, he stopped at a drugstore and picked up a couple of prescriptions. We didn't know for what. But at this time, I had asked Joel to give me the rundown on all his staff. What was everyone's situation? Anyone having financial trouble? He told me what he could, which wasn't much. Anyway, then you made your arrest, and Cutter got a lot more active. He talked to the media, talked to more politicians, and had sort of a clandestine meeting."

"With whom?"

"I don't know. One guy, early thirties. They met in the street five blocks away from Cutter's home. Sat in Cutter's car and talked. Merkel got photos."

"Where are the photos?"

"He emailed them to me. They're on my computer. Back at my place."

"You don't have email on your phone?"

"Hey, I just got my first non-flip phone last year. My fat

fingers can barely text. Anyway, I downloaded the pictures and deleted the email." Eddie shrugged. "You never know who's watching."

Shannon was about to ask that they head over to his house, but her phone was buzzing.

She checked and saw the office calling. "Hang on, I'm sorry, let me take this." She rose from the table and let herself out the front door. "Ames."

"It's me," Agent Reese said.

"What's going on?"

"We got him."

So much had been happening, it took Shannon a second. "The actor?"

"His name is Ryan Sherwood. He lives in Astoria. He advertises himself as an actor for hire online, he's the right height and weight, and I've got a delivery confirmation from USPS of a package from Men's Warehouse on Monday before the fundraiser. I'm ninety-nine percent on it."

"He's our guy at the hotel," Shannon said. "In Nickerson's suit."

"And if so, he's the one in the elevator, playing the senator himself."

"Thank you, Jenna."

She hung up and told Bufort.

He offered her a choice. "I'll stay with this? You go?"

Off she went.

31

R yan Sherwood sat on his couch with the look of a
man who'd finally gotten recognition for his work,
but in the worst way possible. He wanted to crawl
out of his skin, far away from the FBI agent sitting across
from him.

Shannon smiled at his two roommates, carefully groomed
twentysomething men loitering in the adjoining kitchen.
They seemed to think they were in for the show of the
century. "Will you excuse us, gentlemen?"

They left, disappointed.

"So, Ryan," Shannon began. The first-name basis would
hopefully help him feel more at ease. "You're twenty-eight?"

Sherwood's Adam's apple bobbed up and down as he
swallowed. "Yes, ma'am."

"Originally from Ohio."

"Yes, ma'am. Dayton."

"Did you move here to be an actor?"

"Sort of. I actually moved here because my older brother
lives here, and he was able to get me a job. He works for a 3D

printing company. He was actually one of its founders. He, ah ... yeah." Sherwood was all nerves.

"Interesting. So you're doing all right."

"Um ..."

"You have a steady job. You're not struggling."

"Well, I mean ..."

"I'm just wondering why you'd take a job like this. Is that how it went? Did someone call you up for some acting work?"

His posture tightened as he blushed. "I, ah – should I get a lawyer?"

"You can, absolutely. Right now, I'm just hoping to establish some basic facts. I'm not here to arrest you. I just want to know what happened."

She waited, but he only gripped his knees and looked unsure.

She handed Sherwood her phone, which showed Fain posing for her professional headshot. "A woman is missing. This woman."

His worry seemed to deepen, but he kept the phone, kept staring at Fain's image. "I saw her on the news," he said.

"Did you recognize her?"

"No. Why would I?"

After giving him another few seconds to look, Shannon took her phone back. "Ryan, why do you think I'm here?"

He studied her. "I guess something happened to her in relation to the project? The film?"

"The film ... Ryan, why don't you tell me about this job you took. Okay? Start at the beginning."

He sighed and rubbed his palms on his knees some more before answering. "Okay. So, I haven't worked for my brother in over six months. I knew if I had that job, I wouldn't be motivated, I wouldn't be hungry. And he and I weren't getting along anyway. So I quit. And I've been struggling for acting jobs all the while. When this thing came up, I thought it was weird – obviously – but this is New York. I've heard all kinds of stories about weird acting gigs. Guys who show up, do a scene, never even see the cameras. You take what you can get."

"Sure."

"I went where they told me. To the Takano Hotel. They said the camera was in the elevator. It was very specific. I had to be there at an exact time and get into the elevator. I'd meet another actor there."

"And do what?"

He looked like he wanted to fold up in shame, but he remained seated, keeping eye contact. Shannon guessed he was proud of his trade. Even if he was depicting something unsavory, it was just that – a depiction. It was acting. "I was supposed to act like I was assaulting her."

"Did you wonder why? Why anyone would ask you to do that?"

"Yes. But like I said, there are stranger gigs. Some actors I know spend the night at parties, pretending to be some other person. Some directors don't have permits and steal scenes wherever they can. I was told that this was an indie film, and I was a day player. That's someone who just does one day's work. There was a scene in an elevator, they said, and they were going to use the house cams – the surveillance cams. And I don't know ... Like I said ..."

"How much?"

Sherwood hesitated. "Two thousand dollars. For five minutes' worth of work, I mean ..."

"And have you been paid?"

He nodded. "Half up front, half after. They used Venmo."

She noted it. "And who hired you? How did they contact you?"

"Through my website. I have a Squarespace page. People can reach me through the contact form."

"Can I see it? The message?"

"Sure. It forwards to my email. Here, let me get my phone." He dug into his pocket, and she tensed, just reaction, her hand going to the grip of the Glock at her back.

It was a smartphone, nothing more. "Um, it was a company. Luminosity Pictures. The woman's name was Sasha Rei. R-e-i. She was the producer I dealt with."

"Did you speak with this person directly?"

"Only email and text. There was her initial contact, and then I had some questions, and she got back to me with more details, and then I said yes. Payment came through that night."

Luminosity Pictures. Sasha Rei. Shannon Googled for details.

As it turned out, there was an actual company based in New York, LA, and Miami. Small, though, from the looks of it. "And there's Sasha," Shannon said after navigating to the company's *Who We Are* page. "I'm going to call them, okay?"

Sherwood suddenly seemed like he was about to get emotional. "All I did was try to get an acting job."

"I understand."

"I know I shouldn't have. I didn't want to perform an assault, anyway. I don't want to contribute to any sort of culture of violence against women, fiction or not. Honestly, I was hoping maybe it was a PSA, or a commercial, something for a woman's organization. But the communication was very brief."

"I understand, Ryan. You're just trying to get work."

He gave her a wounded look. "And now you're doing the REID technique on me ..."

"Where did you hear about that?"

"About a year ago I had a walk-on on *CSI: New York*. I was a guy getting questioned, just like this. And the cops in the scene were using the REID technique. You're taking the morality out of what I did. Making it seem like it's all okay."

"Ryan – I'm really not judging you – you're doing that. But if you want to feel better, and this is no bullshit, just keep doing what you're doing. Cooperating, helping. Right now, you need to let me make this call."

He stopped talking and slumped back as she clicked the call number on the website. A moment later, she was listening to the line ring in Los Angeles. A young woman answered. Shannon explained who she was, and asked if Sasha Rei was available. Rei wasn't – she was currently on location. Shannon had the assistant forward the call, and a minute later was talking to a producer somewhere in the Mojave Desert, filming a commercial.

"I've never heard of Ryan Sherwood," Rei said. "I'm sorry."

"And your production company has never worked on something like I described?"

"Never. We have some small-scale shoots, some tight productions, but nothing like that, not in New York. Not ever, really. I'm sorry, but this wasn't us."

Shannon thanked her and ended the call. Ryan had put it together just from listening to Shannon's end. He hung his head and shook it back and forth. "Oh my God," he said.

"Whoever you corresponded with was someone else, it sounds like."

Ryan lifted his head, frustration coming into his eyes. He poked at his phone. "How? I've got emails from her. It's Luminosity Pictures. Says right here ..."

Shannon sat beside him. She had the company website open on her phone and compared their contact page with his emails.

"That's not her actual email address. There's an extra hyphen there – see that?"

He did and became maudlin, hanging his head again. "Ah, man ..."

Shannon said, "Ryan, I'm going to need these emails, okay? I'll need your phone, your laptop."

"Okay."

"I'm sure they scrambled their IP through the deep web. And the phone is probably a burner. But we still have to try. Do you still have the suit?"

"I do. God, I thought it was weird that they didn't want it returned. Ah, man ..."

"And I'm going to need you to come in and give an official statement."

"Okay. All right. I mean, what happened? What is this?"

"I think you were part of a deepfake. You played someone assaulting a woman in an elevator – you were turned into Senator Joel Nickerson, and she was supposed to be his aide. The missing woman, Kristin Fain."

Every last bit of color left his face. "Oh my God ..."

Sherwood put his head in his hands and sobbed.

Shannon patted him on the back. A somber moment for Ryan Sherwood, but adrenaline was lighting her up: his statement, the emails, the suit – it would free Joel Nickerson.

32

Things were tumbling out now, happening fast. She checked in with Bufort, who had gotten the pictures from Eddie Caprice – Cutter meeting this mystery person – and was headed back to the office.

"This guy Merkel is no ace photographer."

"Why?"

"The photos of Cutter and the unknown subject are distanced, telephoto lens, not the greatest detail. We'll try facial recognition on the unknown subject, but I'm not gonna bet on it. Too blurry."

She had a thought. "Listen, if you can't pull facial, try something."

"What?"

"Look through the fundraiser images. See if any of the guests resemble our mystery person, even a little."

"The fundraiser?"

She shrugged. "It's as good a place as any to look. If the mystery person is involved with the deepfake, maybe they wanted to be there that night. Anyway, we'll talk later – I'm about to formally interview Ryan Sherwood in front of the lawyers."

"Good luck."

Once she had Ryan in a room at Federal Plaza, he described the evening at the Takano Hotel. Now that he knew the situation, he was even more willing to cooperate. At the same time, he'd brought a lawyer, apparently his brother's boyfriend.

"It got even weirder the night of the gig. They wanted me at there at 10:00 p.m. Well, not at the hotel, but a block away. There's a coffee shop on Park and Thirty-Ninth. I sat and waited for a text when they were ready for me."

He never saw the actor playing Fain while awaiting the moment, but he suspected she was lurking around Midtown east somewhere like he was, waiting for the same cue. "If anything, she had more reason to be nervous than I did. But when we hit the scene, she was a real pro."

"Did you get her name?"

He shook his head. "No. Uh-uh. All I can give you is a physical description." And he did, providing a picture of a young woman roughly Fain's age and body type, with the same hair but notably different facial features.

The whole thing, he said, was over very quickly. Like a blur. At 10:38, he had received the text from "Sasha Rei" that it was time. He'd been given careful instructions in the email about how to play the scene, and further instruction that, on his way to the elevator, he move quickly and not interact with anyone.

"They said to just get in, meet the female actor in the lobby, and head to the elevator. Then we would do the scene."

"And what exactly was the scene?" Shannon asked. "I know it's uncomfortable, but I need you to take me through it, in detail."

"I was supposed to talk to her a little bit, tell her she

looked nice, if she was enjoying the evening. She would say yes, she was. I would ask her if she wanted to come with me to my room. She would say no thank you. Then I would say, 'Come on ...' you know." Sherwood steeled himself. "And then I would force myself on her. Sasha had said to really sell it, make it as believable as possible, take it right to the edge."

Sherwood's lawyer interrupted. "Ryan, did she tell you more about the project? How it was going to be used? Anything about the real intention behind this?"

"I never even spoke to her, never heard her voice. It could have been a man, for all I know. But she said the project was under wraps."

Shannon asked, "And the other actor with you – how did she seem?"

"We only had seconds together. A minute, maybe. I assumed she'd been given all the same information. I had asked for some character background. Sasha said I was a lawyer, and the woman in the elevator was my paralegal, and we were on a big case in the city. We'd been working together for months, and I was strongly attracted to her, and I just couldn't ... Ugh. I'm sorry."

"Take your time."

Sherwood worked through his remorse and finally completed the story. Despite all his doubts and concerns, he'd tried to do the best job he could. Once they had acted out the scene and the elevator stopped – they'd been instructed to go to the top floor – it was simply over. They were to ride the elevator back to the lobby and go their separate ways.

"That was the longest ride of my life," Sherwood said. There were tears in his eyes. "You do a scene like that, and this poor woman ... she was a trooper, but it was ... ah, God. That was a long ride back down."

Shannon asked, "What if someone else had needed the elevator?"

"Sasha said that we shouldn't get on the elevator if anyone else was on. And if someone jumped in at the last second, we should abort, but then go back and try again. But it went smoothly. We got it in one take."

"And you never had a chance to get her name. The other actor."

"No."

"Was there any chat? Any conversation outside of your roles?"

He shook his head. "I'm not exactly a method actor, but I just ... I needed to put my head down, to do the scene. I didn't even say hi to her."

"Okay. Ryan, I need to ask you one last question. Were there any other instructions? Regarding the camera?"

"Yes, actually. Sasha was very clear about that. I was supposed to make sure my face got in the camera. I was really nervous about that part, because I didn't want to look at the camera, which would blow it, but I needed to know where it was. I mean, she told me how it was positioned, but still. Mostly it was how we had to block the scene. How our bodies had to be. She – the other actor – *wasn't* supposed to get her face on camera. Just me. Sasha wanted to make sure the camera saw me, and only me."

"Thank you, Ryan."

Shannon faced the one-way glass, knowing Tyler and the others were behind it.

As far as she was concerned, Ryan Sherwood was genuine. And as far as his statement exonerating Nickerson, he'd just hit it out of the park.

"So? Are we going to let Nickerson go?" Shannon was in Tyler's office, Galloway with them.

Tyler stood at the window overlooking the city, his back to the room. He didn't answer.

Shannon said, "Sir, I think we have a pretty clear picture now. Actors were hired to play Nickerson and Fain. Nickerson's face was then digitally mapped onto the actor – Sherwood. The effect is a very convincing video that appears to show Nickerson sexually assaulting Fain. And the motive is clear – coerce him into voting yes on Monday."

Tyler finally turned. "But who? Who is coercing him?"

"We don't know. But that's next. Nickerson's private investigator might have a lead."

Tyler scoffed. "The pictures of Nickerson's chief of staff sitting in a car with someone."

"Caprice thinks Cutter is connected to this." She knew how it sounded, but kept her back straight, her chin up. "I know it's just conjecture. But it's a reasonable place to start."

Someone knocked at the door. Bufort came in when Tyler told him to enter. He greeted Galloway and said, "I made an ID on the guy. The one Cutter was having his clandestine meeting with two nights ago."

"Well, you're right on time," Tyler said.

"Who is it?" Shannon was on the edge of her seat.

"Cutter was talking to someone named Zach Handler," Bufort said. "He's an independent contractor, a software guy, and he's worked for Plexus."

"How did you ID him?"

"You were right. I found matching pictures from the fundraiser. And those I could run against the system."

Tyler held up a hand. "You matched Merkel's terrible PI photos to someone from the fundraiser dinner? By eye?"

"Yeah. It's him."

"I'd like to see." Tyler crossed his arms.

"Sure, come on down to Reese's office."

"I will. But even if – so what? He could be hiring him for a job for all we know."

"Handler has worked for Plexus for several years."

"As a contractor – you said. So he's not someone tied into the success of Plexus. He's a free agent in a gig economy." Tyler looked back and forth between Bufort and Shannon. "You're going to need more than that if you want us to take a run at Cutter, let alone put him up on a wire."

Galloway nodded. "It could take weeks to get the proper documentation for that."

"We don't have weeks," Shannon said. She pressed her palms together, as if in prayer. "Sir, I think Fain is alive. She's being held by the same people who deepfaked the senator, who hired these actors and made that video. She was taken because she could have obviously challenged the authenticity of that video. She would have said she was never in the elevator."

"Ames ..." There was an unusual tension in Tyler's voice. Something different from his typical stress. "You need to take a step back."

"A step back? We're right there, sir. I don't understand ..."

Tyler asked Bufort and Galloway that they be left alone. The two men walked out, and Bufort gave her a worried look before he closed the door.

Tyler reached into his desk drawer and pulled out a file, dropped it on his desk. "Do you know what this is?"

She hesitated, looking at him a moment, then moved to the file, icicles forming in her stomach. She flipped through it. It didn't take long before the icicles started jabbing.

"It's a preliminary report from the Office of the Inspector General," she said.

"Correct. They're investigating you for embezzlement."

"Sir?"

"Money is missing from one of our accounts. A significant amount. As you can see, your bank generated a SAR for nearly the same amount."

He meant Suspicious Activity Report. Banks generated them automatically when a large enough amount of money was deposited or withdrawn. She managed to keep from fainting, but barely. How had she not seen this? Well, she had, but she'd been so focused on Kristie Fain ...

Tyler said, "Your bank records show a recent deposit of nearly fifteen thousand dollars. Fifteen thousand lodged in your account, then a debit for the amount of a recent purchase. Your doorman said a package arrived from Christian Dior. The jewelry company."

Now her skin crawled. So this was what it was like to be in the center of a hoax. She had a newfound compassion for Nickerson. She opened her mouth, closed it, then shook her head. "This isn't what it looks like."

"What it looks like is that you're under investigation by the OIG. And I can't have you working this case while they conduct theirs."

"Don't you see?" She could feel herself losing control. It didn't often happen, but if there was ever a time ... "This all started happening because I'm getting close. As soon as I thought Nickerson might be telling the truth, this happened."

"What? What happened and when, Shannon?"

She swallowed. "I got the package. The Dior jewelry. Expensive jewelry. I didn't know where it came from. I didn't even think to check my own account for a debit. But it's going to look like I bought it. Why would I do that? That's conspicuous consumption, and you know me, sir. This is not me." She glanced at the door, wishing Bufort were there to back her up.

Tyler said, "What I know is that when this started happening to you, you didn't tell me. You didn't come to me."

It all broke her. "This is *them*. Cutter, Plexus – I'm being set up!"

Tyler lost his cool, too. "Shannon, you sound like a fucking conspiracy theorist. You're suspended. Suspensions usually happen on Fridays, but this is an extreme situation. It's effective immediately."

She felt explosive now, unable to stop. "Mark – listen to me. Nickerson showed us the video. We arrested him, and now we've got reason to let him go. But he might still fear the public release of that video. Do you understand? He may fear further – maybe irreparable – reputational damage. The end of his career. He said no one bounces back from that, whether it's true or not." She took a steadying breath. "Fain hasn't been able to challenge the video – that's *part* of why she was taken. But she's also their insurance policy. *Having her is their currency*. The same situation is still in play. Nickerson can still be coerced to vote. Nothing has changed." She added, emphasizing each word: "Unless we get to her."

Tyler was listening, but his eyes were distant. After a moment, he held out his hand. "Special Agent Ames, I need you to leave your badge and your gun. I'll give you a moment to collect your things, and then I'm asking you to leave. Someone from the OIG will be in touch."

For a moment, she thought she might cry. But she complied with Tyler's orders and set down her Glock on his desk, laid her badge holder on top of it.

She didn't cry, and she didn't lose it. She only looked Tyler square in the eye and left.

33

By a week, Kristie had learned all their names. Mahdi was her nursemaid. Kahleel was the quiet one, the one with the thick mustache. Rafiq was the leader. At least, when he spoke, the other two men seemed to listen, and never challenged him. His eyes were glassy and dark, his mood volatile. He'd received a call just moments ago; Kristie could detect the vibration of his voice as he stood on the deck, though could not make out any words.

Was this finally it? Some kind of demands were being made? Perhaps a negotiation for her release? She'd had plenty of time to develop theories as to why she was here – none of them were good.

Rafiq turned and looked at her through the glass.

Something is definitely happening ...

When he ended the call, he spoke to the others. This time it was Mahdi who gave her a look from outside.

The pity in his eyes was unmistakable, and cold dread invaded her bones. *Oh God ...*

The men dispersed, and Mahdi entered the house. The

TV was on – she'd been allowed it since Wednesday, after she'd had a kind of nervous breakdown. Though they'd been avoiding all other appliances in the house – including lights – they'd brought in a mid-sized flatscreen and plugged it in. She was only allowed one channel, Cartoon Network, and only for an hour in the morning and an hour in the afternoon. It was just past eight now, Sunday morning, ten minutes into her hour. Mahdi shut it off.

"What's going on?" Her voice trembled even as she tried to stay calm.

He didn't answer. He only came closer and started to undo her binds. The other two men were nowhere in sight. She thought she heard an engine turn over.

"Mahdi, what happened?" Pleading in her voice now, despite her better intentions.

He stayed mute and freed her ankles from the chair. When he started on her wrists, he said, "Moving you."

"What? Why? Can you talk to me?"

Was that a good thing? Moving her? Was someone about to pay the ransom? Were the cops getting close?

"Just be quiet."

He seemed upset with her – but, no – he was upset with the situation, maybe. Rafiq was demanding and exerted lots of pressure.

"Please," she whispered. "You can tell me."

But her captors were disciplined. Meticulous. They seemed careful even that the electric meter didn't betray their existence here; the two hours of Cartoon Network was as lavish as they'd gotten. Judging by the weather outside and the general temperature, she figured she was still on the east coast – New York or maybe south of there, Virginia – but that was all she knew for sure.

Mahdi had her completely free now and got her up on

her feet. Before she could plead further, his companions entered the room, both of them walking fast.

She glimpsed something in Kahleel's hands.

"No!"

He was fast and forcible, stuffing the gag in her mouth, choking her, cutting off the word. As she coughed and sputtered behind the wadded fabric, one of the men pulled a black bag over her head.

Kristie instantly started to struggle. There was no thought to it – this was survival. But the men held her by the arms and by the legs and carried her through the house as she convulsed in their grip. When one of them hit her, the blow to the head stopped her from moving at once.

As she struggled to stay conscious, she sensed a change in the air – they were outside. Feet crunched over gravel. A moment later, hinges squealed, then a door banged closed. The place they entered smelled like chemicals, fuel.

She was sat down, a rough drop that sent a bolt from her tailbone up her spine.

Mom, she thought. *Mommy, I love you ...*

Her legs were bound again. Her wrists lashed behind her. This was a hard, straight-backed chair. The men started speaking in low tones, talking in Arabic again. They seemed to argue.

"Don't," she tried to say. *Don't kill me.* But the gag prevented her, and she could only moan.

Mahdi, she thought. *I know you're good. Please help me.*

But she no longer could sense the big man near her. No longer sense his protective, more amiable presence at all.

The other two men seemed to be arguing in front of her, about five yards away. Feet scraped hard ground; the noises sounded canned. Something in their voices reminded her of people in a relationship, frustrated by close quarters. Only, these two were likely arguing about which way to kill her, and how to keep it quiet without too much mess.

Then someone yanked off her hood, and Kristie screamed in terror.

34

When her phone rang, Shannon was already awake. She'd tossed and turned all night, unable to slow the racing thoughts. She took the call as she swung her legs out of the bed. "Hello, Charles."

"The new guy sucks," Bufort said.

"Tyler replaced me already?" But then, she shouldn't be surprised. The OIG had opened a case on her the same day her bank had received the deposit. Tyler had a lot riding on this. "Who is it?"

"Kilburn."

"From Domestic Terrorism?" She remembered him; he'd given a presentation on TIK and Drexel Murphy. "Isn't he a friend?"

"He started in DT after I left. All I know is, he just left my office and he's headed over to Reese. Shannon ... he was drinking a decaf latte."

Funny, but there were more pressing concerns. "What was the decision on Nickerson?"

"That's why I'm calling. Tyler listened to you. Nickerson is no longer in custody. He's free. Did you throw away your TV?"

That woke her up. She left the bedroom for the living room and clicked on her set, turned it to one of the twenty-four-hour news channels.

"I needed to clear my head," she told Bufort distractedly. Nickerson was the main story. Cameras captured him leaving a squat, nondescript government building as he got into the rear of a black SUV and it drove away. The chyron read: *New Twist in Senator Assault Case.* She flipped to the next news channel. *Was Nickerson Framed?*

Bufort said, "It's everywhere. I mean, it's a huge story."

She flipped again. On a Sunday morning talk show, the women gathered around a table discussed it with vigor. "The biggest concern is how this is going to be ammunition for anyone against the women's movement," one said.

"Yeah, but she's missing," responded another. "It's almost like this is saying, the only way something like this works is to get rid of the woman entirely. Because women tell the truth."

A third co-host was frowning. "I'm confused. How do we know she wasn't assaulted and abducted? I think we're taking a big leap here ..."

"Because an actor has admitted posing as Senator Nickerson for this elevator video."

"Are we ever going to get this video? I think the American people need to see it ..."

The audience clapped and cheered.

"Good times," Bufort said in Shannon's ear. She walked away from the TV to the kitchen, suddenly parched. He talked some more about Kilburn while she guzzled a glass of water. She appreciated Bufort's call – he was both attempting to cheer her up and keep her in the loop – but she needed to think.

"All right," he said when she asked him to let her go. "Keep in touch."

She hung up and went to her terrace with a fresh glass of water and looked out at Queens. The day was humid, hazy, a few birds tweeting unseen. Jasper joined her and jumped up onto one of the two wrought-iron chairs at the small metal table.

The same thoughts that had been plaguing her all night were still there. But they were incomplete, inchoate. Her mind felt like a skipping record:

You were close.

Then they went after you.

Now you're being investigated.

You may not bounce back from this.

After a moment of blank despair, it repeated:

You were close.

Then they went after you ...

Whoever they were – they were good. She understood that money was mostly digital in the modern world, and it wasn't like thieves had heisted cash from an FBI evidence room and stuck it under her mattress. But still – to hack the FBI? To penetrate the top law enforcement body's digital defenses in order to move fifteen thousand dollars? It was no small feat. From what little she knew, the heisted account funded overtime and other agency expenses.

The hackers had breached her personal account, too, and used the FBI money to make a purchase. Just to make it look good – she was stealing and then hiding the money in expensive items.

Shannon went back into the apartment and sat at her desk, an antique rolltop that had come with the partly furnished space. She opened the package, gazed at the finely crafted rose gold jewelry. She held it in her hand, again sensing the paradox of its strength and fragility.

When her phone buzzed in the other room, it startled her. She put the jewelry back in the box – she'd be taking it to her meeting with the OIG first thing tomorrow morning – and returned to the kitchen, where she'd left her phone sitting on the countertop.

She checked the screen before answering. "Eddie?"

"Special Agent Ames, I'm outside your apartment. Would you come down and talk to me?"

It was unexpected. "You're at my *home*?"

"Seems like more of an older generation around here. I like it. Yes, I'm downstairs in my car. I have something to show you."

"What?"

He cleared his throat. "You need to come see."

35

The young woman was tied up and gagged.

She looked rough, her auburn hair frizzed, her wet eyes ringed with dark fatigue. She was in the same clothes from a week ago: black stretch pants and a simple T-shirt, the white looking dingier, spotted. Kristie Fain.

Shannon sat in the passenger seat of Eddie Caprice's car, watching. He'd handed her his phone and pressed play just moments before.

On the video, a man stepped into view, his head out of frame. Then he stooped low to look into the camera. Exaggerated black eyebrows arched high onto his white forehead. His mouth was lengthened with black paint, curled up at the ends. He seemed be checking to make sure the angle of the camera was right by slowly waving his hand up and down.

Fain had been crying. Tears streaked her dirty face. She stared into the lens, as if pleading for help. But then the man said something – Shannon heard a mumbling voice, too low to discern the words – and Fain looked up at him as he approached, and nodded quickly.

Finally, he reached in and pulled the gag out of her mouth. He said one more word, and Shannon understood it: "Go."

Fain managed a couple of words and started coughing. Then she recovered and began again. "My name is Kristin Elizabeth Fain. This is really me, this is not a fake." Her body jumped with a sob. She continued by providing her birth-date, social security number, and mother's maiden name.

As she spoke, the man stood beside her, half in the image. Shannon watched as he slowly moved a gun towards Fain until the barrel was pressing against her temple.

"This is not a fake," she repeated, and began crying. "What you're seeing is re–"

The image went black, and then five words appeared in bold white:

VOTE YES OR SHE DIES

Shannon released a shuddering breath. She tried to put the emotion aside and quiet the clamoring thoughts; there was no time to process what she'd just seen – no time for Fain, anyway – she needed to act. Eddie Caprice's phone had to get to video forensics for any clues in the image, and they had to trace the source.

When she said as much to Eddie, he just looked at her. "You should think about that."

"What are you talking about?" She added, "And when did you get this?"

"An hour ago. Joel sent it. I drove straight here."

"Has anyone else seen it?"

"No."

"Not Cutter?"

"Not Cutter. Joel showed me and was about to call your people. I advised him to wait. I wanted to talk to you first."

"Well, I'm off the case. I'm suspended as of yesterday."

"I heard. I called your office first."

"What did you tell them?"

"Nothing. I spoke to the clerk, asked if you were in, he said no. I asked for the covering agent, he said, 'Let me check,' and then came back two minutes later and said you weren't. But his tone had changed, and I knew what it meant." Caprice gave her a look like he already knew the answer. "They got to you, didn't they?"

For a moment, she made no response. They sat parked on the street in front of her apartment building, Eddie's SUV idling. A light rain started to sprinkle against the windshield.

"I'm being investigated for embezzlement."

He whistled. "Ouch. That could take a while. And you're probably still taking heat for arresting Joel in the first place, not letting him turn himself in. Am I right?"

"You're not wrong."

"What's the max penalty short of being fired?"

"Forty-five days. Listen – thank you for bringing this to me. But Senator Nickerson's instincts are right –this needs to get into the proper hands."

"Okay, so let your people work on it. But what are *you* gonna do?"

"I just told you. There's nothing I can do."

"Did you find anything on Cutter? On who he was meeting with?"

"I can't answer that."

"It was Plexus, wasn't it?"

She studied Eddie. "What do you know about them?"

"I know what you know. That they almost certainly stand to gain from a yes vote. And I think Cutter needs money, so he's a perfect middleman."

"Why does he need money?"

"I asked Joel last night. Cutter hasn't exactly been forthcoming, but Joel thinks he's got some medical problem. He's had days where he couldn't come into work, made up an excuse. He almost lost his balance once, almost fell over in front of Joel."

Cutter's trip to the drugstore came to mind; Merkel had witnessed him picking up multiple prescriptions. "Does Joel suspect Cutter?"

Eddie shook his head. "Cutter has been with Joel from the beginning. So even if his rational mind has an inkling, he quashed it right away."

"Then why didn't he share the video with Cutter? We're talking about his number-two man, practically his consiglieri."

"Careful. *I'm* his consiglieri. I'll tell you why he didn't share it with Cutter – because regardless of how he feels about the guy, Joel doesn't trust anyone right now. Anyone but me. And I only trust you. Especially now that they got to you."

She waved a hand. "I appreciate you coming to me with this. But it needs to go to the right people. And the pictures of Cutter meeting with Zach Handler from Plexus, it's interesting, but it's not enough to act on. Same with his possible medical issue. It's all circumstantial. You know that."

"Yeah, and it could never be used in court; it's fruit of the poisonous tree, yadda yadda." He watched Shannon a moment. "But what do you think is going to happen to this girl?"

She thought about Fain's tear-streaked face, her choked words. There was no performance there, no deepfake – Shannon was sure it was a hundred percent real. "I don't know. Has Joel said what he's going to do in terms of the vote? Is he going to give them what they want tomorrow?"

Eddie gazed through the rain-specked windshield. He turned on the wipers. "I didn't ask him that."

She considered what the public knew – that Nickerson had been arrested in connection to Fain's disappearance. Rumors of his having assaulted her at a New York City hotel fundraiser.

People were discussing the possibility Nickerson had been set up, but as far as Shannon knew, the motive of coercing his vote was not yet part of the public discourse. That aspect was under wraps, but barely. What would happen when people found out a senator had been extorted into changing his vote?

Nickerson had a dilemma. Vote according to his principles and possibly sentence Fain to death. Vote according to the demands of criminals and the whole system of democracy was upended.

She wanted to talk to him, discover his intentions. Did he think it was a bluff? Was he going to put first principles ahead of everything else, to adopt a firm, no-negotiating-with-terrorists position?

And what if he did vote as directed – would they even let Fain go after all was said and done? Or had she seen and heard too much; was she too much of a liability? Why would they risk it?

Shannon suddenly felt far away from home. From her roots. Her family, the farm, her church. The larger world felt run by greed and a lust for power. And not the kind of healthy interests for progress and prosperity, but a kind of superstorm of technology, money, and global reach that had implications beyond what she wanted to consider.

It didn't matter.

She needed to focus on getting to Kristie Fain. Before it was too late.

"Putting pressure on Cutter is not the way," she told Eddie. "If we press him, it could further jeopardize Fain."

"Agreed. You can't take a run at him directly, no. But you

need to have eyes-on, see what he does."

"*I* can't do anything," she said with frustration. "The Washington field office won't respond to my requests, not when I'm suspended. And even if I could influence my office here ... the new lead agent is too gung ho. Cutter will see him coming a mile away."

Eddie sat quietly. She sensed him awaiting her decision.

"Where do you think they took her? Is she in New York? Or DC?"

"It's a good question." Eddie replayed the video, holding the phone so they could both watch, and turned the sound down to study the image with less distraction. The oil-stained concrete floor suggested a basement or garage. But residential, not industrial, and not an apartment building. That didn't narrow it down much. There were tools partly in view, hanging from a pegboard behind Fain. Not immediately helpful either. It was summer, so whether she was in New York or DC, she could be sweating. And she was; a shimmer of perspiration coated her face and arms. Shannon could barely handle watching her, seeing the pain in her eyes, hearing the desperation in her voice. By all accounts, Kristin Fain was a strong, independent woman. But she'd been broken.

"All right," Shannon said quietly. The video had ended.

"All right?"

"Let's go."

Eddie put the SUV in gear. "Yes, ma'am. And where exactly are we going?"

"We need to find Keith Cutter."

"I was hoping you'd say that. And the good news is, we won't need to look very hard."

"Why?"

"Because I had Tom Merkel put a tracker on him three days ago."

36

Interstate 95 teemed with motorists, people returning home from a leisurely August weekend. The noon sun starred off all the glass and chrome. Eddie weaved through traffic, pushing the Ford up to eighty.

Going after Keith Cutter with a civilian – and while actively suspended – was exceedingly bad judgment. But it was her best shot. It was Fain's best shot. And if, at most, it got them information she could pass on to her colleagues, it was worth it.

But it plagued her.

Eddie said, "So, forty-five days that you could be suspended before they drop the hammer?"

"Yeah."

He shook his head. "In my day, the department would pass the hat to try to make up some or all of an officer's missed wages."

He meant other cops contributing to a kind of informal fund for the suspended officer. Shannon wondered if the NYO would do that for her – she'd barely been there a week.

But wages were the last thing she was concerned with at the moment.

"So where you from, Shannon?"

"I'm sorry ... I don't feel like talking."

"Come on, we're only twenty minutes in; a good two and a half hours left. It'll go quicker if we get to know each other."

She sighed, nodded; he was right. "Upstate New York, in the Adirondacks."

"Ah, beautiful up there. God's country, they say."

"It is." For a moment she thought of Caldoza, whose family had left him property not far from where she'd grown up. For a short time, she and Caldoza had made plans together. Maybe they'd even retire up there together one day. But it had been fantasy. Their work was too consuming, too dangerous.

God – was this her life? In the morning, she would have to submit to rounds of questioning from the OIG. Her world was about to be turned upside down, and here she was, speeding south to Washington, DC, with an ex-cop who moonlighted as a US senator's personal fixer. Talk about digging the hole deeper.

"I've been to a farm a few times," Eddie said. "Cows and all of that. Jersey actually has a lot of rural areas." He gave her a sideways look. "You're not gonna ask me where I grew up – you already know."

"Kearny. The same place you live now."

"Beautiful place. When I was growing up, mostly no crime, no drugs." His mood seemed to darken. "All the opioids now – I know somebody's getting rich. A *lot* of some-bodies are getting rich. My son-in-law, Joe, was hurt in a traffic accident while in a high-speed pursuit. Messed up his legs, both of his knees. They prescribed him hydrocodone." Eddie sounded remorseful. "They never should've given him that shit. Some strong Tylenol would've done it. But they had to push this stuff. Had to get it out there. And he didn't know any better. None of us did. He got hooked. And then, to keep things together, the marriage, the family, Tammy would bring it home from the hospital."

He glanced at Shannon, an apology in his eyes. "She regrets it to her core. Because when she eventually said 'no more,' Joe started copping off the street. Using the badge. And ... he had drugs in his system when he got shot in the line of duty. So when he died, the insurance investigation turned up that he was an addict, and Tammy and Zoe got nothing. She works around the clock to pay the bills. There's some money for day care, but she works odd hours that day care doesn't cover."

"So you step in."

"I do what I can. It's not much. They deserve a lot more than me. A lot better." He changed lanes after passing a tractor-trailer. The bruises on his knuckles had faded some, but not entirely.

A minute passed in silence. Shannon had texts from Bufort, who was the only one who knew what she was doing. Nickerson had sent the video to the FBI after Eddie had contacted him, and now the techs were studying it for clues. Kilburn had spoken with Nickerson and discussed strategies. But Bufort texted her:

No one knows what the fuck to do.

EDDIE'S FRIEND Tom Merkel was how she expected: in his sixties with saggy eyes and a PI's stomach hanging over his pleated pants. He met them in a Burger King parking lot ten minutes from the Capitol, to update them on Cutter.

Shannon and Eddie stayed in the car while Merkel stood

beside the open driver's-side window. "I followed him around all morning, seemed like the usual slate of errands," Merkel said about Cutter. "Now he's at the office. Been there for the past three hours." He ducked his head to get another look at Shannon. "So ... it's just the two of you?"

Eddie sidestepped the question. "How does the tracking work?" He had an app open on his phone.

Merkel took it. "Here. So, basically, the subject has a GPS dot. I'll put in the number on it and you'll have it on your phone. See? I give you the number for the GPS dot; now you can track it on your own app. That's it." He poked at the screen a moment and handed it back. "Modern tech, huh?"

"I hear you."

Merkel sniffed and looked off into the distance. "He sent his wife and daughter away this morning."

Shannon leaned over to get a better look at the ex-cop. "What do you mean?"

"I mean, I put a dot on both of Cutter's vehicles, his and hers. Sometimes he takes hers – it's a Honda Fit, better gas mileage, maybe. I was on the house this morning, she and the daughter – fourteen – left with bags. A little while later, they were in Bethesda, and they've been there since."

"Thanks, Tommy," Eddie said. The men shook hands.

SHANNON AND EDDIE waited on East Capitol Street, parked in front of the Supreme Court. They had a straight view of the Capitol Building down the street: pillared, alabaster white, dome topped with the colossal bronze *Statue of Freedom* – the one she'd seen replicated inside. The sun descended behind it.

She felt restless, but they needed to wait. Wait for what

the techs might find, for what Kilburn decided to do. And to see what moves Cutter made.

When he left that evening, they tracked him to his house in Forest Hills, a residential area in the northwest of the city. Once parked, his SUV was the sole vehicle in the driveway. The house was two stories, redbrick with black shutters, plenty of shrubs and trees. A first-floor window glowed yellow as the world dissolved into darkness.

"Looks like he's all alone," Caprice said. "Are you ready to do this? I'd say it's now or never."

But she didn't move. Her phone sat on her lap – her last text to Bufort had asked for an update, but he'd had nothing earth-shattering to report. While agents studied the video content, techs from the WFO had cloned Nickerson's phone and were trying to source the video. As expected, it had been routed through the deep web, rendering it untraceable. Same with the money paid to Ryan Sherwood, the actor.

She thought of Fain: beaten, terrified, abused as a political bargaining chip. Waiting in purgatory while dozens of law enforcement figured out what to do.

The least she could do was talk to Cutter. She was here. Nothing illegal about a little conversation. Nothing that would alarm him, she hoped, and endanger Fain. If, in fact, there was even a real connection there.

Shannon closed her eyes a moment, seeking guidance. The response was quiet, just the sound of Eddie breathing beside her, a little whistle in his nose.

"Okay," she said, eyes open. "But we do this my way."

WHEN SHE WALKED UP to the house, she was alone. She knocked on the door and rang the buzzer, suddenly self-conscious of her appearance. Did you wear a T-shirt, jeans, black boots and a small golden crucifix when you were about to interrogate a suspect off the books? Maybe she should've worn the rose gold ...

Multiple dogs were barking. Beneath their racket, a beeping sound.

When the door opened, Cutter stared out at her. "Special Agent Ames. What's ...? How can I help you?"

"I was in the neighborhood."

He didn't smile back.

She switched to blunt tactics: "Mr. Cutter, I have information I need to share with you – and a few questions that won't take long. Can I come in?"

"Of course."

He opened the door wider, allowing her to pass, then closed it. A red light flashed on a wall panel – it appeared Cutter had deactivated an alarm to let her in. His two large gray dogs, Neapolitan mastiffs by the look of their wrinkly faces and drooping jowls, came trotting over, nails clicking the marble floor. He grabbed their collars and put them in a separate room, then led Shannon into a living area where the décor was more cozy than formal. A gas-burning fireplace with fake logs, two couches that faced each other, a large potted plant in each corner.

"I'd give you the tour," Cutter said, "but it seems urgent."

"It is."

Cutter was still dressed in work clothing, though his jacket and tie were removed. She saw them draped over the one hardback chair in the room, situated at a small desk against the far wall. An open door on that same wall led to a kitchen.

"Do we have time to sit?" Cutter asked.

"That's okay." She took her phone out and queued up the video as she continued: "When is the last time you spoke to Senator Nickerson?"

"Just before I left work," Cutter answered. "He's at home, trying to avoid the media. Agent Ames, I have to say – your good work finding that actor – Senator Nickerson is incredibly grateful. We all are."

She held his eye a moment. "Did the senator seem to behave strangely at all today? Let me clarify: Have there been any developments you know about, anything since his release?"

Cutter looked puzzled. "Developments ... I don't know, I didn't see him a lot today. But obviously he has a lot on his mind. When we did speak, yeah, I suppose you could say he seemed distracted." Cutter's gaze ticked to the window, like he saw something outside, or was expecting to. "Are you here on your own?"

"I'm the only agent here, yes. Mr. Cutter, let me ask you – what is the senator going to do?"

"You mean how is he going to vote? I honestly don't know. I'm sure you can imagine – this has just been a whirlwind."

"What I meant to ask – how serious has Senator Nickerson considered this threat? To release the video? Do you think – whoever is doing this – it's enough now? He's been released from custody. The papers are saying he was framed, that it's a deepfake hoax. The people behind this, you'd think they'd need to raise the stakes."

Cutter gave her a shrewd look. She regretted her choice of words; she might be laying it on too thick. He was already suspicious of her presence, perhaps slightly confused, but if she pushed too far, he'd sense her trying to trap him into admitting something. If there was anything to admit.

"Which question would you like me to answer?"

"How have you counseled him to vote?"

"I've counseled the senator to vote yes. The way the terrorists – that's what I call them – have demanded. And that's not a reputational strategy. That's an effort to save

Kristie Fain's life. Do they need to up the stakes, as you put it? I'm not sure. I think the implication is clear. Why would they just let her go, even if the senator votes how they've asked? We've considered that eventuality from the very beginning, Special Agent Ames. But you being here, now, and on your own – I wonder. Something's happened. I think maybe I'm out of the loop."

Shannon took out her phone. Continuing to evaluate Cutter's sincerity, she opened a picture. "Just to be clear, you're saying to me that you have no knowledge that anything has been sent to Senator Nickerson since the text demanding his vote. No follow-up video, nothing."

He was straight-faced. "Not to my knowledge, no."

Now or never. She handed her phone to Cutter, open to the picture of him and Zach Handler. "Does this look familiar to you?"

She watched him review the image.

Cutter said, "Where did you get this?"

"That's your car?"

His eyes met hers. "It appears to be."

She moved closer, retrieved the phone from him, and swiped through more images. "The man you're talking to has been identified as a contractor for Plexus."

"I obviously know who he is. Mr. Handler is a friend. He's been a huge supporter – he was at the fundraiser dinner in New York."

"Yes, he was." She put her phone away. "Why were you meeting?"

"I went to Georgetown with Zach. We're friends, and this meeting was of a personal nature. Unless I'm legally compelled, I think I've said everything I'm going to say about that." Cutter frowned at her. "Have you been following me? The FBI is watching me?"

"You're saying that meeting has nothing to do with Kristie Fain? The deepfake, her disappearance – none of it?"

"Are you kidding me? That's why you're here?" His face was blooming red.

"You're saying it's a coincidence that you happen to be talking to a Plexus contractor in the middle of an extortion scheme against Senator Nickerson – when Plexus is the front-runner to earn a multimillion-dollar contract for the new federal surveillance system?"

"I told you – he's a *friend*. And no contractors have been selected yet. Plexus is a huge company, thousands of employees, thousands more subcontractors. I don't like where this is headed. I think I'm going to ask you to leave."

"So 'yes' is your answer? Yes, it's a coincidence?"

He was fuming. "Yes," he said at last.

A voice emanated from the back of the room. "You're gonna have to do better than that."

37

The moment Eddie spoke, Shannon's dilemma peaked. She already felt wrong being here, a suspended agent interrogating a suspect, on her own. And Cutter's story wasn't unreasonable. He could have been meeting with Handler for any number of reasons. Would a multibillion-dollar company truly resort to such brute tactics? And without guarantee they'd even get a contract? She felt foolish, flushing her career down the drain. And while she'd agreed to it, she'd hoped it wouldn't have come to this – seeing Eddie meant they were headed into even worse territory, with consequences unfathomable.

He emerged from the shadowed corner of the room, wearing black leather gloves that squeaked when he flexed his hands.

"How did you get in here?" Cutter sounded both angry and scared.

"Through the back door."

Cutter seemed unsure of where to go next, and stood in a kind of frozen limbo between Shannon and Eddie. Eddie had stopped, too. "When you turned off your alarm," he explained.

Cutter took his gaze off Eddie and glared at Shannon. "You're working with this guy?"

"Mr. Cutter," Shannon said, trying to maintain some air of professionalism, of calm, "this is Edward Caprice."

"I know who he is." Cutter stared at Eddie some more. "Joel hired you. I know he did. He just told me he had *someone* working on it, but I knew it was you."

Eddie nodded somberly, studying the floor. When his eyes came up, they had gone darker, distant. He raised one black-gloved hand and patted the air. "Why don't you sit down a minute, Keith?"

Cutter took out his phone. "Why don't I call the cops?" He nodded at Shannon. "There's no way she's here on a sanctioned visit. She's off the reservation, I can see it. And I'm going to take her d–"

In a couple of quick strides and one swift move, Shannon snatched Cutter's phone out of his hand. Cutter lunged for it, but Eddie was there – he was damn fast for an older guy – and wrapped his arm around Cutter's neck.

The dogs started barking in the other room as Cutter fought back against Eddie. Shannon watched with mounting horror. Every nerve in her body protested what she was seeing – a crime in progress. A crime she was *part* of. They were in a man's home, where they had no right to be, no jurisdiction, and they were assaulting him. And she was staking it all on hunches and a couple of photographs.

It got worse: He managed to slip the hold. When he started running for the kitchen, Eddie went the other way, around the couch, and was able to block his escape.

"You sons of bitches," Cutter mumbled. "You're both going to go to fucking prison for this. Your lives are over. Do you realize what you're doing? Who I am?"

Eddie kept the doorway blocked, ready if Cutter made a move. The dogs continued their deep, upset barking in the other room. Each bark seemed to rattle her rib cage. Those were Neapolitan mastiffs. If they got out and defended their master, she and Eddie were probably dead.

Nickerson's chief of staff stood, fuming, then turned around, facing Shannon still by the second couch. "I'll make sure you never work in law enforcement again. Not a Podunk town deputy, not a meter ma–"

"Where is she?" It felt like something took over inside Shannon. There was no more time to debate this, to worry about the consequences. She was here; she was already in it; now she had to commit.

"How the hell should I know?"

Shannon moved closer, picking her way past the furniture. "Where is she? Where are they keeping her?"

"Get out of my house."

"You've worked with her for three years. Are you even going to let her go, regardless of how Nickerson votes? You said it yourself – you considered it. Because you set it up." Having gotten just a few feet away from Cutter, Shannon studied his eyes. "Talk to me. Keith, I know you have reasons for doing this. But it's got to stop."

"I don't know what the fuck you're talking about." Cutter had backed against the wall. "You're both insane."

Shannon had cut off his route to the front of the house, and Eddie his way into the kitchen. Cutter was like a cornered animal. When he came for her, she put her arms up to defend herself, but he managed to get a handful of her hair and slammed her head off the wall as he shoved his way past her.

Eddie was again quick and caught him. As Shannon stumbled back from the wall to find a place to sit, stunned by the blow, Eddie hit Cutter in the face. Cutter went down.

Eddie loomed over him. He turned to Shannon. "You okay?"

"Yeah," she said, her head throbbing.

Eddie turned back to Cutter and stared down at the man. Then he kicked him in the stomach.

Shannon yelled, "No! Stop!"

But it was too late. Eddie bent low, grabbed Cutter by the shirt with one gloved hand, and smashed him in the nose with the other. "Talk!" His face was turning red, spit flying from his lips. "Talk, you motherfucker! Or I'll beat you to death!"

Shannon closed her eyes. She wanted to escape, to be somewhere else, but she couldn't be. She'd chosen this.

God forgive me.

She took a steadying breath, then got to her feet. One phone call and it would all be over.

"Talk to me, now!" Eddie bellowed. He was strong for an older man and raised Cutter to his feet. Cutter's head lolled on his neck. Blood ran from his nose. The dogs barked.

Cutter's eyes fluttered as Eddie cocked his fist for another blow.

"Okay!" Cutter said.

Shannon paused, her finger hovering over the send button, about to call Tyler. To put an end to this. To confess what she'd done. To give up.

"Okay," Cutter said again, breathless. "I'll tell you. I'll fucking tell you ..."

38

With a bleeding nose and rapidly swelling, tearful eyes, Cutter explained how it all had come together. "Zach came to me six months ago. At first, it was just talk. There was a forthcoming bill and, in it, a chance for Plexus to win big. Then he offered me money."

"How much?"

"Two and a half million."

The dogs were still barking. Shannon was still shaking. Cutter's admission was major; now she had to regroup, to be smart. "Two and a half million, just to persuade Nickerson?"

"But Joel wouldn't budge. Not for months. I told Zach I couldn't do it."

"What gives Zach Handler, some freelance software engineer, the ability to make an offer like that?"

Cutter hesitated, but then looked at Eddie, as if deciding where the hesitation might lead. "McWilliams. He was sent by Brian McWilliams, the CEO. I wanted proof of that – that the company was behind it – and I threatened to walk if I didn't get it. So there was one time. One Zoom we had on Zach's phone."

She wondered if there would be any record of that. Most likely not.

This thing was huge. And horrific.

Cutter said, "But I still told Zach no. I couldn't do it, no way. And I thought they'd let it go ... but then I had an idea. I was watching Joel and Kristie together, it was just work, they were chatting, she looked nice, and the sexual assault occurred to me. We could make an accusation, say that he assaulted someone. Done deal. But there were two problems. The woman would have to be in on it. And still, an accusation alone was probably not enough. It had to be something that, if it got out, he couldn't come back from. Something that would really motivate him. So I met with Zach. We always met in the car, and he made me turn off my phone. Zach asked if Kristie would go along for a cut of the money, but I knew she wouldn't."

Cutter paused. "Zach had an idea. He said it wouldn't need to involve us, we'd use actors. We would digitally map the faces of Joel and Kristie. I provided the high-definition footage of Joel. But we didn't have enough for Kristie – she's not usually on TV. Zach said we could arrange things so we didn't have to see her face, just her hair, her outfit. I thought of the fundraiser. The elevator. And I could know in advance what everyone was wearing – I always know what Joel is planning, and we used a rental company for several of the men's tuxes and women's dresses – Fain was going to be one of them. I could provide physical descriptions of my staff, right down to their wardrobe, so hotel and waitstaff would be sure to recognize them. Zach liked it. He said it was good, because she'd be seen that night by hundreds of eyewitnesses. Anyone who saw the video would definitely assume it was her."

Shannon knew where it was headed and said, "But Fain

could just deny any video when it came out. So you had to remove her from the equation."

Cutter closed his eyes. For a moment, he looked like he might be sick. "I didn't want it that way. But I knew the first person he'd call would be Kristie. To have her debunk it as a hoax. Trust me, I thought of every other way to get around that. Send her out of the country on assignment. Just steal her phone, hack her email, shut down all her communications for a week. But none of that would have worked. The only way was for her to disappear."

Shannon said, "Which had the extra benefit of making it look like Nickerson kidnapped her so she couldn't talk about the assault."

Cutter's silence confirmed it.

"So who took her? Who did you hire?"

"I didn't hire anyone. Zach did. Listen – when I tell you I was against this, I was. I told Zach no, for the second time. When it came to kidnapping her, I said forget it. I went home that night and couldn't sleep."

Cutter lowered his head again. "I have lung cancer," he said, almost too quietly to hear. "Stage 3. Just diagnosed three months ago."

Shannon looked at Eddie, who stood a couple of yards away in the doorway. The dogs had finally stopped barking, but gave the occasional whine. Cutter said, "I'm over-leveraged. And my insurance won't cover the costs. By the time I'm dead, my wife and daughter will have nothing. They'll be in debt. I needed to fix it. To leave them *something*." His sadness hardened into anger. "And Joel is just so fucking *stubborn*. I knew he'd never change his mind. It was the only way ..."

The one thing left had been to create a smoke screen. To give the police someone to chase until voting day arrived.

Which was when Cutter had his next big brainchild –

using TIK as the red herring. A libertarian group who'd been publicly rebuked by Fain.

"She'd called them conspiracy theorists on Twitter," Cutter reminded them. "They threatened her. And they wore that makeup ..."

In a city where everything was captured on video, they'd be on camera, individually anonymous but easily associated with TIK because of the makeup – the perfect bait for law enforcement to take.

Shannon asked, "Did you worry about them being ideologically allied with Nickerson?"

"They're well hidden. The idea was for police to chase them, not to talk politics with them. You went farther than I thought the police would get."

She had everything she needed – the important thing now was getting Fain to safety.

But Cutter was despondent. "I don't know where she is. I really don't. That wasn't my department – that was Zach's."

SHANNON AND EDDIE sped out of Cutter's neighborhood with Cutter in the back seat. She'd had no choice but to bring him, keep an eye on him, and to take his phone. She couldn't risk having him call Fain's captors, tipping them off. He claimed to have no contact with them, but he could be lying.

Zach Handler's house was dark. No cars in the driveway, nothing in the garage. An area light snapped on as she approached the front door. She rang the doorbell and waited. No barking dogs here, nothing. It was almost midnight. Where was he?

Even if she weren't suspended and could put out a BOLO right now – get every cop and agent in DC looking for him – that would pose a grave risk to Fain. As long as everybody thought things were going according to plan, Fain was relatively safe. At least, she was the bargaining chip until Nickerson cast his vote. Police action could tip off the abductors that it was game over.

On the other hand, if she didn't have direct access to Fain, a wide search might be her only hope.

It was time to call it in.

To his credit, Tyler listened to the whole story before laying into her: "Ames, you're killing me. I never would have expected you to go off the deep end like this."

"Sir, if there had been any other way."

"You're not *seeing* the other way. This isn't like you. And it's not why I brought you with me. I know all the stuff with the bank will get sorted out – you're not a thief. But *this*? How did you get this information from Cutter? Torture him? I mean, Jesus Christ, Shannon! Do you realize where this goes from here?"

"I'm sorry. But this is what it is."

"It's *nothing* right now, except you turning around and going home. Getting up tomorrow and facing your investigation."

"Please listen to me. They'll kill her. Okay? They'll use her and kill her either way. No matter what Nickerson does. That's my gut feeling."

"Shannon, you're an FBI agent! You don't have a gut!" He was so loud she pulled the phone from her ear. Eddie watched her from behind the wheel of the Ford. "You're not a private eye, you're not a *vigilante* – you work for the federal fucking *government*. Or – maybe you *did*. Because you're an inch away from getting fired. Right here, right now."

"We need Zach Handler. If you don't help me, I'll get people who will."

"Is that a *threat*? Ames, you're done. And I'm done."

She looked at the phone. He'd hung up.

She felt cold, her stomach twisted in knots. But she noted the lack of guilt. She'd always been a bit driven by the need for approval; she knew that. She didn't like confrontation, not with her superiors. Part of that was being a woman – you could only get away with so much in the real world. And part of it was her own nature.

But that nature was changing.

Still in the street in front of Handler's house, she called Bufort. She called Reese. And she called Matheson, with the WFO. She didn't know if it would work. She didn't know if they would tell her she was crazy. But she had to try.

39

DAY EIGHT: MONDAY, VOTING DAY

J ust before 1:00 a.m., Virginia State Police pulled over a green Dodge Challenger headed south out of the city. The driver was Zachary Louis Handler, supposedly on his way to Richmond.

Matheson was the first agent on the scene. The state police had done as instructed – after detaining Handler as if it were a traffic stop, they seized his phone. He hadn't been able to place any calls from the moment he'd been pulled over.

Matheson had put Handler in the back of his BuCar, where he grilled him. When Handler denied any connection to Kristie Fain's disappearance, he called Shannon.

"We got him," Matheson said. "He was on his way to a consulting job, he says. Everything else, he's stonewalling."

Shannon said, "I have Keith Cutter with me. Can you put your phone on speaker? We'll have the two of them talk directly."

"Good idea."

Cutter was pale and morose, but he agreed. "It's over," he said to Handler. "You have to tell them. Or she'll die. And for nothing – you're not going to get what you want. And neither am I."

After a considered pause, Handler said, "I can't say anything. If they see someone coming, she's dead, too."

Shannon spoke. "Who are they?"

"They're men available for hire. I knew the right places to look; I called in some favors. But I can't say any more about that until I know my family is safe. My parents, my sister. These are people who don't forgive a confession."

"How many?"

"There are three of them. And they're very good at what they do. They leave nothing to chance. They don't even use the stove."

"Give me the address."

"I rented a house," Handler said. "And I had them remove any traces of the owners so she would never know where she was. She was supposed to live through this."

"*Give me the address ...*"

Handler did.

"THAT'S LESS THAN AN HOUR AWAY," Shannon said after putting it into the GPS. The Broadlands were almost due west, the deep suburbs of Washington.

Matheson came back on the line. "What do you want to do?"

"I can be there in forty-five minutes," Shannon told him.

"Forty," said Eddie, already pouring on the gas. He took Highway 190 out of Forest Hills, driving in the fast lane.

"I don't know what I can do," Matheson said. "I can run it up the flagpole, see if we can scramble a team ..."

"Thank you." But she felt heavy with doubt. Suspended, she'd gone off with a civilian on paper-thin evidence and beaten information out of Keith Cutter. He might've said anything for fear of traumatic brain injury at the hands of Eddie Caprice. Handler, for that matter, could have also lied. And she was a rogue agent.

"All right," Matheson said. "Call you back."

She thought to try Tyler, maybe even contact the Bureau director himself. But there was a risk they'd want her to come in. She could wind up a fugitive if she kept pushing. Better to let Matheson handle it. But it would have to be soon. With dawn approaching, the vote just hours away, a human being was about to become a political casualty unless everyone acted swiftly.

40

Matheson had bad news. "I talked to my SAC. Had to wake him up, actually. He, ah ... he basically told me to proceed at my own risk. That putting my neck on the line when this intelligence on Fain could be bunk was a bad move. I just ... I've got seven years to retirement. I'm sorry, Ames."

Eddie had taken 190 to I-495, then 267, to bring them within a few miles of their destination. Things here were quiet and dark, the openness broken by sections of tract housing strung like necklaces alongside the highway.

"It's all right. I understand. I'll keep working on it from my end." She hung up.

She had Eddie, and maybe he was all she needed.

After the tract-housing sections, Broadlands looked more like a real neighborhood with wide streets and stately homes set back into wooded properties. Eddie found a dead end and pulled his Ford off the asphalt and partway into the woods. If it was someone's property, the nearest house was a good hundred yards away, too far to notice. A creek babbled somewhere in proximity in the dark; maybe this was a section of state land. At any rate, the neighborhood was quiet, and it was the ditch hours of the night. It would have to do.

Eddie opened the back and returned with bailing twine and duct tape. He tied Cutter's hands and ankles, then attached him to the metal bar beneath the front seat.

"I won't be able to breathe," Cutter said as Eddie neared with a length of tape. "Only breathing through my nose – it's not enough." He looked at Shannon. "I have cancer, for chrissakes."

Eddie hesitated, then withdrew a knife from his pocket. He cut a slash in the center of the length of duct tape, then stretched the tape across Cutter's mouth, connecting the ends around the back of his head. The slash was in the middle, where his mouth was. "There," Eddie said. "You can breathe but can't yell."

Shannon turned and threw up. It was such a sudden, violent purging that she couldn't move for a moment. She stayed bent over, staring at what had come out of her, tallying up all the laws she was breaking and the number of civil rights violations. The immorality. Eddie, meanwhile, pulled a bag from the SUV and slipped the straps over his shoulders.

"You good?"

She nodded, took a breath, then she was walking alongside Eddie as they moved back up the dead-end street on foot. They took a left, jogged fifty yards past another big beautiful house, white with black trim, and then went right. Her body shivered though the night was warm. Her hip felt like bones grinding to dust. Down a long road, past two more Southern-style homes, the pain crawled up her side and circled her pelvis. She had to stop running.

And then the house. Just a sketch of it in the darkness. It sat a good hundred yards away from their last turn, at the end of the road. Wide, mostly one-story, dark, surrounded by forest. And she knew from the map there was a lake just beyond the scrub. A reservoir.

The house was exactly as Handler had described: large but understated, the vinyl siding cobalt gray, the shutters black. A detached garage was partly visible to the rear and the right.

The sight of it emboldened her, chased out the cold, made her feel solid again. Shannon stepped off the road and into the trees, and Eddie followed. The woods were sparse and mostly free of detritus. They were able to move quietly and mostly maintain a visual.

Close enough, she stopped and hunkered down to watch, unsure of what to expect – perhaps a man with a high-powered rifle pacing a widow's walk. But the home had neither a widow's walk nor an obvious guard. It appeared completely dark inside. Only the walkway was lighted, small, possibly solar-powered lamps throwing starred light on the ground.

Eddie quietly opened his bag and handed her a Kevlar vest. He had black, oil-based face paint, and they both smeared it on, camouflaging them in the night. He pulled out two ArmaLite AR-15 rifles. He'd brought it all from home; she was using a civilian's weapons on top of everything else. But she glassed the scene with the mounted scope, carefully checking each window and door, her pulse working in her neck.

There seemed to be no one here. No lights, no sounds, no car in the driveway, nothing. The garage, too, was still and dark. A raised deck was mostly visible, a section of it concealed behind the house.

She pulled the scope away and gestured to Eddie that they get a little closer. He nodded, and they pushed toward the house, keeping concealed in the forest, moving slowly and as silently as possible. When Eddie stepped on a twig and broke it, they both froze.

They waited. When she swallowed, her throat felt dry. Sensing no obvious danger, they continued on, creeping closer, until they were alongside the house.

In the video, Fain had appeared to be in a basement or garage. At least, there'd been a concrete floor and possibly a pegboard for tools. But that was the video, and it could have been taken at any time; they could have moved her since. Eddie had suggested they separate once they reached the place, one checking the house, one the garage. But Shannon decided that they remain together. Eddie was a help, but also a risky variable. And he was her responsibility. She was already deep into extrajudicial territory, no need to further–

Moving steps ahead of Eddie, she froze and made a tight fist in the air so Eddie could see it. He stopped when she stopped, and her heart started banging against her ribs.

She smelled a cigarette.

The raised deck covered most of the territory between them and the garage. She'd caught a whiff of smoke on the night breeze, and now she spied the tendril of it rise in the moonlight. From her angle on the ground beside the deck, she couldn't see the smoker, just the smoke. But he was there. A mere few yards away from them.

Eddie's eyes shined amid the dark streaks of makeup as he looked up at the same smoke, which rose and dissipated into the blackness. The only way to get eyes on this person was to ease away from the deck to gain perspective. Or to continue moving around behind it, where the land sloped higher. But to get eyes on him meant he could see them, too.

She waited, breathing shallow, sensing Eddie behind her.

She heard the hiss of a cigarette butt dropped in water.

A moment later, the back door opened and closed.

Shannon let herself exhale. She caught Eddie's gaze and

knew they were thinking the same thing: someone was here. Yet they were no closer to confirming Fain's location or justifying the call for backup – the backup she would only get if she had ironclad proof.

They needed to get to the garage. But, knowing someone was here, she decided to modify their plan. She gestured to Eddie that he return to the woods and cover her. He understood and quietly left the perimeter of the house and dissolved into the shadows. Now she was alone.

The deck was shaped like two-thirds of an octagon. As the land sloped up, she would become gradually more visible.

She started around, moving as quietly as possible. The nearby water made soft lapping sounds. Insects buzzed in the trees. At first, the deck was at her eye line. Then, as the ground shifted upward, more of her body rose into view. If anyone was looking out, she could be spotted.

She kept moving in a crouch, holding the rifle in the low-ready position at her side. Traces of the cigarette hung in the humid air. A curtain drawn across the sliding glass doors concealed the interior of the house. Another door, a few feet from the sliding glass door, was windowless. If anyone could see her, she didn't know where they'd be watching from.

She glanced back in the direction she'd come, just able to make out Eddie's shape where he crouched in the trees, monitoring her progress. Then the deck blocked her view as she kept moving. She focused on the ground in front of her, careful not to bump into something, make a noise.

The strip of driveway stretched in from the street and widened to an end. A freestanding basketball hoop stood at its terminus. Directly in front of her was the garage. It was two bays – two garage doors, each with a bank of small dark windows.

She would have to cross the asphalt to get a look inside. There would likely be a separate entrance, a door on either the right or left. Maybe that door had a window; it was unlikely she'd find a view of the interior from anywhere but there. She'd be entirely visible to someone on the south or west side of the house, or anywhere on the deck. But she had to risk it. She had to see.

She was steeling herself for it, ready to sprint across the driveway, when she heard a door open and close. And then voices.

Huddled there, a mere three-foot height of decking to conceal her, she stayed motionless, listening.

Men walked this way, their footfalls creaking over the boards. At least two of them. They spoke quietly, audible but not discernible. After a moment, they descended the steps on the west side of the deck.

Shannon backed up. She started reversing around the deck, putting distance between herself and the men. She stopped just short of losing the view, and in time to see them as they moved toward the garage.

Two men.

She could see the area light attached above the garage, but either the bulbs were dead or the motion sensor deactivated; neither man triggered it as he crossed the driveway. One of them was clearly armed – a handgun stuck out from the back of his pants. She wasn't sure about the other one, but she bet he was, too.

They disappeared into the shadows along the right side of the building. A set of keys jangled, then inserted into a lock; a door opened and shut.

Had they both gone inside? Was one standing guard? She watched the windows over each garage bay door. She studied the shadows.

Her heart banging, she eased her phone out of her pocket and quickly tapped out a mass text to Tyler, Bufort, Matheson – everyone:

*Confirming at least two armed men 423 Waxpool Road,
Broadlands. Send help.*

She talked herself down as she waited for a response –
and then she saw a light come on inside the garage. Not
much, maybe a flashlight or a lamp.

Her phone buzzed. Tyler.

Need visual confirmation of victim.

Shannon exhaled. At least he was listening to her. But
what sort of confirmation? An image? Sure, maybe she'd just
waltz right up and snap a cell pic.

No, Tyler would take her word. But it needed to be
authentic. She needed to see.

She waited just another few seconds in case someone had
remained outside. Her heart was going hard enough to crack
a rib. She'd trained at Quantico, but real-life situations like
this rarely ended well, and she never got used to it. Every cell
in her body sought to avoid confrontation. She wanted to
wait, but waiting was a gamble. If Fain was in there, they
could be doing something to her. Hurting her again, torturing
her for another video. To make sure Nickerson followed
through.

She eased out from beneath the deck and quickly and
quietly crossed the driveway.

Stay, stay, stay.

But she had to ignore the instinct. Perhaps later, if she
made it through all this, she could reminisce how handling a
missing persons case seemed perpetually at cross-purposes
with all reason, procedure, and self-preservation. Probably,
she'd have to do it in a courtroom, facing charges. For now,
she headed for the spot between the two bay doors, a narrow
strip of wall about two feet wide, directly beneath the dark-

ened area light. The windows in the garage doors were just about eye level.

She took a breath, prepared to get a look inside.

She's not in there. This is all a wild-goose chase.

Or a trap ...

Shannon stretched up onto the balls of her feet and peered through the dusty glass.

41

A moment after, she dropped back to the ground, ice in her veins, holding a breath in her lungs. Fain was in there. Tied up, just like the video. God, she'd been like that for going on twenty-four hours.

The small light clamped to the workbench beside her had illuminated the bruised side of her face. She'd been wearing the same clothes she'd been in a week ago, walking to Penn Station. Like Shannon had feared, her captors seemed in the process of another video. They wore the clown face paint. One of them had held Fain by her hair, a knife to her throat, while the other one manned the camera.

His gaze might have flicked up to the windows. Maybe he'd only seen the light reflected back?

Or maybe he'd been able to make out a woman's face.

She didn't have long to wonder – the side door opened. She ran back across the driveway, towards the deck. When she dared to look back, the man emerged from the shadows, holding his gun, eyes locked on her. He fired.

The projectile hit the side of the deck flooring, just beside her head. Shannon ducked but kept running. She had the rifle; she could stop and return fire. But it was too dangerous – she risked hitting Fain. Or returning fire might cause the men to abort. To kill their hostage – the chief witness to their crime – and get the hell out of there.

Maybe things were past that point. Now knowing someone was here, maybe they could guess who it was. And one of them was firing. The neighborhood homes were sparse, but someone might hear the gunshots and call the police.

It all passed through her mind in a couple of seconds. Shannon stopped running and turned around. As soon as she located the man – the white paint of his face stood out in the gloom – she squeezed the trigger. The rifle had a decent kick, but she held on. The rounds chased him off, running up the driveway, past the basketball hoop and into the woods.

A door opened at her right. She swung the rifle in that direction and fired again. The explosions blew out the shadows, lighting up the area just beside the garage, where lush vegetation had encroached. The man there pointed his weapon, but the rounds from her AR-15 cut him down.

Shannon moved in, keeping the weapon aimed. Her head felt like it was on fire from the adrenaline, her lungs working double time. She kicked the door open and cleared the room. No one else in the garage except for Kristie Fain. The woman's eyes were wide and alert as Shannon approached.

"I'll be right back for you," Shannon said. "I have to make sure–"

Glass exploded. One of the small square windows of a garage door had been punctured by a round and shattered. More rounds punched into the door – they came through. Shannon flipped the rifle onto her back and dove for Fain. She took the woman down to the floor, chair and all, and stayed on top of her as the hail of gunfire continued.

They couldn't stay here. Shannon jumped up and dragged Fain and the chair toward a second room.

More gun reports from outside, but nothing that hit the garage this time. It sounded like the gunman out there was firing in a different direction.

Eddie ...

With Fain pulled back to a hopefully safer spot, Shannon removed the gag from her mouth. The woman gasped for breath.

"How many?" Shannon asked. Cutter had given a number, but could've been lying, or it had changed.

"Three," Fain answered. She lay on her side, plastic zip ties fastening her to the wooden chair.

Shannon needed a knife or snips. "I'll be right back."

Gunfire continued to pop off in the background as Eddie and one or both of Fain's remaining captors waged a small war. In the main room, Shannon scanned the pegboard wall of tools until she found tin snips.

She returned to Fain and snapped through the restraints. "Who are they?"

"They might be Israeli. They speak Arabic. I know their names, but they're obviously code. I don't know more than that. Are they terrorists?"

"They were hired by Plexus."

A look of fresh horror spread across Fain's face. Before she could ask anything else, the door banged open to the garage.

Someone was inside with them.

Shannon held a trembling finger to her lips. Fain nodded her understanding. Shannon got the AR-15 swung around into the ready position again. Her finger now rested against the trigger.

There was no door to the back room of the garage. If someone appeared, there was nothing stopping him from coming in.

Gunshots rang out in the distance. It sounded like Eddie's shoot-out was moving south, toward the lake.

The man who stepped into view wasn't wearing any makeup. He had an olive complexion, soulful dark eyes. He aimed his pistol at Shannon, and she aimed back.

Fain spoke. "Mahdi ..."

Shannon stared. She kept the AR-15 trained on him. "I'm an FBI agent."

He looked at her, like he was thinking. "Just two of you?"

"You're surrounded. They're moving in."

His gaze switched between the women, then stayed on Fain. "If you don't stay, I don't get paid."

He fired and jumped away. Shannon was hit in the chest and returned fire, but the impact of Mahdi's round threw her off balance, and her own shot went high.

She stumbled back, gasping for air, but somehow managed to stay on her feet. When she saw Mahdi reach around the doorway to fire again, she leapt out of the way.

His shots were rapid, reverberating off the concrete. Her ears rang from all the noise; the pain in her chest felt like a heart attack. She squeezed the trigger as she moved toward the main room.

She would outshoot him; she had more ammo.

Stopping at the doorway, she put her back to the wall. If he was still there, he was right on the other side of it. She strained to listen, but everything sounded like it was underwater.

She spun into the room, rifle ready, finger on the trigger. Mahdi's pistol was aimed at her head. She dropped low as he fired, and she squeezed again. His bullet missed her, hers hit him in the chest, and he dropped.

Shannon advanced quickly and put another round in him. Standing over him, she aimed at his forehead. He stared up, his lips moving silently as his dark eyes focused on her.

She kicked his gun away. She pulled her finger out of the trigger loop.

Fain emerged from the back room. "Mahdi," she said, crying.

Shannon moved to block her, but Fain just went around. She dropped to her knees, bent toward him and put her head on his chest. Mahdi lifted a hand, dirty and streaked with blood, and petted her hair.

"I'm sorry," he said.

42

"He's gone," Eddie said about the third man. "He left by the lake. For all I know, he dove in and swam away."

As soon as Eddie delivered the news, he put a hand against his abdomen and grimaced. He was wearing black, so Shannon had missed it at first – the blood. A bullet had pierced him just below the vest.

"I'm okay."

Fain swayed on her feet in the driveway, staring at the dead man outside the garage. Her tears had already dried. Inside, the one called Mahdi was also dead, his last breath bubbling out seconds after he'd made his apology to her.

Despite the lack of vehicles, the men had to have gotten here somehow. Maybe they'd ditched the van, the one seen on the video when they'd abducted Fain. Whatever they'd switched to was likely hidden somewhere nearby. The third man could get to it and escape.

Fain didn't remember anything. She only knew she'd awakened in the house.

Shannon had sent out updates, and help was on the way.

But she needed to get Eddie and Fain to safety. She beckoned them down the driveway to the street, then limped ahead of them, aiming the rifle, checking windows on the house, places in the surrounding trees, the street ahead.

The first of dawn lightened the horizon. A breeze rustled the trees, and then there was nothing except the sirens rising in the distance and the sound of their feet as Shannon led them. Fain was helping Eddie to walk now.

They kept to the edge of the street, ready to take cover in the trees if Shannon got the slightest hint of danger.

The sirens grew louder. They might not make it to Eddie's SUV before being intercepted. Shannon slung the rifle over her shoulder and took out her phone. She found the contact and connected.

Nickerson sounded like he'd been awake for a while despite the early hour. "Agent Ames? I just got to the Capitol ... I heard you were off the case?"

"I've got her," Shannon said. The emotion came unbidden, unexpected, and her vision blurred with tears. "I've got Fain."

"You – what? You have her?"

"I'm with Eddie."

They moved beside her as she spoke, Fain still helping Eddie along, his arm up over her neck. What a sight the two of them made. But when Shannon saw the blood trail he was leaving, she forced them to stop. Any further movement was only causing Eddie more harm. Kristie, too. All of them.

Eddie gritted his teeth and grimaced as Shannon and Kristie helped him to lie down, propped against an embankment on the side of the road.

The nearest house was close enough now that Shannon could see someone standing on the porch, watching. The police were just around the corner, by the sound.

Nickerson had been asking, "Eddie Caprice? He's with

you?"

Now she could answer. "He is. He's been shot. Police are coming. Senator – you can vote however you want."

———

WHEN THE FIRST black-and-whites pulled up to the scene, Shannon had her hands in the air, the rifle on the ground beside her. They still went through the motions, as she'd expected, having her lie down on the pavement and put her hands behind her back. They cuffed her and got her to her feet. They held her, and they questioned her. She told them about Cutter, back in Eddie's vehicle, and two officers went in search of him. Finally, ambulances arrived. Eddie went in one. Shannon tried to speak with him before he was taken, but there were too many cops, too much going on.

Mark Tyler finally got through to the Washington Police, and they took the cuffs off Shannon. She held Kristie's hand as the paramedics wheeled her to the back of the ambulance. Shannon let go as they lifted her gurney and folded the legs and loaded her in. The doors closed. The lights twirling, the vehicle drove off.

It was fully morning now. The house at the end of the street, where Fain had been held captive for one week, belonged to a wealthy businessman, a second home he rented out as an Airbnb. The renter was Zach Handler. Shannon wanted to ask Handler how he slept at night. She wanted to ask him lots of things. She wanted to speak to McWilliams, to the press, to shed some light on this whole sinister fiasco.

But when she lost her balance and dropped to one knee, the paramedics swooped in on her. And then she, too, was being placed in the back of an ambulance, and she was driven away.

43

S he was treated for dehydration, cuts and bruises, a mild concussion. When the doctor came in to follow up, she read the concern on his face.

"I had an injury last year," she said. "It affected my hip and lower back."

"I've seen that. You had inflammation above your hip, a lateral abdominal wall hematoma. It's been bothering you?"

"A little."

The understatement of the year ...

He nodded, flipping through her chart. "Well, from what I can tell, that's muscle strain, and maybe a little tendonitis. You're a runner?"

"I run, yes."

"I'm going to prescribe you some NSAIDs, 800 milligrams. Okay? And you need to ice that area." His concern deepened. "But what's got me more worried than your hip was the fainting. We don't take fainting lightly. You've had a mild concussion, for one thing, but your records also indicate you had a subdural hematoma when you had the original trauma. And some neurological issues as a result."

"My head feels fine."

"Well, I'd like to run some tests ..."

WHEN TYLER SHOWED up a little later, she was dozing.

"Renegade work makes you tired, huh?"

Shannon stirred as he sat down on the bed beside her.

"You missed your appointment with the OIG this morning."

She became self-conscious, looking down at herself dressed in the requisite hospital gown. The white bedsheet covered her from the waist down, her feet tenting the fabric at the end of the bed. "Everyone looks the same in hospitals," she said.

Tyler agreed. "It's the great equalizer. So what should I tell them? You couldn't make your first interview for an embezzlement investigation because you were freewheeling your way through a kidnapping extraction?"

"Plexus," she mumbled. She searched for water; her mouth was like cotton.

He found her cup and helped her to drink. "You don't need to worry about that right now. You need to take care of your health." After he put the empty cup aside, he used a nearby napkin to wipe her mouth. "I'm sorry, Shannon."

"For what?"

"I don't know ... maybe for putting too much on you too soon." He sighed. "There's going to be a lot of questions now. You know the drill. Some you might want to wait until you speak to your lawyer. But some are urgent – there's still a guy running around out there, and the world is turned upside down by this story." He shook his head. "This is one big fucking mess."

A PAGEANT OF INVESTIGATORS ENSUED. Agents from FBI headquarters, plus more agents from the WFO. They wanted her account of the events leading up to the showdown in Broadlands, and she gave it. Tyler stayed in the room, mostly in the corner, his arms folded, listening as she explained the sequence leading to Kristie Fain's location. She didn't sugarcoat it. She was forthcoming when it came to Cutter and the physical assault he'd sustained.

When the FBI was done with her, including Tyler, a woman from OIG arrived to ask about the money in Shannon's account. Again, Shannon gave her the story exactly as it had happened: she'd come home to find the package containing the jewelry, and the next day she'd received the deposit notification. She'd never stolen anything in her life. "You need to talk to Keith Cutter and Zach Handler," she said. "Either one or the other did this because I was getting too close."

"We have," the investigator said. "At this point, both men have retained counsel and are not speaking about the matter. We can compel them – and we will – but for now, all we have is the evidence and your story."

"I didn't do this," Shannon said. She got out of bed.

"Should you be doing that?"

"I'm fine." She started pulling on her clothes. "So I'm still suspended?"

"That's up to Tyler. Our investigation will proceed. There will be a hearing ..."

The OIG investigator continued talking, but Shannon tuned it out. When it was over, she picked up her bag and left the room. She limped to the nurses' station and asked for Eddie Caprice's room. Eddie was in surgery and couldn't be visited at the moment. But the nurse was confident he'd pull through.

She visited Kristie next, but realized the woman was sleeping. Not wanting to disturb her, Shannon went back to the nurses' station and asked for a pen. She jotted a note on the back of a business card she kept in her wallet, and left the card on a chair just inside Kristie's room.

She checked herself out of the hospital. Tests could be run some other time – she'd gone this long, what was a couple more days?

She'd been texting Bufort for several hours – he'd come down with Tyler, but had most recently been at the house in Broadlands. He was close enough to pick her up. He was waiting in a rented car when the orderly wheeled her to the front entrance.

It was dark out and disorienting. She was aware she'd been at the hospital for most of the day, but still hadn't expected to walk out into darkness.

Multiple reporters and their camera crews were in proximity. They recognized Shannon and moved in. "Miss? Are you Special Agent Ames? Can you comment on Kristin Fain? How is she doing? How did you know where to find her?"

Bufort shooed them off. "This is still an active investigation, folks. We can't comment at this time."

He helped Shannon into the passenger seat and hurried around to the driver's side as the reporters continued to lob questions and the cameramen jockeyed for a better shot.

"Déjà vu," Bufort said as he slid into his seat.

"What do you mean?"

He kept the car in park a moment. "A year ago, I picked you up from New York Presbyterian Hospital. I figure you're just trying different hospitals in different states?" He joked, but concern shone in his eyes.

Without expecting it, she reached across the seat and hugged him. He seemed surprised at first, then hugged her back. The tears were hot and sudden. She let them fall.

He rubbed her arm. "Hey," he said. "Hey, we're gonna fix this. It's gonna be all right."

I DIDN'T DO THIS ...

Her words to the OIG inspector echoed Nickerson's own, days before.

She worried for a world where nothing people saw or heard could be trusted.

"That house looked like a Wild West shoot-out." Bufort was beside her, driving back to New York. The road was dark and wet with rain. "I kind of wish I'd been there to see you in action."

Shannon opened her shirt collar and examined her chest in the visor mirror. A purple-yellow bruise mottled the flesh where her Kevlar vest had absorbed the shot.

"Talk to me," Bufort said. He was no longer joking around. "If you want to."

"I do."

She told him everything, starting with that first sign of smoke. Of particular clarity: the moment the one called Mahdi had said, *If you don't stay, I don't get paid.* It underlined that these were contractors, men hired to keep Fain captive until Nickerson cast his vote the way he was supposed to.

After she finished, Bufort paused. "That's rough. I'm sorry you were in that position. I'm sorry I wasn't able to do more."

"It's okay. What's the story on the house? Is there a solid connection to Handler? Or Cutter?"

"The guy who owns it, named Howard Finker, is a hedge fund manager. As soon as he was called and questioned, he clammed up. He'd already seen something on the news, I guess. He's got a lawyer and isn't talking."

The story was in every major newspaper from coast to coast: *Kristen Fain Found in Broadlands, Virginia.* She'd been kidnapped by men suspected to be outside hires. Two were dead; one was at large. Fain was recuperating at Inova Fairfax Trauma Center, where Shannon had been, and was expected to make a full recovery.

As Shannon skimmed the articles on her phone, Bufort summarized the coverage: "Possible reasons for her abduction vary: She was being kept by Nickerson's chief of staff so she'd be unable to come forward with sexual assault allegations. She was abducted by the Time Keepers as part of some grander scheme yet to be revealed. Or it all had to do with her boyfriend's father, a celebrity spokesperson in favor of a Peruvian government hydroelectric project that would further displace the Ashaninka people."

No one suspected Fain had been used to coerce Nickerson's vote. In all the major papers and across social media, there was nothing about Plexus.

Shannon shook her head with incredulity. "What's Tyler saying? He was at the hospital most of the morning, but he disappeared."

"It's what he's *not* saying. Tyler and I go back a little ways, and we have our issues, as you know. He's a good guy, but he's an admin. He's got to think about budgets; he's got to think about us having the resources we need."

"Charlie, you've never been one to talk around a subject ..."

"I'm saying Plexus is getting treated with kid gloves. For the same reason Tyler wanted to tread lightly with Nickerson. Plexus is worth more than the GDP of most countries on the planet. They shape culture. They have political clout." Bufort glanced at her. "And I'm underselling it."

"I understand the too-big-to-fail concept." She was feeling frustrated and didn't want to take it out on Bufort. "Sorry."

"It's okay."

"But what's going on with McWilliams?"

"He's completely distancing himself, as you can expect. Zach Handler was just some freelance contractor who did work for them. And not even good work. They didn't rehire him, according to McWilliams's PR person. And there are hints that Handler is unstable."

"So if he does make any accusations, Plexus is already teeing it up to discredit his character."

"You got it."

"But that can't be their entire narrative if Handler *does* throw Plexus under the bus. 'Oh, he's just crazy ...'"

"That's most of it, honestly. But they'll probably say something like he did this to get back in their good graces. He was Hinckley Jr. shooting President Reagan in order to impress Jodie Foster. That sort of thing. 'Look what I did, guys – I got Nickerson to pass the bill that will make you rich. Aren't you proud of me?'"

"That's weak."

"Maybe. But it happens every day. You don't like someone's accusations, you attack their character. You know how it goes."

He was right – she did know, and she didn't like it. Shannon was of the mindset to let politics be politics and to focus on helping people. Serving the public by solving crimes and hopefully preventing them before they happened. But politics had swelled to have an outsize presence in everyday life. What was once something boring and back-room had become a national pastime. Almost a religion. You couldn't escape it.

"We should be putting pressure on Plexus," she said.

"I agree. But this is what it is. Listen, we're an hour away from home. You want to stop and get something to eat while prices are still reasonable?"

She was lost in thought, remembering something Nickerson had said. "Oh," she answered Bufort after a moment. "Yes. Food." The hospital had provided some jiggly, amorphous substance that hadn't touched her hunger. It had been more than a week of nearly nonstop activity, and she was a bottomless pit.

"All right," Bufort said. "We're stopping. We'll find a midnight diner, something."

"Good," she said distractedly, remembering Nickerson's words:

The harder I fight, the tighter the noose gets. There's no coming back from this.

44

B eing in Tyler's office felt like standing before the firing squad. She was soon to be executed.

After waking up in the hospital Monday afternoon, talking to doctors, Tyler, and FBI investigators, and after Bufort had driven her home, she'd fallen asleep – this time in her bed – for a solid twelve hours. It was the kind of sleep that rendered everything before it somewhat hazier, like a past life.

For a short time, anyway. Returning to the office brought it all rushing back.

Agents had clapped for her as she'd come in. Smiles and pats on the back and offers of "congratulations" were balanced by nervous looks, subtle expressions of pity. Her colleagues knew she'd found Fain, knew that the way she'd found her was controversial, and that she now had to face the consequences.

But those consequences – a forced resignation, most likely – didn't bother her. Being an FBI agent meant a lot. It wasn't that she took it lightly. But she'd find another job.

She'd find ways to serve her community, one way or the other.

What bothered her was Plexus.

When Bufort burst into the room, Tyler was immediately annoyed; he'd barely gotten started dressing her down. But Bufort ignored him and strode to the TV on Tyler's wall, flicked it on.

"What are you doing?"

"Nickerson is holding a press conference."

Shannon crowded in next to Bufort and Tyler in front of the screen.

"Turn it up," Tyler said, then realized the remote was on his desk.

Senator Joel Nickerson stood in front of reporters at the Capitol Building. Behind him, the American flag hung solemnly on its pole. "... for all of us," Nickerson was saying. "Because when something like this happens, it can't be about any one person. It can't be about any one career. It can't be about self-preservation – it has to be about the preservation of our democracy. Our nation. Our way of life."

Shannon felt gooseflesh break out on her arms. She thought she knew where this was headed. She hoped.

"Today, I'm going to share a video that was sent to me over a week ago. And the text message I received almost four days later, in the middle of the night, with instructions on how to vote on the infrastructure bill that was just passed."

"It passed?" Shannon asked. She'd had yet to hear.

"Yeah. It passed," Bufort said.

Nickerson said, "But before I do, I want you to know that I didn't vote the way they told me. And that fact is owed to the DOJ, the FBI, the NYPD, and the WPD. Liberty was preserved, thanks to capable law enforcement. Liberty was preserved thanks to a very close friend of mine." He looked into the camera. "And thanks to one FBI agent in particular. Because of her, Kristie Fain was safe, I knew she was safe, so I voted my conscience." He paused to let the implication settle in; he'd voted no. "But this isn't about policy. This isn't about my view of government. Or about left- or right-leaning politics. This is about preserving our democratic process. And that no one – no politician and no *corporation* – is above the law. We have to be vigilant now. Because we live in a world where ..."

Tyler lowered the volume with the remote at his desk. He stared into a corner for a moment while Nickerson's lips moved soundlessly on-screen.

Then Tyler looked at Shannon. "You realize this doesn't change anything."

"I understand."

"You were suspended. You acted above the law. You and a civilian physically assaulted a man. A *chief of staff* for a US senator."

Bufort interjected, "A chief of staff who wound up responsible for the *whole thing* ..."

"Zip it," Tyler snapped. He held a finger at Bufort. "I've got multiple bones to pick with you, too."

"So pick them," Bufort said, moving closer to Shannon. "But I want you to know something, Mark. If she goes, I go."

Tyler stared, then shook his head, as if with pity. "Charlie, you are just ..."

Shannon grabbed the remote from Tyler and raised the volume on the TV. "Shh. Watch."

"All right," Nickerson said on the screen. "What you are about to see has been carefully and meticulously studied. Multiple law enforcement agencies with forensic experts have determined this is fake. The man you are about to see is not me. And the woman is not Kristin Elizabeth Fain."

The air around Nickerson darkened, and a screen bright-
ened behind him. A split second later, the TV feed switched
to the elevator video. The scene played out; Tyler and Bufort
watched it silently. Arms crossed, Shannon bit her fingernails. Realizing it, she stopped. Nickerson doing this was
important. The public knowing that this technology existed,
and could be deployed at this level, was important. But
Shannon was preoccupied by thoughts of Fain. And what
she'd written to her on the business card, and how the
woman might've taken it.

When the video ended, Shannon could feel the collective
hush of the world. Nickerson paused a moment before
leaning toward the microphone and saying, "What you just
saw was not real. That was not me. And it was not Kristie
Fain."

The scrum of reporters became excited. Someone
stepped onto the dais, and cameras swung in her direction.
Kristie Fain, being helped by her mother and her friend
Rachel Lockhart, walked slowly to the lectern. She cleared
her throat, everything fell silent, and she said, "He's right. I
was never in that elevator."

The reporters erupted with questions. *Where have you
been? What happened to you? What can you tell us about your
escape?* Someone thought to ask, *How can we believe you now?*

But Fain wasn't taking questions and moved away from
the lectern. She stopped at Senator Nickerson, who looked at
her with pity and compassion. She hugged him, and he
hugged her back, and the media lost their mind.

Tyler shut it off. He glared at Bufort a moment before
walking behind his desk and sitting down. Shannon took her
cue and sat across from him while Bufort remained standing.

"Listen," Tyler said to her. "You've got multiple investigations this week. The Broadlands investigators are trying to
reconstruct those events and didn't grill you to the extent they

could have yesterday – I told them to back off. You were recovering."

"Thank you."

"Same thing with Fain – they talked to her, but need to do so again." He picked up his phone and read something on it. "Apparently, you left her a note? It said, 'Take care of yourself now. Do whatever you need to do.'"

"Yes, sir."

He set his phone down. "What does that mean?"

"It just means ... I hoped she didn't feel like she had to make any choice other than the one that was best for her. Especially after all she'd been through. The thought of any pressure on her ... I was just giving her my two cents."

Tyler seemed to absorb this. "Well, I'm hoping maybe you could be there and talk to her. In particular – we need everything on this third man who escaped. There's not much information on the two decedents – they're not in any database we have. Whoever they worked for, if it was Mossad, there's no link to that, of course; it's like they never existed. No fingerprints, no dentition, nothing. But we need the third man. If we get him, we have a better chance of linking this back to Handler and then to McWilliams and Plexus. And I know that means a lot to you."

After a moment's hesitation, he glanced at Bufort. "It means something to me, too."

"We're also looking for the woman," Bufort said. "The one who played Fain in the elevator."

"Good, yes." Tyler's gaze came back to Shannon. "Listen to me. No one is getting fired today. You can stick yourself in some cozy job with the sheriff's department back home in farm country, but it isn't going to be because I fired you. All the same, there are consequences – penalties – for your conduct on this case. There have to be."

"I understand, sir."

"But right now, I need you to help me with these loose ends and submit to your investigations. In the meantime, think it all over. And let me know what you decide."

"Thank you. I will."

45

Bufort walked beside her as they left the office. "How passive-aggressive is that? What are you supposed to *think* about? I don't understand. Does he want to fire you or not?"

Shannon didn't answer right away. They walked half the block and turned down Duane Street to pick up her Impala.

Driving uptown a few minutes later, she said, "There's no way we're ever going to find the third man."

"No. We're not. He's in the wind forever."

"Tyler doesn't want me to quit."

"No, I don't think he does."

She glanced at Bufort. "You two need to settle whatever it is between you."

He was silent, watching the city outside the car. They undulated over a bumpy road uptown. "Fair enough. Where are we going, anyway?"

She drove them to an area with a hipster bar on one corner and an organic market on another. She parked the Impala.

"Okay," Bufort said. "Time to let me in on it."

"That night at the club, La Jeunesse ran out. Eddie Caprice was watching. He saw this guy in face paint flee the scene. He followed him. And this is where La Jeunesse came."

She got out; Bufort followed. They walked two blocks until they reached a handsome brownstone and climbed up the stoop, rang the buzzer.

A male voice answered after a few seconds. "Hello?"

"Special Agent Shannon Ames. I'm here with Special Agent Charlie Bufort."

For a while, nothing happened. Then the buzzer rang.

The inside was ostentatious. Wide red carpet in the hallway, suits of armor between the massive apartment doors. One of the doors opened, and La Jeunesse peeked out.

"Ms. Ames," he said, "Mr. Bufort, good to see you again."

"You look different than I remember."

"Ah, yes." La Jeunesse touched his bare face. No black diamond eyes, black-painted mouth, just the pinkish-beige of Caucasian skin. "Can we come in?"

"Absolutely."

His place was impressive, a main clerestory room with a balcony encircling half the space. Rooms off the balcony, rooms below. Furniture placed to create communal spaces. "Kind of like the downstairs at the old grist mill," Shannon observed, when they were seated.

"I do like my open spaces." He put his hands between his legs and leaned forward. "I was interested in your phone call."

Shannon took a breath and said, "I think we can work together."

He studied her with inquisitive eyes.

She said, "I think we have similar goals. We want people to be free. And we want this country to come together. Part of that is removing the illusions. Things like deepfakes that are only going to get worse. People need to know what's real and what's not."

"You're right."

"And we need to hold companies like Plexus to account."

His eyes narrowed. "We need to keep them under control, if that's what you mean."

She paused, then reached across the space toward him.

He shook her hand. "What have you got in mind?"

THE END

WE HOPE YOU ENJOYED THIS BOOK

If you could spend a moment to write an honest review on Amazon, no matter how short, we would be extremely grateful. They really do help readers discover new authors.

And feel free to connect with TJ... he'd love to hear from you!

www.tjbrearton.net

Not long ago, a reader wrote to me to say he appreciated the procedural detail in these Shannon Ames stories. As it turns out, he was a former FBI Special Agent. Zing!

I wasted no time imploring him to answer my questions as I developed the next book. Wonderfully, graciously, he accepted. So, to the next reader, any details you find compelling and authentic, you have Xgboy Phil Lorge to thank. (Including the use of "Xgboy!") As do I. Thank you, Phil.

Thank you, of course, to my illustrious editor, Jodi Compton. In some ways, her work feels like the literary equivalent of shaking her head at me with a sly smile. "Not on my watch," she says, and there go any foolish or out-of-character moments, plot holes, and superfluous ornamental breaks.

Thanks to Pauline Nolet for once again doing her amazing hummingbird-like job of buzzing around to get every single thing right in the book. And thank you to Claire Milto for bringing it all home — not to mention, making sure I write my acknowledgements...

If you didn't like this book, Brian Lynch told me it would be tricky. If you did like this book, credit goes to him anyway for letting me write it. Thank you, Brian and Garret, for helping me bring this series to life.

ALSO BY TJ BREARTON

INKUBATOR TITLES

THE KILLING TIME

(Book 1 in the Special Agent Shannon Ames series)

HIDE AND SEEK

(Book 2 in the Special Agent Shannon Ames series)

IN TOO DEEP

(Book 3 in the Special Agent Shannon Ames series)

NOWHERE TO HIDE

(Book 4 in the Special Agent Shannon Ames series)

NO WAY BACK

(Book 5 in the Special Agent Shannon Ames series)

ROUGH COUNTRY

T.J.'S OTHER TITLES

HABIT

SURVIVORS

DARK WEB

HIGH WATER

DARK KILLS

DAYBREAK

GONE

DEAD GONE

BURIED SECRETS

BLACK SOUL

GONE MISSING

NEXT TO DIE

TRUTH OR DEAD

THE HUSBANDS

WHEN HE VANISHED

DEAD OR ALIVE

Made in the USA
Middletown, DE
20 October 2023

41118914R00201